Avon Books by
Teresa Medeiros

Yours Until Dawn
One Night of Scandal

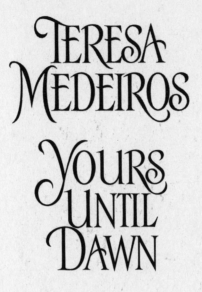

TERESA MEDEIROS

YOURS UNTIL DAWN

AVON BOOKS

An Imprint of HarperCollinsPublishers

This is a work of fiction. Names, characters, places, and incidents are products of the author's imagination or are used fictitiously and are not to be construed as real. Any resemblance to actual events, locales, organizations, or persons, living or dead, is entirely coincidental.

AVON BOOKS
An Imprint of HarperCollins*Publishers*
10 East 53rd Street
New York, New York 10022-5299

To my Michael, one of my greatest blessings is waking up to your sweet face every morning.

To my very own Axis of Angels—you know who you are . . .

To all of the angels of mercy at Western State Nursing Facility. May God bless you for all you do to take care of my mom.

And for my sweet Lord, who healed the lame and made the blind to see.

Who ever loved, that loved not at first sight?

CHRISTOPHER MARLOWE

≈ Chapter 1 ≈

England, 1806

My dear Miss March,

I pray you'll forgive me for being presumptuous enough to contact you in this rather unconventional manner . . .

"So tell me, Miss Wickersham, have you any experience?"

From somewhere deep in the sprawling Jacobean mansion, a tremendous crash sounded. Although the portly butler who was conducting the interview visibly flinched and the housekeeper standing at rigid attention beside the tea table let out an audible squeak, Samantha refused to so much as blink.

Instead, she drew a neat packet of papers from the side pocket of the battered leather portmanteau resting at her feet and held them out. "I'm sure you'll find my letters of reference are in order, Mr. Beckwith."

Although it was midday, the light in the modest breakfast parlor was abysmal. Shafts of sunlight bled through the cracks in the heavy velvet drapes, striping the rich ruby weave of the Turkish carpet. The wax candles scattered across the occasional tables filled the corners with flickering shadows. The room smelled musty and close, as if it had gone unaired for ages. If not for the absence of black swags over the windows and mirrors, Samantha would have sworn someone very dear to the household had recently died.

The butler took the papers from her white-gloved hand and unfolded them. As the housekeeper craned her long neck to peer over his shoulder, Samantha could only pray the dim light would work to her advantage, preventing them from studying the scrawled signatures too closely. Mrs. Philpot was a handsome woman of indeterminate age, as sleek and narrow as the butler was round. Although her face was unlined, silver frosted the black chignon anchored at her nape.

"As you can see, I served two years as governess for Lord and Lady Carstairs," Samantha informed Mr. Beckwith as he gave the papers a cursory thumbing-through. "Once the war resumed, I joined several other governesses in volunteering to treat sailors and soldiers who returned from sea or the front with debilitating wounds."

The housekeeper could not quite hide the faint tightening of her lips. Samantha knew there were still those in society who believed women who nursed soldiers to be little more than glorified camp followers. Immodest creatures who wouldn't even blush to look upon a strange man's nakedness. Feeling heat rise to her own cheeks, Samantha lifted her chin another notch.

Mr. Beckwith examined her over the top of his wire-rimmed spectacles. "I must confess, Miss Wickersham, that you're a trifle bit . . . *younger* than what we had in mind. Such strenuous duty might require a woman of more . . . maturity. Perhaps one of the other applicants . . ." At Samantha's arch look, he trailed off.

"I don't see any other applicants, Mr. Beckwith," she pointed out, sliding her own ill-fitting spectacles up her nose with one finger. "Given the generous, even extravagant, wages you offered in your advertisement, I fully expected to find them lined up outside your gates."

Another crash came, this one even closer than the last. It sounded as if some sort of massive beast were lumbering toward its den.

Mrs. Philpot hastened around the chair, her starched petticoats rustling. "Would you care for some more tea, my dear?" As she poured from the porcelain pot, her hand trembled so violently that tea splashed over the rim of Samantha's saucer and into her lap.

"Thank you," Samantha murmured, surreptitiously dabbing at the spreading stain with her glove.

The floor beneath their feet visibly shuddered, as did Mrs. Philpot. The muffled roar that followed was peppered by a string of mercifully unintelligible oaths. There could no longer be any denying it. Someone—or something—was approaching.

Casting a panicked look at the gilded double door that led to the next chamber, Mr. Beckwith lurched to his feet, his prominent brow glistening with sweat. "Perhaps this isn't the most opportune time . . ."

As he shoved the letters of reference back at Samantha, Mrs. Philpot whisked the cup and saucer out of her other hand and deposited them back on the tea cart with a noisy rattle. "Beckwith is right, my dear. You'll have to forgive us. We may have been entirely too hasty . . ." The woman pulled Samantha to her feet and began to tug her away from the door and toward the heavily curtained French windows that led to the terrace.

"But my bag!" Samantha protested, casting the portmanteau a helpless glance over her shoulder.

"Don't worry, child," Mrs. Philpot assured her, gritting her teeth in a kindly smile. "We'll have one of the footmen bring it out to your hack." As the thunderous crashing and cursing swelled, the woman dug her nails into the sturdy brown wool of Samantha's sleeve and yanked her into motion. Mr. Beckwith dashed around them and whipped open one of the floor-to-ceiling windows, flooding the gloom with bright April sunshine. But before Mrs. Philpot could urge Samantha through it, the mysterious racket ceased.

The three of them turned as one to gaze at the gilded doors on the opposite side of the room.

For a moment there was no sound at all except for the delicate ticking of the French gilt clock on the mantel. Then came a most curious noise, as if something were fumbling, or perhaps even scratching, at the doors. Something large. And angry. Samantha took an involuntary step backward; the housekeeper and butler exchanged an apprehensive glance.

The doors came flying open, striking the opposite walls with a mighty crash. Framed by their wings was not a beast, but a man— or what was left of one after all the genteel veneer of society had been stripped away. His tawny hair, shaggy from neglect, hung well past his shoulders. Shoulders that came close to filling the breadth of the doorway. A pair of buckskin pantaloons clung to his lean hips and hugged every curve of his muscular calves and thighs. Several days' growth of beard shadowed his jaw, lending his visage a piratical aspect. If he'd have had a cutlass gripped between his bared teeth, Samantha would have been tempted to bolt from the house in fear for her virtue.

He wore stockings, but no boots. A rumpled cravat hung loose around his throat, as if someone had attempted to knot it several times, then given up in frustration. His lawn shirt was untucked and missing half its studs, revealing a shocking slice of well-muscled chest lightly dusted with golden hair.

Poised there in the shadows of the doorway, he cocked his head at an odd angle, as if listening for something only he could hear. His aristocratic nostrils flared.

The downy hair on Samantha's nape prickled. She could not shake the sensation that it was *her* scent he was seeking, *her* he was stalking. She had almost convinced herself she was being ridiculous when he started forward with the grace of a natural predator, heading straight for her.

But an overstuffed ottoman stood in his path. Even as a cry of warning caught in her throat, he tumbled right over the ottoman and went crashing to the floor.

Far worse than the fall was the way he just lay there, as if there really weren't any particular point in getting up. Ever.

Samantha could only stand paralyzed as Beckwith rushed to his side. "My lord! We thought you were taking an afternoon nap!"

"Sorry to disappoint you," the earl of Sheffield drawled, his voice muffled by the rug. "Someone must have forgotten to tuck me into my cradle."

As he shook off his servant's grip and staggered heavily to his feet, the sunlight streaming through the outside door struck him full in the face.

Samantha gasped.

A fresh scar, still red and angry, bisected the corner of his left eye and descended down his cheek in a jagged lightning bolt, drawing the skin around it taut. It had once been an angel's face with the sort of masculine beauty reserved only for princes and seraphim. But now it was marked forever with the devil's brand. Perhaps it wasn't the devil, Samantha thought, but God Himself who had been jealous that a mere human could aspire to such perfection. She knew she should have been repulsed, but she couldn't look away. His ruined beauty was somehow more compelling than perfection could ever be.

He wore his disfigurement like a mask, hiding any hint of vulnerability behind it. But he could do nothing to disguise the lingering bewilderment in his sea-foam-green eyes. Eyes that didn't gaze at Samantha, but *through* her.

His nostrils flared again. "There's a woman here," he announced with utter conviction.

"Of course there is, my lord," said Mrs. Philpot brightly. "Beckwith and I were just enjoying a spot of afternoon tea."

The housekeeper tugged at Samantha's arm again, silently begging her to make her escape. But Gabriel Fairchild's sightless gaze had riveted her to the floor. He began to move toward her, slower now, but with no less determination than before. Samantha realized in that moment that she would be a fool to mistake his caution for weakness. His desperation only made him more dangerous. Especially to her.

He advanced on her with such resolve that even Mrs. Philpot melted back into the shadows, leaving Samantha to face him all alone. Although her first instinct was to shrink away from him, she forced herself to stand straight and tall. Her initial fear that he might run into her—or even over her—was unfounded.

With uncanny perception, he halted a mere foot away from her, sniffing warily at the air. Samantha wouldn't have thought the tart, clean fragrance of the lemon verbena she'd dabbed behind her ears would be all that enticing to a man. But the look on his face as he filled his lungs with her scent made her feel like some scantily clad harem girl awaiting the sultan's pleasure. Her skin tingled with awareness. It was as if he were touching her everywhere at once without lifting a finger.

When he began to circle her, she turned with him, some primitive instinct refusing to trust him behind her. He finally stopped, so close she could feel the animal heat radiating from his skin and count every one of the gilt-tipped lashes ringing those extraordinary eyes.

"Who is she?" he demanded, fixing his gaze just over her left shoulder. "And what does she want?"

Before either servant could stammer out an answer, Samantha said firmly, "*She,* my lord, is Miss Samantha Wickersham and *she* has come to apply for a position as your nurse."

The earl adjusted his empty gaze downward, quirking his lips as if amused to find his quarry so small. A snort escaped him. "Nursemaid, you mean? Someone who can sing me to sleep at bedtime, spoon porridge into my mouth, and wipe my"—he hesitated just long enough to make both servants cringe with dread— "*chin* if I dribble?"

"I haven't the voice for lullabies and I'm sure you're perfectly capable of wiping your own . . . *chin*," Samantha replied smoothly. "My task would be to help you adjust to your new circumstances."

He leaned even closer to her. "What if I don't want to adjust? What if I just want to be left the bloody hell alone so I can rot here in peace?"

Mrs. Philpot gasped, but Samantha refused to be shocked by his casual profanity. "You needn't blush on my behalf, Mrs. Philpot. I can assure you that I am no stranger to dealing with childish outbursts. During my stint as a governess, my young charges often delighted in testing the limits of my forbearance by throwing tantrums when they didn't get their way."

At being compared to an obstinate three-year-old, the earl softened his voice to a menacing growl. "And I suppose you cured them of that habit?"

"With adequate time. And patience. At the moment it seems that you're blessed with one and I the other."

He startled her by wheeling toward the general direction of Mr. Beckwith and Mrs. Philpot. "What makes you think this one will be any different from the others?"

"The others?" Samantha echoed, arching one brow.

The butler and housekeeper exchanged a guilty glance.

The earl wheeled back around. "I suppose they neglected to mention your predecessors. Let's see, first there was old Cora Gringott. She was nearly as deaf as I was blind. We made a fine pair, we did. I spent most of the time groping for her ear trumpet so I could bellow into it. If memory serves me, I believe she lasted less than a fortnight."

He began to pace back and forth in front of Samantha—his long strides carrying him precisely four steps forward, four steps back. It was only too easy to imagine him pacing the deck of a ship with such effortless command, his golden hair blowing in the wind, his penetrating gaze fixed on the distant horizon. "Then came that chit from Lancashire. She was a rather timid creature from the start. Barely spoke above a whisper. She didn't even bother to collect her wages or pack her belongings when she left. Just fled screaming into the night as if some madman had taken after her."

"Imagine that," Samantha murmured.

He paused briefly, then continued pacing. "And only last week we lost the dear widow Hawkins. She seemed to possess a sturdier constitution and quicker wit than the others. Before she went huffing out of here, she recommended that Beckwith hire not a nurse, but a zookeeper, since his master obviously belonged in a cage."

Samantha was almost glad he couldn't see her lips twitch.

"So you see, Miss Wickersham, I am beyond any assistance, especially yours. So you might as well trot yourself back to the schoolroom or the nursery or wherever it was you came from. There's no need to waste any more of your precious time. Or mine."

"Really, my lord!" Beckwith protested. "It's hardly necessary to be rude to the young lady."

"Young lady? Ha!" The earl threw out a hand, nearly decapitating a potted ficus tree that looked as if it hadn't been watered in over a decade. "I can tell from her voice that she's a tart, vinegary creature without an ounce of womanly softness about her. If you were going to hire me another woman, you could have probably found one down on Fleet Street who would have suited me far better. I don't need a nurse! What I need is a good—"

"My lord!" Mrs. Philpot shouted.

Her master might be blind, but he wasn't deaf. The woman's scandalized plea silenced him more effectively than a blow. With the ghost of a charm that must have once come second nature to him, he pivoted on one heel and bowed to the wing chair just to the left of where Samantha was standing. "I pray you'll forgive me my *childish outburst*, miss. I bid you a good day. And a good life."

Reorienting himself in the general direction of the parlor doors, he charged forward, refusing to break stride or feel his way along. He might have achieved his destination if his knee hadn't slammed into the corner of a low-slung mahogany table with enough force to make Samantha wince in sympathy. Grunting out an oath, he gave the table a savage kick, sending it smashing against the far wall. It took him three tries to find the ivory door-knobs, but he finally managed to slam the doors behind him with an impressive bang.

As he retreated deeper into the house, the sporadic crashing and swearing eventually faded into silence.

Mrs. Philpot gently closed the French window, then returned to the cart and poured herself a cup of tea. She perched on the edge of the sofa as if she were a guest herself, her cup rattling violently against the saucer.

Mr. Beckwith sank down heavily beside her. Drawing a starched handkerchief from his waistcoat pocket, he mopped at his damp brow before shooting Samantha a contrite look. "I'm afraid we owe you an apology, Miss Wickersham. We weren't entirely forthcoming."

Samantha settled herself into the wing chair and folded her gloved hands in her lap, surprised to discover that she, too, was trembling. Thankful for the refuge the shadows provided, she said, "Well, the earl is not quite the gentle invalid you described in your advertisement."

"He hasn't been himself since he returned from that wretched battle. If you only could have known the dear lad before . . ." Mrs. Philpot swallowed, her gray eyes glistening with tears.

Beckwith handed her his handkerchief. "Lavinia is right. He was a gentleman cut from the finest cloth, a true prince among men. Sometimes I fear the blow that blinded him may have addled his mind as well."

"Or at least his manners," Samantha noted dryly. "His wit doesn't seem to have suffered unduly."

The housekeeper dabbed at her narrow nose. "He was always such a bright boy. Ever so quick with a quip or a sum. I rarely saw him without a book tucked under his arm. When he was small, I used to have to take his candle away at bedtime for fear he would sneak a book into his bed and set his blankets afire."

Samantha was shaken to realize he had been deprived of even that pleasure. It was difficult to imagine a life without the solace books could provide.

Beckwith nodded fondly, his eyes glazed with memories of better times. "He was always his parents' pride and joy. When he took that absurd notion to join the Royal Navy, his mama and his sisters went into hysterics and begged him not to go, and his papa, the marquess, threatened to disown him. But when it came time for him to sail, they all gathered at the dock to shout their blessings and wave their handkerchiefs at him."

Samantha plucked at the back of her gloves. "It's rather uncommon for a nobleman, especially a firstborn son, to seek a naval career, is it not? I thought the Army attracted the wealthy and the titled, while the Royal Navy was the refuge of the poor and the ambitious."

"He would never explain his choice," Mrs. Philpot interjected. "He just said he had to follow his heart wherever it would lead him. He refused to buy his way up the ranks as most men did, but insisted on arriving there on his own merits. When they received word that he had been promoted to lieutenant aboard the HMS *Victory*, his mama wept tears of joy and his papa was so proud he nearly busted the buttons right off his waistcoat."

"The *Victory*," Samantha murmured. The ship's name had proved to be prophetic. With the help of her sister ships, she had routed Napoleon's navy at Trafalgar, destroying the emperor's dream of ruling the seas. But the cost of victory had been high. Admiral Nelson had won the battle, but lost his life, as had many of the young men who had fought so valiantly at his side.

Their debts were paid in full, but Gabriel Fairchild would go on paying for the rest of his life.

She felt a surge of anger. "If his family is so devoted to him, where are they now?"

"Traveling abroad."

"Staying at their London residence."

The servants blurted out their answers in unison, then exchanged a sheepish glance. Mrs. Philpot sighed. "The earl spent most of his youth at Fairchild Park. Of all his father's properties, it was always his favorite. He has his own town house in London, of course, but given the cruel nature of his injuries, his family thought it might be easier for him to recuperate at his childhood home, away from society's prying eyes."

"Easier for who? For him? Or for them?"

Beckwith averted his eyes. "In their defense, the last time they came calling, he all but chased them off the estate. For a minute there, I feared he was actually going to order the groundskeeper to set the hounds on them."

"I doubt they were that difficult to discourage." Samantha closed her eyes briefly, struggling to regain her composure. It wasn't as if she had any right to judge his family for their lack of loyalty. "It's been well over five months since he was injured. Has his physician offered any hope that his sight might someday be restored?"

The butler shook his head sadly. "Very little. There have only been one or two documented cases in which such a loss has reversed itself."

Samantha bowed her head.

Mr. Beckwith rose, his fleshy cheeks and drooping countenance making him look like a melancholy bulldog. "I do hope you'll forgive us for squandering your time, Miss Wickersham. I realize you had to hire a hack to bring you out here. I'll be more than happy to pay for your return to the city out of my own pocket."

Samantha stood. "That won't be necessary, Mr. Beckwith. I won't be returning to London at the moment."

The butler exchanged a baffled glance with Mrs. Philpot. "Excuse me?"

Samantha moved to the chair she had originally occupied and scooped up her portmanteau. "I'll be staying right here. I'm accepting the position as the earl's nurse. Now, if you'll be so kind as to have one of the footmen fetch my trunk from the carriage and show me to my room, I'll prepare to commence my duties."

He could still smell her.

As if to taunt him by reminding him of what he'd lost, Gabriel's sense of smell had only sharpened in the past few months. Whenever he rambled past the kitchens, he could tell with a single sniff whether Étienne, the French cook, was preparing fricandeau of veal or a creamy béchamel sauce to tempt his appetite. The faintest whiff of wood smoke would inform him whether the fire in the deserted library had been freshly stoked or was dying to embers. As he collapsed on the bed in the room that had become more lair than bedchamber, he was assailed by the stale smell of his own sweat that clung to the rumpled sheets.

It was here that he returned to nurse his bruises and scrapes, here he tossed his way through nights distinguished from the days only by their suffocating hush. In the still hours between dusk and dawn, he sometimes felt as if he were the only soul left alive in the world.

Gabriel flung the back of his hand over his brow, closing his eyes out of old habit. When he had stormed into the parlor, he had immediately identified the lavender water favored by Mrs. Philpot and the musky hair pomade Beckwith lavished on his few remaining strands. But he hadn't recognized the crisp, sunlit fragrance of lemons scenting the air. It was an aroma both sweet and tart, delicate and bold.

Miss Wickersham certainly didn't smell like a nurse. Old Cora Gringott had smelled of mothballs, the widow Hawkins like the bitter almond snuff she was so fond of dipping. Nor did Miss

Wickersham smell like the shriveled spinster he envisioned when she spoke. If her withering tones were any indication, her pores should have emitted a poisonous fog of day-old cabbage and grave dust.

As he had drawn near to her, he had made an even more startling discovery. Underlying that cleansing breath of citrus was a scent that maddened him, clouded what little was left of both his senses and his good sense.

She smelled like a woman.

Gabriel groaned through gritted teeth. He hadn't felt a single stirring of desire since awakening in that London hospital to discover his world had gone dark. Yet the warm, sweet smell of Miss Wickersham's skin had evoked a dizzying jumble of scarlet-hazed memories—stolen kisses in a moonlit garden, husky murmurs, the heated satin of a woman's skin beneath his lips. All pleasures he would never know again.

He opened his eyes only to find the world still enveloped by shadows. Perhaps the words he had hurled at Beckwith were true. Perhaps he needed to engage the services of another sort of woman altogether. If he paid her handsomely enough, she might even be able to look upon his ruined face without recoiling. But what would it matter if she did? Gabriel thought, a harsh bark of laughter escaping him. He would never know. Perhaps, while she squeezed her eyes shut and pretended he was the gentleman of her dreams, he could pretend that she was the sort of woman who would sigh his name and whisper promises of eternal devotion.

Promises she had no intention of keeping.

Gabriel shoved himself off the bed. Damn that Wickersham woman! She had no right to taunt him so bitterly, yet smell so sweet. It was fortunate he had ordered Beckwith to send her away. As far as he was concerned, she need never trouble him again.

Chapter 2

My dear Miss March,

Despite my reputation, I can assure you that I'm not in the habit of striking up a clandestine correspondence with every lovely young woman who catches my fancy . . .

As Samantha groped her way down the curving staircase that descended into the heart of Fairchild Park the next morning, she almost felt as if she'd been struck blind. Not a single window of the mansion had been left unveiled. It was as if the house, as well as its master, had been cast into some dark realm of eternal night.

A lone torchière burned at the foot of the stairs, casting just enough light for her to see that the fingertips she'd trailed down the banister were furred with dust. Grimacing, she brushed them off on her skirt. Given the drab gray of the kerseymere, she doubted anyone would notice.

Despite the stifling gloom, it was impossible to completely cloak the legendary Fairchild wealth that had made the noble family the envy of the *ton*. Trying not to be intimidated by the centuries of privilege on display, Samantha stepped off the stairs and into the foyer. The house had long since been updated from the dark paneling and Tudor arches of its somber Jacobean roots. Shadows danced over the gleaming expanse of rose-veined Italian marble beneath her feet. Every graceful arch of molding and cornice, every papier-mâché relief scroll of flower or vase adorning the wainscoting, had been bronzed or gilded. Even the modest bedchamber Mrs. Philpot had assigned Samantha possessed a stained-glass fanlight over the door and walls hung with silk damask.

Beckwith had insisted that his master had once been "a prince among men." Gazing about her at the overblown opulence, Samantha sniffed. Perhaps it wasn't so difficult to claim such a title when one was raised in a palace.

Determined to locate her new charge, she decided to employ one of the tools in his own arsenal. Cocking her head to the side, she grew very still and listened.

She didn't hear any crashing or shouting, but she did hear the musical clinking of dishes and glassware. A sound that grew distinctly less musical when an explosion of shattering glass was followed by a savage oath. Although Samantha winced, a triumphant smile touched her lips.

Gathering her skirts, she sailed through the breakfast parlor where her interview had been conducted and out the opposite door, following the noise. As she strode through one deserted chamber after another, she was forced to veer around several signs of the earl's passing. Her sturdy half-boots crunched over broken porcelain and splintered wood. As she paused to gently right a delicate Chippendale chair, the cracked china face of a Meissen figurine laughed up at her.

The destruction wasn't surprising given Gabriel's penchant for charging recklessly through the house with no regard for his lack of sight.

She passed beneath a graceful arch. The dining room's lack of windows denied the cavernous chamber even a hint of daylight. If not for the branches of candles blazing at each end of the majestic table, Samantha might have feared she'd wandered into the family crypt.

A pair of footmen in navy livery guarded the mahogany sideboard, standing at rigid attention beneath Beckwith's watchful eye. None of them seemed to notice Samantha standing in the doorway. They were too preoccupied with scrutinizing every move their master made. As the earl's elbow nudged a crystal goblet toward the edge of the table, Beckwith made a discreet signal. One of the footmen rushed forward, catching the teetering goblet before it could fall. Shards of china and glass littered the floor around the table, evidence of their earlier failures.

Samantha studied Gabriel's broad shoulders and muscled forearms, struck anew by what an imposing man he was. He could probably snap her delicate neck between thumb and forefinger. If he could find her, that is.

His hair gleamed in the candlelight, its wild tangle combed by nothing more than impatient fingers since he'd rolled out of bed that morning. He wore the same rumpled shirt he'd worn the night before, but now it was spotted with grease and smeared with chocolate. He'd unceremoniously shoved the sleeves up to his elbows, sparing the ruffled cuffs from being dragged through his plate.

He brought a rasher of bacon to his mouth, tearing off a hunk of the tender meat with his teeth, then groped at the plate in front of him. Samantha frowned at the table. There wasn't a piece of cutlery in sight. Which might explain why Gabriel was scooping shirred eggs out of a porcelain ramekin with his cupped hand and doling them into his mouth. He polished off the eggs, then tucked a steaming crossbun into his mouth. He swept his tongue around his lips, but still managed to miss the dollop of honey at the corner of his mouth.

Although she felt like the worst sort of spy, Samantha couldn't tear her gaze away from that single golden drop of honey. Despite

his appalling lack of table manners, there was something un-
abashedly sensual in the way he ate, in his raw determination to
appease his appetites, convention be damned. As he plucked up a
fresh chop and began to gnaw the meat directly from the bone,
juice trickled down his chin. He looked like some sort of ancient
warrior fresh from routing his enemies and ravishing their
women. Samantha half expected him to wave the bone at her and
bellow, "More ale, wench!"

He suddenly froze and sniffed at the air, his expression feral.
Samantha flared her own nostrils, but all she could smell was the
mouthwatering aroma of bacon.

Lowering the chop back to the plate, he said with ominous
calm, "Beckwith, you'd best inform me that you've just brought in
some fresh lemon for my tea."

As he spotted Samantha, the butler's eyes widened. "I'm afraid
not, my lord. But if you'd like, I'll go fetch some immediately."

Gabriel lunged across the table, making a blind grab for the
butler, but Beckwith was already disappearing through the opposite door, the tail of his coat flashing behind him.

"Good morning, my lord," Samantha said smoothly, sliding
into a chair across from him, but well out of his reach. "You'll have
to forgive Mr. Beckwith. He obviously had more pressing duties."

Scowling, Gabriel settled back into his chair. "Let's hope they
include forging some letters of reference and packing his bags.
Then the two of you can return to London together."

Ignoring the jibe, Samantha smiled politely at the frozen footmen. With their naturally blushed cheeks, freckled noses, and tousled brown curls, neither of them looked to be much older than
sixteen. On closer examination, she realized they were not just
brothers, but twins. "I'm famished this morning," she said. "Might
I have some breakfast?"

Even without his sight, Gabriel must have sensed their hesitation. After all, it was hardly *de rigueur* for a servant to dine at his
master's table.

"Serve the lady, you fools!" he barked. "It wouldn't be very hospitable to send Miss Wickersham on her journey with an empty stomach."

The footmen scrambled to do his bidding, nearly knocking heads as they whisked a china plate and silverware in front of Samantha and filled a tray from the sideboard. Offering one of them a comforting smile over her shoulder, she accepted a ramekin of eggs, a crossbun, and several rashers of bacon. She had a feeling she was going to need all of her strength.

As the other footman poured her a cup of steaming tea, she told Gabriel, "I spent last night getting settled into my room. I didn't think you'd mind if I waited until morning to begin my duties."

"You don't have any duties," he replied, raising the chop back to his lips. "You're dismissed."

She smoothed a linen napkin across her lap and took a dainty sip of the steaming tea. "I'm afraid you don't have the authority to dismiss me. I don't work for you."

Gabriel lowered the chop, his gilt-dusted eyebrows forming a thunderous cloud over the bridge of his nose. "Pardon me? My hearing must be going as well."

"It seems that your devoted Mr. Beckwith hired me on the instructions of your father. That would make the marquess of Thornwood, one Theodore Fairchild, my employer. Until he informs me that my services as your nurse are no longer required, I shall endeavor to perform my duties to *his* satisfaction, not yours."

"Well, that's fortunate for you, isn't it? Since the only thing that would satisfy me is your imminent departure."

Using knife and fork, Samantha sawed a tender bit of bacon off a rasher. "Then I fear you are doomed to remain unsatisfied."

"I realized that the moment I heard your voice," he muttered.

Refusing to dignify the provocative insult with a retort, she tucked the bacon between her lips.

Bracing both elbows on the table, he let out a gusty sigh. "So tell me, Miss Wickersham, as my new nurse, which duty would you like to assume first? Would you like to feed me, perhaps?"

Eyeing the wolfish white flash of his teeth as they tore another hunk of meat off the chop, Samantha said, "Given your . . . um . . . *unbridled enthusiasm* for your victuals, I'd be a little worried about getting my fingers that close to your mouth."

One of the footmen suffered a sudden coughing fit, earning an elbow in the ribs from his scowling brother.

Gabriel sucked the last of the meat from the chop and tossed the bone to the table, missing his plate entirely. "Am I to surmise that you find my table manners lacking?"

"I just never realized that blindness precluded the use of napkins and cutlery. You might do just as well eating with your feet."

Gabriel went very still. The taut skin around his scar blanched, making the devil's mark look even more forbidding. In that moment, Samantha was rather glad he didn't have a knife.

Draping one long arm over the back of the chair next to him, he angled his entire body toward the sound of her voice. Although she knew he couldn't see her, his focus was so intent Samantha still had to fight the urge to squirm. "I must confess that you intrigue me, Miss Wickersham. Your tones are cultured, but I can't quite identify your accent. Were you raised in the city?"

"Chelsea," she offered, doubting he'd had much occasion to frequent the modest borough on the north side of London. She took an overly generous gulp of the tea, burning her tongue.

"I'm quite curious to know how a woman of your, um . . . *character* came to seek such a post. What was it that drove you to answer such a calling? Was it Christian charity? An overwhelming desire to help your fellow man? Or perhaps your tender compassion for the infirm?"

Carving a spoonful of egg out of its china cup, Samantha said crisply, "I provided Mr. Beckwith with several letters of reference. I'm sure you'll find them in order."

"In case you haven't noticed," Gabriel replied, his voice gently mocking, "I wasn't able to read those. Perhaps you could enlighten me as to their contents."

She laid aside her spoon. "As I informed Mr. Beckwith, I served as governess for Lord and Lady Carstairs for nearly two years."

"I know of the family."

Samantha tensed. He might know *of* them, but did he *know* them? "After the hostilities with the French resumed, I read in *The Times* how so many of our noble soldiers and sailors were suffering from lack of care. So I decided to offer my services to a local hospital."

"I still don't understand why you'd trade spooning pabulum into the mouths of babes for dressing bloody wounds and holding the hands of men half out of their minds with pain."

Samantha struggled to purge the passion from her voice. "Those men were willing to sacrifice everything for king and country. How could I not offer a small sacrifice of my own?"

He snorted. "The only thing they sacrificed was their good judgment and common sense. They sold them to the Royal Navy for a starched bolt of blue broadcloth and a shiny bit of gold braid on their shoulders."

She frowned, appalled by his cynicism. "How can you say such a cruel thing? Why, the king himself lauded you for your own valor!"

"That shouldn't surprise you. The Crown has a long history of rewarding dreamers and fools."

Forgetting that he couldn't see her, Samantha rose halfway out of her chair. "Not fools! Heroes! Heroes like your very own commander—Admiral Lord Nelson himself!"

"Nelson is dead," he said flatly. "I can't say if that makes him any more of a hero or less of a fool."

Defeated for the moment, she sank back into her chair.

Gabriel rose, using the backs of the chairs to feel his way around the table. As his powerful hands closed around the carved finials of her own chair, it was all Samantha could do not to bolt. Instead, she stared straight ahead, each shallow breath audible to her own ears as well as his.

He leaned down so far his lips came dangerously close to brushing the top of her head. "I'm sure your devotion to your calling is sincere, Miss Wickersham. But as far as I'm concerned, until you come to your senses and resign your post here, you have only one duty." He spoke softly, each word more damning than a shout. "To stay the bloody hell out of my way."

He left her with that warning, brushing past the footman who scrambled forward to offer his arm. Although she supposed it shouldn't surprise her that he would choose to blunder his way through the dark rather than accept a helping hand, she still flinched when a loud crash resounded from somewhere in the house.

Samantha was left with nothing to do with her morning but wander the darkened chambers of Fairchild Park. The hush was nearly as oppressive as the gloom. There was none of the efficient bustle one might expect from a thriving Buckinghamshire country house. There were no chambermaids briskly running feather dusters over the banisters and wainscoting, no red-faced laundry maids trudging up the stairs with baskets of fresh linen, no footmen bearing armloads of firewood to stoke the fireplaces. Every hearth she passed was cold and dark, its embers crumbled to ash. Carved cherubs gazed at her dolefully from ornate marble chimneypieces, their plump cheeks smudged with soot.

The handful of servants she encountered seemed to be creeping about with no particular task in mind. Upon spotting her, they would melt back into the shadows, their voices never raised above a whisper. None of them seemed to be in any rush to fetch a broom to sweep up the splintered furniture and broken shards of porcelain that littered the floors.

Samantha swept open a pair of double doors at the end of a

shadow-draped gallery. Marble stairs spilled down into a vast ballroom. She had allowed herself little enough time for whimsy during the dark winter months, but for just a heartbeat she couldn't resist closing her eyes. She imagined the room awash in a swirl of colors and music and merry chatter, imagined herself being swept around the gleaming floor in a man's strong arms. She could see him smiling down at her, see herself laughing up at him as she reached to tweak the gold braid adorning his broad shoulders.

Samantha's eyes flew open. Shaking her head at her folly, she slammed the ballroom doors. This was the earl's fault. If he would allow her to perform her duties as she was hired to do, she might be able to keep her treacherous imagination in check.

She was marching through a spacious drawing room, paying no more heed to her surroundings than Gabriel would have, when her foot slammed into an overturned pier table. Letting out an infuriated yelp, she hopped up and down on one foot, massaging her throbbing toes through the scuffed leather of her boots. If she had been wearing kid slippers, the blow probably would have broken them.

Eyeing the slivers of sunlight fighting to penetrate the smothering weight of the velvet drapes, Samantha rested her hands on her hips. Gabriel might choose to entomb himself in this mausoleum, but she most certainly did not.

Catching a flash of white out of the corner of her eye, she whirled around to discover a mobcapped maid tiptoeing past the door.

Samantha called after her, "Girl! You there!"

The maid stopped and slowly turned, her reluctance palpable. "Yes, miss?"

"Come here, please. I need your help to get these drapes open." Grunting with effort, Samantha shoved a fat brocaded ottoman toward the window.

Instead of rushing to assist her, the maid began to back away, wringing her pale, freckled hands and shaking her head in dismay. "I don't dare, miss. What would the master say?"

"He might say you were doing your job," Samantha ventured, clambering up on top of the ottoman.

Growing impatient with the maid's dallying, she reached up, grabbed two fistfuls of curtain, and yanked with all of her might. Instead of gliding open, the drapes tore right out of their moorings. They billowed down in a choking cloud of velvet and dust, making Samantha sneeze.

Sunlight came streaming through the floor-to-ceiling French windows, weaving the dust motes into sparkling fairy glamour.

"Oh, miss, you shouldn't have!" the maid cried, blinking like some forest creature that had been living underground for a very long time. "I'm going to fetch Mrs. Philpot right away!"

Swiping her hands on her skirt, Samantha hopped off the ottoman and surveyed her handiwork with satisfaction. "Why don't you do just that? I'd like nothing better than to have a little chat with the dear woman."

With one last inarticulate cry, the wild-eyed girl went dashing from the room.

When Mrs. Philpot came sailing into the drawing room a short while later, it was to find the earl's new nurse balanced precariously on the seat of a delicate Louis XIV chair. The housekeeper could only look on in horror as Samantha gave the drapes she was holding a fierce tug. They collapsed on her head, burying her in a cloud of emerald green velvet.

"Miss Wickersham!" Mrs. Philpot exclaimed, lifting a hand to shield her eyes from the blinding sunshine that came streaming through the French windows. "What is the meaning of this?"

Climbing down from her perch, Samantha batted away the heavy folds of fabric. Following the housekeeper's scandalized gaze, she gave the pile of drapes heaped in the center of the floor an apologetic nod. "I was only going to open them, but after I saw all the dust, I realized they could use a good airing out as well."

Resting her hand on the ring of keys at her waist as if it were the pommel of a sword, Mrs. Philpot drew herself up. "*I* am the head housekeeper at Fairchild Park. *You* are the master's nurse. Airing things out is hardly within the jurisdiction of your duties."

Eyeing the woman warily, Samantha unlatched the window and shoved it open. A gentle breeze, scented with lilac, wafted into the room. "Perhaps not. But the well-being of my patient is. Light might be lost to your master, but there's no reason fresh air should be. Clearing out his lungs might just improve his condition . . . and his disposition."

For a moment, Mrs. Philpot looked almost intrigued.

Encouraged by her hesitation, Samantha began to circle the room, enthusiastically pantomiming her plans. "First, I thought we'd have the maids sweep up all the glass while the footmen cart away the broken furniture. Then, after we've stored away the breakables, we could shove the heavy furniture against the walls, clearing a path through each room for the earl to traverse."

"The earl spends the majority of his time in his bedchamber."

"Can you blame him?" Samantha asked, blinking incredulously. "How would you feel if every time you stepped outside your own bedchamber, you risked barking your shins or cracking open your skull?"

"The master was the one who ordered that the drapes be kept drawn. He was the one who insisted that everything be left as it was before . . . before . . ." The housekeeper swallowed, unable to finish. "I'm sorry, but I can't be a party to defying his wishes. Nor can I order my staff to do so."

"So you won't help me?"

Mrs. Philpot shook her head, genuine regret darkening her gray eyes. "I cannot."

"Very well." Samantha nodded. "I respect your loyalty to your employer and your devotion to your job."

With those words, she turned on her heel, marched to the next window, and began to tug at the heavy drapes.

"What are you doing?" Mrs. Philpot cried as the curtains came cascading down.

Samantha tossed the armful of velvet on top of the heap, then wrenched open the window to invite in a flood of sunshine and fresh air. She turned to face Mrs. Philpot, briskly dusting off her hands. "*My* job."

"Is she still at it?" whispered one of the scullery maids to a rosy-cheeked footman as he entered the expansive basement kitchens of Fairchild Park.

" 'Fraid so," he whispered back, stealing a steaming sausage from her tray and popping it into his mouth. "Can't you hear?"

Although darkness had fallen nearly an hour ago, mysterious noises continued to echo through the first floor of the house. The bumping, jingling, grunting, and the occasional scrape of a heavy piece of furniture being dragged across a parquet floor had been going on since morning.

The servants had spent that day as they'd spent most of their days since Gabriel's return from the war—huddled around the old oak table in front of the kitchen fire in the servants' hall, remembering better times. On this chilly spring evening, Beckwith and Mrs. Philpot sat directly across from each other, drinking one cup of tea after another, neither one speaking or daring to meet the others' eyes.

After a particularly jarring thump that made them all flinch, one of the upstairs chambermaids whispered, "Don't you think we should—"

Mrs. Philpot turned a basilisk glare on her, paralyzing the poor child where she stood. "I think we should tend to our own affairs."

One of the young footmen stepped forward, daring to ask the one question they'd all been dreading. "What if the master hears?"

Drawing off his spectacles to polish them on his sleeve, Beckwith shook his head sadly. "It's been a long time since the master has paid any heed to what goes on around here. There's no reason to believe tonight will be any different."

His words cast a cloud of dejection over them all. They had once prided themselves on their devotion to the great house entrusted to their care. But with no one to see how the woodwork gleamed beneath their loving attentions, no one to praise their efficiency in keeping the floors swept or the fireplaces laid with fresh kindling, there was little reason to bestir themselves from their moping.

They barely noticed when one of the youngest housemaids came creeping into the kitchens. Going straight to Mrs. Philpot, she bobbed one curtsy, then another, plainly too timid to ask for permission to speak.

"Don't just stand there bobbing up and down like a cork on the water, Elsie," Mrs. Philpot snapped. "What is it?"

Wringing her apron in her hands, the girl curtsied again. "I think you'd best come, ma'am, and see for yourself."

Exchanging an exasperated glance with Beckwith, Mrs. Philpot rose. Beckwith shoved himself away from the table to follow. As they left the kitchens, they were both too preoccupied to notice when the rest of the servants fell in behind them.

At the top of the basement stairs, Mrs. Philpot suddenly stopped, nearly creating a disastrous chain reaction. "Shhhhh! Listen!" she commanded.

They all held their breath, but heard only one thing.

Silence.

As their hushed parade passed through room after room, their shoes no longer crunched over shattered and splintered debris. Moonlight streamed through the unveiled windows, revealing that the floors had been swept clean and the broken furniture separated into two tidy piles—one with the pieces considered salvageable and the other useful for nothing but kindling. Although some of the heaviest pieces remained, a path had been cleared through most of the rooms, with all of the fragile objects banished to the highest perches of mantel and bookshelf. Any rug whose braided hem or fringe might catch an unsuspecting foot had also been rolled up and shoved against the wall.

It was in a pale puddle of moonlight in the library that they found their master's new nurse curled up on an ottoman, sound asleep. The servants gathered around her, openly gawking.

The earl's previous nurses had been content to occupy that rather murky social strata usually reserved for governesses or tutors. They certainly weren't considered equal to their employer, but nor did they deign to lower themselves by associating with the other servants. They took their meals in their rooms and would have gasped with horror at the prospect of turning their soft white hands to such menial tasks as sweeping floors or dragging heavy curtains out into the yard for an airing.

Miss Wickersham's hands were no longer soft or white. The pale ovals of her fingernails were broken and rimmed with dirt. A bloody blister had formed on her right hand, between thumb and forefinger. Her spectacles sat askew on her nose and as they watched, a gentle snore sent the limp tendril of hair that had fallen over her nose floating up, then back down again.

"Should I wake her?" Elsie whispered.

"I doubt that you could," Beckwith said softly. "The poor child is plainly exhausted." He crooked a finger at one of the larger footmen. "Why don't you carry Miss Wickersham up to her room, George? Take one of the maids with you."

"I'll go," Elsie said eagerly, forgetting her shyness.

As the footman gathered Miss Wickersham into his burly arms, one of the scullery maids reached up to gently correct the angle of her spectacles.

After they were gone, Mrs. Philpot continued to stare down at the ottoman, her expression unreadable.

Sidling closer to her, Beckwith awkwardly cleared his throat. "Shall I dismiss the rest of the servants for the night?"

The housekeeper slowly lifted her head. Her gray eyes had gone steely with determination. "I should say not. There's much work yet to be done and I won't have them loafing about any longer, leaving their duties to their betters." She snapped her fingers at the two remaining footmen. "Peter, you and Phillip take that chaise longue and shove it against the wall." Exchanging a grin, the twins hastened to take up each end of the heavy couch. "Careful, now!" she chided. "If you nick the rosewood, I'll take the cost of repairs out of your wages *and* your hides."

Rounding on the startled maids, she clapped her hands, the sound echoing through the library like a gunshot. "Betsy, Jane, fetch us a pair of mops, some rags, and a bucket of hot water. My mum always said that there's no point in sweeping if you're not going to mop. And now that we've got the curtains down, the windows will be that much easier to wash." When the maids just stood gaping at her, she began to shoo them toward the door with her apron. "Don't just stand there with your mouths hanging open like a pair of beached trout. Go. *Go!*"

Mrs. Philpot marched to one of the casement windows and threw it open. "Ah!" she exclaimed, her chest expanding as she drew in an intoxicating breath of the lilac-scented night air. "Perhaps by morning this house won't smell like an open grave any longer."

Beckwith trotted after her. "Have you lost your wits, Lavinia? What are we going to tell the master?"

"Oh, we're not going to tell him anything." Mrs. Philpot nodded toward the doorway where Miss Wickersham had disappeared, a sly smile curving her lips. "*She* is."

⇜ Chapter 3 ⇝

My dear Miss March,

*I must confess that since I first laid eyes on you, I've thought of
nothing—and no one—else . . .*

Gabriel came creeping down the stairs the next morning, sniffing
at the air with each step. He flared his nostrils, but couldn't detect
so much as a whiff of lemon. Perhaps Miss Wickersham had
heeded his warning and taken her leave. With any luck, he would
never again have to tolerate her impertinence. The thought left him
feeling curiously empty. He must be hungrier than he realized.

Abandoning any attempt at stealth, he charged toward the
drawing room, already bracing himself for his shins' first impact
with some immovable piece of furniture. In truth, he welcomed
the pain it would bring. Every fresh bruise or scrape only served to
remind him he was still alive.

But there was no preparing himself for the blow to come. As he
crossed the drawing room without encountering so much as a
wayward footstool to break his stride, a lance of sunlight struck
him full in the face. Gabriel staggered to a halt, throwing up a

hand to shield his face from its dazzling warmth. He instinctively squeezed his eyes shut, but could do nothing to defend against the cheery lilt of birdsong or the lilac-scented breeze caressing his skin.

For a minute he believed he was still dreaming in his bed. Believed he would open his eyes and find himself lying in a shimmering green meadow beneath the silky white blossoms of a pear tree. But when he opened them, it was still night, despite the treacherous warmth of the sun on his face.

"Beckwith!" he bellowed.

Someone tapped him on the shoulder. Without thinking, Gabriel swung around and made a grab for his assailant. Although his hands closed on empty air, the tart tang of lemon still tickled his nostrils.

"Hasn't anyone ever told you it's extremely bad form to sneak up on a blind man?" he snarled.

"Dangerous, too, it would seem." Although that all-too-familiar voice lacked none of its usual asperity, there was a breathless quality to it that made his pulse quicken.

Struggling to tame more than just his temper, Gabriel took several steps backward. Since it was impossible to escape the seductive warmth of the sunlight, he deliberately turned the left side of his face away from the sound of her voice. "Where in the devil is Beckwith?"

"I'm not sure, my lord," his nurse confessed. "There seems to be some sort of curious malady going around this morning. Breakfast isn't prepared and most of the servants are still abed."

He spread his arms wide and executed a full turn, not hitting a single object in any direction. "Then perhaps the more appropriate question should be: *Where is my furniture?*"

"Oh, don't worry. It's still here. We just pushed most of it against the walls so it wouldn't be in your way any longer."

"*We?*"

"Well, mostly me." For a rewarding second, she sounded

nearly as confounded as he felt. "Although it seems the servants must have decided to lend a helping hand after I was abed."

Gabriel blew out a sigh fraught with exaggerated patience. "If all of the rooms are exactly the same, how am I to know whether I'm in the drawing room or the library? Or in the compost heap out behind the house, for that matter?"

For one blissful moment, he actually succeeded in rendering her speechless. "Why, I never thought of that!" she finally said. "Perhaps we should have the footmen drag a few pieces toward the middle of each room to serve as landmarks." Her skirts rustled as she paced around him, plainly engrossed in her plans. Gabriel turned with her, keeping his right side to the sound. "If we pad the sharp corners with quilts, then you would still be able to negotiate the house without risking an injury. Especially if you learn to count."

"I can assure you, Miss Wickersham, that I learned to count in the nursery."

It was her turn to sigh. "I meant to count your steps. If you memorize the number of steps it takes to get from room to room, you'll be able to keep your bearings."

"That would be a refreshing change. I've certainly lost them since you set foot in my house."

"Why do you keep doing that?" she suddenly asked, genuine curiosity softening her voice.

He frowned, struggling to follow the gentle tap of her footsteps as she circled him. "Doing what?"

"Turning away from me when I move. If I go left, you turn right. And vice versa."

He stiffened. "I'm blind. How can you expect me to know which way I'm turning?" Eager to deflect her questions, he said, "Perhaps you should be the one explaining why someone deliberately defied my orders and opened the windows in here."

"I was the one who defied your orders. As your nurse, I thought a little sunshine and fresh air might improve your . . .

your . . ."—she cleared her throat as if something had gotten hung in it—"your circulation."

"My circulation is just fine, thank you very much. And a blind man has little need of sunshine. It's nothing but a cruel reminder of all the beauties he'll never see again."

"Perhaps that's true, but it's hardly fair of you to drag your entire household down into the darkness with you."

For a stunned minute, Gabriel couldn't speak at all. Since he'd returned from Trafalgar, everyone had been tiptoeing and whispering around him. No one, not even his family, had dared to address him so bluntly.

He turned fully toward the sound of her voice, allowing the ruthless rays of sunshine to sear his face. "Did it never occur to you that I kept the drapes drawn not for my benefit, but for theirs? Why should they have to look upon me in the daylight? At least I have the blessing of blindness to shield me from my hideous disfigurement."

Miss Wickersham's reaction to his words and his face was the last one he expected. She burst out laughing. Her laugh wasn't what he expected, either. Instead of a dry cackle, it was a bawdy, full-throated song that both mocked and stirred him, proving his circulation was even better than he realized.

"Is that what they told you?" she asked, merry little ripples of laughter still escaping her as she fought to catch her breath. "That you were 'hideously disfigured'?"

He scowled. "No one had to tell me. I may be blind, but I'm not deaf or stupid. I could hear the physicians whispering over my bed. When the last of the bandages came off, I heard my mother and sisters gasp in horror. I could feel the cruel stares on my skin when the footmen carried me from the hospital bed to my carriage. Even my own family can hardly bear to look upon me. Why do you think they've locked me away here like some sort of animal in a cage?"

"As far as I can tell, you're the one who locked the cage doors and barred the windows. Perhaps it's not your face your family fears, but your temper."

Gabriel groped for her hand, capturing it on the third try. He was startled by how small, yet firm, it felt in his grip.

She let out a startled yelp of protest as he yanked her into motion. Instead of her leading him through the house, he led her, halfway dragging her up the stairs and down the long hallway that housed the family portrait gallery. He had learned every nook and cranny of Fairchild Park as a boy and that knowledge still served him well. He marched her down the gallery, measuring his long strides until they reached the end of the hall. He knew exactly what she would find there—a large portrait, veiled by a linen sheet.

He was the one who had ordered the portrait covered. He couldn't bear the thought of anyone gazing upon it and wistfully remembering the man he had been. If he hadn't been such a sentimental fool, he would have had it destroyed, just as he had been.

He groped for the edge of the sheet, then snatched it away. "There! What do you think of my face now?"

Gabriel stepped back to lean against the gallery rail, allowing her to study the portrait without him breathing down her neck. He didn't need his sight to know exactly what she was seeing. He had gazed at that same face in the mirror every day for almost thirty years.

He knew the way shadow and light played over every beautifully sculpted plane and hollow. He knew the tantalizing hint of a dimple in its rugged jaw. His mother had always sworn he'd been kissed by an angel while still in her womb. At least once a golden haze of beard-shadow had started to darken that jaw, his sisters could no longer accuse him of being prettier than them.

He knew that face and he knew its effect on women. From the maiden aunts who could never resist pinching his rosy cheeks when he'd been a babe to the debutantes who giggled and blushed as he doffed his hat to them in Hyde Park to the beautiful women who had eagerly tumbled into his bed for little more than the price of a dizzying turn around the ballroom and a seductive smile.

He doubted even the prickly Miss Wickersham could resist its charms.

She studied the portrait in silence for a long time. "He's handsome enough, I suppose," she finally said, her voice musing, "if you fancy the sort."

Gabriel frowned. "And just what sort might that be?"

He could almost hear her pondering her words. "His face lacks character. He's someone to whom everything has come too easily. He's no longer a boy, but not yet a man. I'm sure he'd be pleasant enough company for a stroll in the park or an evening at the theater, but I don't think he's someone I would care to know."

Gabriel reached toward the sound of her voice, his hand closing over the soft part of her upper arm through the wool of her sleeve. He tugged her around to face him, genuinely curious. "What do you see now?"

This time there was no hesitation in her voice. "I see a man," she said softly. "A man with the roar of cannons still ringing in his ears. A man bloodied by life, but not beaten. A man with a scar that draws his mouth into a frown when he might actually long to smile." She ran a fingertip lightly along that scar, raising gooseflesh on every inch of Gabriel's body.

Shocked by the intimacy of her touch, he caught her hand in his, drawing it down between them.

She quickly tugged it out of his grasp, the briskness returning to her voice. "I see a man in desperate want of a shave and a clean change of clothing. You know, there's really no need for you to go wandering about looking as if you'd been dressed—"

"By a blind man?" he dryly provided, as relieved as she was to return to familiar footing.

"Have you no valet?" she asked.

Feeling a determined tug on the cravat he'd fished off the floor of his bedchamber and draped carelessly around his neck, he batted her hand away. "I dismissed him. I can't stand to have anyone hovering over me as if I'm some helpless invalid."

She chose to ignore that particular warning shot fired across her bow. "I can't imagine why. Most gentlemen of your station with two perfectly good eyes are quite content to stand with their arms outstretched and be dressed as if they were children. If you won't stand for a valet, I can at least have the footmen draw you a hot bath. Unless you have some objection to bathing as well."

Gabriel was about to point out that the only thing he had an objection to was *her* when a new thought struck him. Perhaps there was more than one way to goad her into giving notice.

"A nice hot bath might be just the thing," he said, deliberately injecting a silky note into his voice. "Of course, there are many hazards in the bath for a blind man. What if I should stumble climbing into the tub and strike my head? What if I should slip beneath the water and drown? What if I should . . . drop the soap? I can hardly be expected to retrieve it myself." He fumbled for her hand again, this time bringing it to his mouth and flowering his lips against the sensitive skin at the center of her palm. "As my nurse, Miss Wickersham, I think it only fitting that *you* should bathe me."

Instead of slapping him for his impertinence as he deserved, she simply wrestled her hand away from him and said sweetly, "I'm sure my services won't be required. One of those strapping young footmen of yours should be only too delighted to retrieve the soap for you."

She had been right about one thing. Suddenly Gabriel did want to smile. As he heard her determined footsteps marching briskly down the stairs, it was all he could do to keep from laughing out loud.

Samantha held her candlestick aloft, bathing the portrait of Gabriel Fairchild in a flickering veil of light. The house lay dark and silent around her, sleeping, just as she hoped its master was.

After their earlier encounter, the earl had spent the entire day barricaded in the stifling gloom of his bedchamber, refusing to emerge even for meals.

Tilting her head to the side, Samantha studied the portrait, wishing she were as immune to its charms as she'd pretended to be. Although it was dated 1803, it might as well have been painted a lifetime ago. The faint hint of arrogance in Gabriel's boyish smile was tempered by the twinkle of self-mocking humor in his light green eyes. Eyes that looked toward the future and all it would bring with eagerness and hope. Eyes that had never seen things they shouldn't have and paid the price with their sight.

Samantha reached up and drew a fingertip down his unblemished cheek. But this time there was no warmth, no staggering jolt of awareness. There was only cool canvas mocking her wistful touch.

"Goodnight, sweet prince," she whispered as she gently draped the sheet over the portrait.

The tender green mint of spring drenched the rolling meadows. Fluffy white clouds frisked like lambs across a sky of pastel blue. Pale yellow sunshine bathed his face in warmth. Gabriel rolled to one elbow and gazed down at the woman napping in the grass next to him. A pear blossom had drifted down to nestle in her upswept curls. His thirsty eyes drank in the warm honey gold of her hair, the downy peach of her cheek, the moist coral of her parted lips.

He'd never seen a hue quite so delectable . . . or so tempting.

As he lowered his lips to hers, her eyes fluttered open and her lips curved in a sleepy smile, deepening the dimples he adored. But just as she reached for him, a cloud came billowing across the sun, its inescapable shadow draining all the color from his world.

Swallowed by darkness, Gabriel sat bolt upright in his bed, the rasp of his breathing harsh in the silence. He had no way of knowing if it was morning or night. He only knew he'd been cast out of his only retreat from the darkness—his dreams.

Tossing back the blankets, he swung his legs over the side of the bed and sat up. He dropped his head into his hands, fighting to get both his breath and his bearings. He couldn't help but wonder what Miss Wickersham might make of his current attire. At the moment, he wore nothing at all. Perhaps he should knot a clean cravat around his neck so as not to offend her delicate sensibilities.

After much fumbling and groping, he finally located the rumpled dressing gown draped across the foot of the bed and slipped into it. Without bothering to knot the sash, he rose and padded heavily across the room. Still disoriented by his abrupt awakening, he misjudged the distance between bed and writing desk. His toes slammed into one of the desk's clawed feet, sending a tingling jolt of agony up his leg. Biting off an oath, he sank down in the desk chair and groped for the center drawer's ivory knobs.

He felt inside the velvet-lined drawer, knowing exactly what he would find—a thick packet of letters tied with a single silk ribbon. As he drew it out, tantalizing tendrils of fragrance wafted to his nose.

This was no penny lemon verbena purchased from some common street vendor, but a woman's scent—rich and floral and seductive.

Breathing deeply, Gabriel tugged loose the silk ribbon and ran his hands over the expensive linen stationery. The paper was crumpled and worn from the many months he'd carried the letters next to his heart. He smoothed one of them open, tracing the graceful loops of ink with his fingertip. If he concentrated hard enough, he might be able to make out a single word or perhaps even a familiar phrase.

Meaningless words. Empty phrases.

His hand curled into a loose fist. He slowly refolded the letter, thinking how ludicrous it was for a blind man to hoard letters he could no longer read from a woman who no longer loved him.

If she ever truly had.

Even so, he painstakingly tied the ribbon around the letters before dropping them gently back into the drawer.

⇐ *Chapter 4* ⇒

My dear Miss March,

Dare I hope that you would allow me to woo you with honeyed words?

When Gabriel emerged from his bedchamber the next morning, desperate for a brief respite from his own company, his suspicious sniffing yielded only the mingled aromas of bacon and chocolate. He cautiously followed them to the dining room, wondering just where Miss Wickersham might be lurking. To his surprise, he was allowed to breakfast in peace without anyone critiquing his table manners or his attire. He ate hastily and with even less finesse than usual, hoping to make it back to the haven of his bedchamber before his overbearing nurse could come springing out at him.

After swiping the grease from his mouth with a corner of the table linens, he went hurrying back up the stairs. But when he reached for the ornately carved mahogany door that led to the master bedchamber, his hands met only air.

Gabriel recoiled, fearing that in his haste he'd taken a wrong turn somewhere along the way.

A cheery voice sang out, "Good morning, my lord!"

"And a good morning to you, Miss Wickersham," he replied through gritted teeth.

He took one tentative step forward, then another, robbed of his confidence by the treacherous warmth of the sunlight on his face, the gentle breeze caressing his brow, the melodic chirping of some bird perched just outside the open window of his bed-chamber.

"I hope you don't mind the intrusion," she said. "I thought we'd air out your chambers while you were downstairs at break-fast."

"We?" he repeated ominously, wondering just how many witnesses there were going to be to her murder.

"Surely you didn't expect me to do all the work by myself! Peter and Phillip are preparing your morning bath while Elsie and Hannah change the linens on your bed. Mrs. Philpot and Meg are out in the yard airing out your bed hangings. And dear Millie is dusting your sitting room."

The splash of water and the brisk flapping of sheets confirmed her claims. Gabriel took a deep breath—a breath poisoned by the sweet tang of lemon verbena and laundry starch. As he exhaled, he heard a rustling from the direction of his dressing room like the sound a rat might make. A very plump, balding rat, wearing a waistcoat.

"Beckwith?" Gabriel barked.

The rustling ceased, fading to stony silence.

Gabriel sighed. "You might as well come out, Beckwith. I can smell your hair pomade."

Shuffling steps informed him that the butler had come creep-ing out of the dressing room. Before his nurse could offer some cheery explanation for his presence there, Beckwith said, "Since you don't wish to have a valet hovering over you, my lord, Miss Wickersham suggested that we group your clothing according to type and color. Then you should be able to dress yourself without the aid of a manservant."

"And you were kind enough to volunteer for the task. *Et tu, Brute?*" Gabriel murmured.

Not only had his new nurse invaded his only remaining sanctuary, she had enlisted his own servants to lead the charge. He wondered how she had managed to earn their loyalty so quickly. Perhaps he had underestimated her charms. She might be a more dangerous adversary than he'd suspected.

"Leave us," he commanded curtly.

A frantic bustle of activity that involved much rustling of sheets and clanking of buckets informed him that the servants weren't even going to pretend to misunderstand him.

"My lord, I really don't think . . ." Beckwith attempted. "I mean, it's hardly proper to leave you alone in your bedchamber with—"

"Are you afraid to be alone with me?"

Miss Wickersham didn't pretend to misunderstand him, either. He was probably the only one who noted her slight hesitation. "Of course not."

"You heard her," he said. "Go. All of you." The air stirred as the servants rushed past him. As he heard the last of their footsteps fade away down the corridor, he asked, "Are they gone?"

"They are."

Gabriel fumbled behind him until he found the doorknob. He dragged the door shut with a thunderous bang, then leaned against it, cutting off her only hope of escape. "Did it never occur to you, Miss Wickersham," he said tautly, "that I might have left my door closed for a reason? That I might have wished for my bedchamber to be left undisturbed? That I might cherish my privacy?" His voice rose. "That I might prefer to keep some small corner of my life free from your meddling influence?"

"I should think you'd be grateful." She sniffed pointedly. "At least it no longer smells as if you've been keeping goats in here."

He glowered in her general direction. "At the moment I would much prefer the company of goats."

He actually heard her open her mouth, then snap it shut. She paused precisely long enough to count to ten before attempting to speak again. "Perhaps the two of us simply got off on the wrong foot, my lord. You seem to have received the mistaken impression that I came to Fairchild Park to make your life more difficult."

"The words 'a living hell' have come to mind more than once since your arrival."

She blew out a gusty sigh. "Contrary to what you may believe, I took this position so I could bring more ease to your life."

"Just when were you planning to start?"

"As soon as you'll allow me," she retorted. "Rearranging the house for your convenience can be just the beginning. Why, I could help alleviate your boredom by taking you for walks in the garden, assisting you with your correspondence, reading aloud to you."

Books were yet another cruel reminder of a pleasure he could no longer enjoy. "No, thank you. I won't be read to as if I were some dull-witted child." As he folded his arms over his chest, even Gabriel knew he was behaving like one.

"Very well. But even so, there are a hundred other things I can do to help you adjust to your blindness."

"That won't be necessary."

"Why not?"

"Because I have no intention of living the rest of my life this way!" Gabriel roared, his control finally snapping.

As the echo of his shout died, the silence swelled between them.

He sank against the door, raking a hand through his hair. "At this very moment, even as we speak, a team of physicians hired by my father is traveling through Europe, gathering all the information they can find on my condition. They're scheduled to return here within the fortnight. At that time they will confirm what I've always suspected—that my affliction isn't permanent, but is only a temporary aberration."

In that moment, Gabriel was almost thankful he couldn't see her eyes. He was afraid he'd find in their depths the one torment she'd spared him thus far—her pity. He would almost prefer her laughter.

"Do you know what the best thing about getting my sight back will be?" he asked softly.

"No," she replied, all of the bravado gone from her voice.

Straightening, he took one step toward her, then another. She refused to give ground until he was almost on top of her. Feeling the air shift as she retreated, he clumsily flanked her until their positions were reversed and she was the one backing toward the door. "Some might believe it would be the joy of watching the sun dip below a lavender horizon at the end of a perfect summer day."

When he heard her back come up against the door, he splayed one palm against the thick mahogany behind her. "Others might judge it to be perusing the velvety petals of a ruby red rose . . ." —leaning forward until he felt the warm tickle of her breath against his face, he deepened his voice to a smoky caress—"or gazing tenderly into the eyes of a beautiful woman. But I can promise you, Miss Wickersham, that all of those pleasures will pale in comparison to the sheer unmitigated joy of being rid of you."

Sliding his hand down until he encountered the doorknob, he flung open the door, sending her stumbling backward into the hallway.

"Are you clear of the door, Miss Wickersham?"

"Pardon?" she snapped, plainly confused.

"Are you clear of the door?"

"Yes."

"Good."

Without further ado, Gabriel slammed it in her face.

* * *

Samantha was passing through the foyer later that day, on her way to retrieve Gabriel's bed hangings from the laundress, when his smoky baritone came floating down from the landing above. "So tell me, Beckwith, just what does our Miss Wickersham look like? It's straining the limits of my imagination to envision such a vexatious creature. All I can see in my mind's eye is some sort of withered crone bent over a cauldron, cackling with glee."

Samantha jerked to a halt, her heart lurching with panic. She touched a trembling hand to her heavy spectacles, then to the dull, reddish brown hair she'd wound into a tight knot at the nape of her neck.

Seized by sudden inspiration, she drifted back into Beckwith's line of vision and pressed a finger to her lips, silently pleading with him not to reveal her presence. Gabriel was leaning against the wall, his imposing arms folded over his chest.

The butler drew out his handkerchief and mopped his damp brow, plainly torn between loyalty to his master and Samantha's beseeching gaze. "As nurses go, I suppose you could describe her as rather . . . nondescript."

"Come, now, Beckwith. Surely you can do better than that. Is her hair icy blond? Or faded gray? Or black as soot? Does she wear it cropped? Or wound around her head in a strangling crown of braids? Is she as shrunken and bony as she sounds?"

Beckwith shot Samantha a frantic look over the banister. In reply, she puffed out her cheeks and drew a huge circle around herself with her hands.

"Oh, no, my lord. She's a rather . . . l-l-large woman."

Gabriel frowned. "How large?"

"Oh, about . . ." Samantha held up ten fingers, then eight. "About eighty stone," Beckwith finished confidently.

"Eighty stone! Good God, man! I've ridden ponies smaller than that."

Samantha rolled her eyes and tried again.

"Not eighty stone, my lord," Beckwith said slowly, his gaze riveted on her flashing fingers. "Eighteen."

Gabriel stroked his chin. "That's odd. She's rather light on her feet for such a large woman, don't you think? When I took her hand, I would have sworn . . ." He shook his head as if to clear it of some inexplicable notion. "What of her face?"

"We-e-e-e-ell," Beckwith said, stalling for time as Samantha closed her fingertips over her pert nose and made a tugging motion. "She has a rather long, pointy nose."

"I knew it!" Gabriel exclaimed triumphantly.

"And teeth like . . ." Beckwith narrowed his eyes in bewilderment as Samantha crooked two fingers over her head. "A donkey?" he ventured.

Shaking her head, she curled her hands into paws and made tiny hopping motions.

"A rabbit!" Finally getting into the spirit of the game, Beckwith stopped himself just short of clapping his plump hands. "She has teeth like a rabbit!"

Gabriel snorted with satisfaction. "No doubt perfectly suiting her long, horsey face."

Samantha tapped her chin.

"And on her chin," the butler continued, his enthusiasm mounting, "there's an enormous wart with . . ." Samantha put her hand under her chin and wiggled three fingers. "Three curly hairs growing out of it!"

Gabriel shuddered. "It's even worse than I suspected. I can't imagine what possessed me to think . . ."

Beckwith blinked innocently behind his spectacles. "Think what, my lord?"

Gabriel waved away the question. "Nothing. Nothing at all. Just a consequence of spending too much time in my own company, I fear." He held up a hand. "Please spare me any more details about Miss Wickersham's appearance. Perhaps some things really are better left to the imagination."

He turned toward the stairs, his tread heavy. Samantha cupped a hand over her mouth to smother her laughter, but despite her best efforts, a squeak escaped.

Gabriel slowly pivoted on his heel. Did she imagine the flare of his nostrils? The suspicious curl of his lip? She held her breath, fearing the slightest move or wayward draft might give her away.

He cocked his head to the side. "Did you hear that, Beckwith?"

"No, my lord. I didn't hear anything. Not even the creak of a floorboard."

Gabriel's sightless gaze scanned the floor below, returning to linger near Samantha with uncanny accuracy. "Are you certain Miss Wickersham doesn't have any of the attributes of a mouse? Twitching whiskers? A passionate fondness for cheese? A tendency to creep about and spy on people, perhaps?"

Beckwith's brow was starting to glisten again. "Oh, no, my lord. She doesn't resemble a rodent in the least."

"That's fortunate. Because if she did, I might have to set a trap for her." Arching one tawny eyebrow, he turned on his heel and started up the stairs, leaving Samantha to wonder nervously just what bait he might use.

Bells were ringing, sweetly caroling their song across the countryside. Samantha rolled over and nestled deeper into her feather pillow, dreaming of a sunny Saturday morning and a church thronged with smiling people. A man stood before the altar, his broad shoulders straining the fawn linen of his morning coat. Samantha started down the long aisle, a bouquet of lilacs gripped in her trembling hands. She could sense him smiling at her, could feel his irresistible warmth tugging her toward him, but no matter how bright the sunshine streaming through the stained-glass windows or how close she drew to him, his face remained in shadow.

The ringing of the bells swelled, no longer melodious, but jarring and off-key. Their harsh, insistent jangle was joined by an even more insistent pounding on the door of her bedchamber. Samantha's eyes flew open.

"Miss Wickersham!" cried a muffled voice tinged with panic.

Samantha scrambled out of bed and rushed to the door, tossing a dressing gown over her plain cotton nightdress. She threw it open to find the earl's harried butler standing in the corridor, clutching a branch of candles in his shaking hand.

"Good heavens, what is it, Beckwith? Is the house afire?"

"No, miss, it's the master. He won't stop ringing until you come."

She rubbed at her bleary eyes. "I should have thought I'd be the last person he'd summon. Especially after all but tossing me out of his bedchamber this morning."

Beckwith shook his head, his quivering chins and red-rimmed eyes making him look only a sniffle away from bursting into tears. "I've tried to reason with him, but he insists that he wants only you."

Although his words gave Samantha pause, she simply said, "Very well. I'll be right there."

She dressed quickly, blessing the simplicity of her dark blue, high-waisted morning gown and the new French styles. At least she didn't have to squander precious time waiting for a lady's maid to lace her corset or wrestle with a hundred tiny silk-covered buttons.

When she emerged from her chamber, still tucking flyaway wisps of hair into her drooping chignon, Beckwith was waiting in the hall to escort her to Gabriel's bedside. As they hurried down a long corridor and up a broad flight of stairs to the third floor of the house, Samantha smothered a yawn with her hand. Judging from the murky light seeping through the freshly washed window on the landing, night was only just beginning its surrender to dawn.

Gabriel's bedchamber door stood ajar. If not for the vigorous jingling, Samantha might have feared finding him collapsed on the floor on the verge of death.

Instead, he was reclining against the carved teak headboard of his towering four-poster, looking in robust good health. He wore no shirt, and judging from the way the silk sheet rode low on his hips, no pantaloons, either. The candlelight cast a glowing patina over skin that already looked as if it had been sprinkled with gold dust. As her gaze was drawn to that impressive expanse of muscle and sinew, Samantha felt her mouth go dry. A sparkling mat of hair tapered to a narrow ribbon on his taut belly before disappearing beneath the sheet.

For a moment, Samantha feared Beckwith might actually drop the candles and clap his hands over her eyes. At the butler's scandalized gasp, Gabriel gave the bell in his hand one last indolent flick.

"Really, my lord!" Beckwith exclaimed, resting the branch of candles on a nearby pier table before returning to stand at rigid attention by the door. "Don't you think you should have at least covered yourself before the young lady arrived?"

Gabriel simply draped one muscular arm over the mound of pillows piled next to him, stretching like some large, lazy cat. "Forgive me, Miss Wickersham. I didn't realize you'd never seen a man shirtless before."

Thankful that he couldn't see the heat flooding her cheeks, Samantha said, "Don't be ridiculous. I've seen plenty of men without their shirts." Her cheeks grew even hotter. "I mean while performing my duties. As a nurse."

"That's very fortunate. But I still wouldn't want to offend your delicate sensibilities." Gabriel fumbled among the bedclothes until he located a rumpled cravat. He draped the scrap of cloth around his neck and tugged it into a clumsy knot before turning a devilish smile in her direction. "There. Is that better?"

Somehow he managed to look even more indecent wearing a cravat but no shirt. If this was the trap he'd set for her, he had baited it well. Refusing to be caught without a struggle, Samantha went marching over to the bed. Gabriel stiffened as she tucked one finger into his poorly made knot, tugging it loose.

Despite his wary stillness and her concerted efforts, the backs of her fingers brushed the heated velvet of his skin more than once as she fashioned the lace-edged linen into a snowy waterfall she would have dared any valet to improve.

"There," she pronounced, giving her handiwork an approving pat. "*That's* better."

Gabriel's gilt-tipped lashes were lowered over his eyes. "I'm surprised you didn't strangle me with it."

"Tempting though the prospect might be, I have no desire to seek other employment right now."

"It's rare to find a woman who can tie a cravat with such skill. Have you a father or grandfather who was a fumble-fingers?"

"Brothers," was all she offered. Straightening, she moved just out of his reach. Despite his blindness, she feared he still saw more than she wanted him to. "Now would you care to enlighten me as to why you dragged half of your household out of their warm, cozy beds before the crack of dawn?"

"If you must know, my conscience was troubling me."

"I can see why such a rare occurrence might rob you of your sleep."

Gabriel drummed his long, elegant fingers on a silk-covered bolster, his only acknowledgment of her riposte. "I was lying here all alone in my bed when I suddenly realized how unfair it was of me to hinder you in the performance of your *duties*." His sulky mouth caressed the word, sending a curious shiver down Samantha's spine. "You're obviously a woman of high moral character. It would hardly be right to expect you to sit back and collect your rather generous wages for doing nothing at all. So I decided to rectify the situation by ringing for you."

"How very thoughtful of you. And just which *duty* would you like me to perform first?"

He pondered for a moment before his face brightened. "Breakfast. In bed. On a tray. Please don't disturb Étienne this early. I'm sure you can manage. I'd like my eggs baked and my bacon lightly charred around the edges. I'd prefer my chocolate to be steaming, but not *too* hot. I don't wish to scorch my tongue."

Bemused by his high-handedness, Samantha exchanged a look with Beckwith. "Will there be anything else?" She had to bite her bottom lip to keep from adding, *Your Majesty*.

"Some kippers and two fresh-baked crossbuns, slathered with honey and butter. And once you've cleared up after breakfast, perhaps you could ring up a bath and finish dusting my sitting room." He blinked in her direction, looking as angelic as that sinister slash of a scar would allow. "If it's not too much trouble, of course."

"It's no trouble at all," she assured him. "It's my job."

"Indeed it is," he concurred.

As the right corner of his mouth curled in a devilish smile, Samantha clearly heard the sound of a trap snapping shut on her tender tail.

≈ *Chapter 5* ≈

My dear Miss March,

If you mock my honeyed words, perhaps I should try to woo you with honeyed kisses instead . . .

"Miss Wickersham? Oh, Miss Wickersham?" That plaintive refrain was accompanied by the merry jingling of Gabriel's bell.

Samantha slowly turned in the doorway of his bedchamber, still breathless from having traipsed up four flights of stairs from the basement kitchens for the third time that morning.

Her patient was propped up among the bed pillows in a pool of morning sunshine. Sprawled there on the rumpled sheets with the sunlight sifting through his tousled hair, he looked less like an invalid than a man who had just enjoyed a passionate tryst.

He held out the Wedgwood cup Samantha had just handed him, a disappointed moue turning down the unscarred corner of his mouth. "I'm afraid my chocolate is lukewarm. Would you mind asking Étienne to make a fresh pot?"

"Of course not," Samantha replied, returning to the bed and

wrenching the cup from his hand with more force than was necessary.

She hadn't even reached the top of the stairs when the bell started jingling again. She stopped and counted to ten beneath her breath before painstakingly retracing her steps. She poked her head around the doorframe. "You rang?"

Gabriel dropped the bell. "When you return, I thought that perhaps you could reorganize my wardrobe. I've decided it might be easier for me to dress myself if you grouped all of my cravats, waistcoats, and stockings together."

"I wasn't aware that you'd stirred yourself from your bed in the past week long enough to dress yourself. And I spent six hours yesterday matching your garments into complete sets because you decided you didn't care to have them sorted by type."

Gabriel sighed, his fingers plucking aimlessly at the satin coverlet. "Well, if it's too much trouble . . ." Ducking his head, he left the challenge hanging in the air between them.

She gritted her teeth in a smile that felt more like a death rictus. "I should say not. On the contrary, it will be both a privilege and a pleasure."

Before he could find the bell among the disheveled bedclothes, Samantha turned on her heel and went stalking down the stairs, wondering if she could talk the French cook into lacing his master's next pot of chocolate with hemlock.

She spent the rest of that day just as she had spent her every waking moment for the past week—at Gabriel's beck and call. Since the first morning he had summoned her, he had refused to allow her a single second to call her own. Every time she so much as thought about sitting down for a few minutes or stealing to her bedchamber for a brief nap, his bell would start ringing again. Its persistent jangling continued morning, noon, and night until the other servants were forced to sleep with their pillows pressed over their ears.

Although she knew exactly what he was trying to do, Samantha refused to let him goad her into resigning her position. She was determined to prove she was made of much sterner stuff than old Cora Gringott or the widow Hawkins. Never had a nurse been so devoted to the well-being of her charge. She bit back her every sarcastic retort and tirelessly played the roles of valet, cook, butler, and nursemaid.

Gabriel was especially peevish at bedtime. She would tuck the blankets around him and draw the bed hangings, only to have him dolefully observe that the room was getting a trifle bit stuffy. She would open the bed hangings, peel back the blankets, and crack open a window, but before she could tiptoe to the door, he would sigh and say that he feared the night air might give him a fatal chill. After covering him again, she would linger in the doorway, just waiting for those gilded lashes of his to settle against his cheeks. Then she would hurry down the stairs to her own bedchamber, already dreaming of her feather mattress and a night of uninterrupted sleep. But before her head could sink into the plush goose down of her pillow, the bell would start ringing again.

Tossing her clothes back on, Samantha would rush back up the stairs, only to find Gabriel propped against the headboard, beaming like a cherub. He hated to disturb her, he would sheepishly confess, but would she mind plumping up his pillows before she retired for the night?

That very night Samantha finally sank down in the overstuffed wing chair in Gabriel's sitting room, thinking only to prop up her aching feet for a few precious minutes.

Gabriel reclined in the bed, pretending to sleep, and waited for the telltale creak of the door. He'd grown accustomed to the cozy rustle of Miss Wickersham's skirts as she bustled about his bedchamber, blowing out candles and picking up whatever objects he'd managed to strew across the floor without actually leaving the bed. As soon as she believed him to be asleep, she would attempt to make her escape. He always knew the moment she went. Her absence left an almost palpable void.

But tonight he heard nothing.

"Miss Wickersham," he said firmly, poking his long feet out from under the blankets, "I do believe my toes are taking a chill."

He wiggled those toes, but got no response.

"Miss Wickersham?"

A gentle snore was his only reply.

Gabriel tossed back the bedclothes. Playing the invalid day and night was growing wearying in the extreme. He couldn't believe how intractable his nurse was turning out to be. The stubborn creature should have tendered her resignation days ago. Despite her gracious responses to his demands, her brittle restraint was showing signs of cracking.

Only tonight, after he had requested that she plump up his pillows for the third time in an hour, he had felt her hovering over him, pillow in hand, and had known he was one querulous demand away from being smothered to death.

He felt his way along the papered panels until he reached the sitting room that adjoined his bedchamber. The siren melody of the snores lured him to the wing chair that crouched in front of the hearth. Judging from the chill in the air, Miss Wickersham hadn't bothered to lay a fire for her own comfort.

Plagued by a stab of remorse, Gabriel knelt beside the chair. Surely only utter exhaustion could have driven his indefatigable nurse to this! He knew he should shake her awake, should insist that she get up immediately and close the window or fetch him a warm brick wrapped in wool to warm his toes. But instead he found himself reaching toward her, touching his fingers to the flyaway wisps of hair that crowned her brow. They were softer than he expected, gliding like gossamer between his fingertips.

The snoring ceased. She shifted in the chair. Gabriel held his breath, but her breathing quickly resettled into a deep and even rhythm.

His hand grazed the icy metal of her steel spectacles. Despite

Beckwith's claims, they seemed to be hanging askew on a nose far too small to bear such a weight. Gabriel gently drew them off and laid them aside, assuring himself he was only seeing to her comfort. But with her face bared to his touch, she presented a temptation too great to resist.

She had only herself to blame, he told himself firmly. If she hadn't coaxed Beckwith into playing that wicked trick on him, his curiosity about her appearance might have been satisfied.

Gabriel ran his fingertips over her cheek, startled by the downy softness of her skin. She must be far younger than her flinty voice had led him to believe.

Instead of satisfying his curiosity, his discovery only deepened it. Why would a genteel young woman choose such a thankless vocation? Had she been the victim of a father with a gambling habit or a faithless lover who had ruined her, then left her to fend for herself? If they couldn't find posts as governesses or seamstresses, such women too often ended up on the streets with no goods to sell but themselves.

His cautious exploration proved that there was nothing long or horselike about her face. Delicate bones shaped it into a perfect heart, broad at the cheek, but tapering to a rather pointed chin that betrayed no sign of a mole, hairy or otherwise. Gabriel's thumb strayed away from his other fingers only to encounter a more enticing softness.

As he ran the pad of his thumb over her plump lips, Miss Wickersham nestled her cheek into his palm, a husky little moan of contentment escaping her lips.

Gabriel froze, paralyzed by the hot surge of blood to his groin. He had boasted that his circulation was just fine, but until that moment, he hadn't realized just how very fine it was. It had been so long since he'd felt a woman's skin warm beneath his touch, felt the caress of her breath as her lips parted in invitation. Even before Trafalgar, he'd spent nearly a year at sea with only a packet of worn letters and his dreams for the future to warm him. He'd forgotten just how powerful that first sweet kick of desire could be. And how dangerous.

He yanked his hand back, thoroughly disgusted with himself. It was one thing to torment his nurse while she was awake, quite another to fondle her while she slept. He reached for her again, this time determined to shake her awake and send her to her own bedchamber before his wits could completely desert him.

She stirred and the delicate snores resumed. Gabriel sighed.

Muttering several colorful oaths beneath his breath, he fumbled his way back into the adjoining room and snatched up a quilt. He returned to the sitting room and awkwardly tucked the quilt around her before stumbling back to his own cold, empty bed.

Samantha curled deeper into her cozy nest, trying to ignore the fact that it felt as if a dozen pesky elves were doing needlework on her right foot. She didn't want to wake up, didn't want to relinquish the delicious dream still clinging to the edges of her consciousness. She couldn't remember the exact details. She only knew that in it she had felt warm and safe and loved and that letting it go would leave her with nothing but a helpless sense of longing.

Her eyes slowly fluttered open. Through the casement window, she could see the pinkish golden haze of dawn streaking the eastern horizon. She yawned and stretched her stiff muscles, trying to remember the last time she'd been allowed a full night's sleep. As she uncurled her tingling foot from beneath her, the quilt draped over her lap slid to the floor.

Samantha blinked down at the eiderdown quilt, recognizing it as just one of the many luxuriant blankets from the earl's bed. Perplexed, she instinctively reached up to pull off her spectacles. They were gone.

Feeling woefully exposed, she groped frantically in the chair around her, thinking they must have slipped off while she slept.

But when she leaned forward, she found them folded neatly on the rug beside the chair.

Suddenly wide awake, Samantha slid them on and peered warily around the sitting room. She barely remembered collapsing in the chair last night, but tantalizing fragments of her dream were returning to her—a man's warm fingers touching her hair, stroking her skin, caressing the softness of her lips. Closing her eyes, she touched two fingers to her lips, reliving both the exquisite sensation and the yearning his touch had evoked.

What if it hadn't been a dream?

Samantha's eyes flew open as she shook away the mad notion. She doubted the man sleeping in the next room was even capable of such tenderness. But that still left her with no explanation for who had covered her and removed her spectacles with such care.

Scooping up the quilt, she rose and slipped silently into the adjoining bedchamber, not sure what she hoped to find. Gabriel was sprawled on his stomach among the rumpled bedclothes, his folded arms cradling his head. The silk sheet had slipped off one thigh—a thigh rippling with muscle and dusted with the same golden hair as his chest. Samantha knew exactly how he had earned those muscles—riding, hunting, swaggering across the deck of a ship, shouting out orders to the men under his command.

She crept closer to the bed. Despite the months he'd spent cooped up in this house, the taut, smooth skin of his back hadn't completely lost its sun-kissed glow. Lured by that spill of molten gold, Samantha stretched out her hand. Although her fingertips barely brushed his flesh, a jolt of awareness sizzled through her, heating her own skin.

Appalled by her brazenness, she snatched back her hand. She tossed the quilt carelessly over him, then went scurrying for the door. She could only imagine what Mrs. Philpot and the other servants would think if they caught her creeping out of the earl's bedchamber at dawn, her face flushed and her eyes still heavy-lidded from sleep.

Clutching the banister, she went tiptoeing hastily down the stairs. She'd nearly reached her own landing when a merry jingling drifted down from the floor above. Samantha froze, seized by the sudden horrifying thought that Gabriel might have only been feigning sleep.

The bell sounded again, its shrill tones even more insistent.

Shoulders slumping, she slowly turned and went trudging back up the stairs.

By early afternoon, the bell's hellish echo seemed to have taken up permanent residence in Samantha's skull. She was on hands and knees on the floor of Gabriel's dressing room, stretching to retrieve a silk cravat that had slithered just out of her reach, when it started jangling again. She reared up, striking her head sharply on the shelf above. The shelf tilted, raining a dozen beaver hats down on top of her.

Knocking them away, she muttered, "I can't imagine why a man with one head would require so many hats."

She emerged from the stifling confines of the dressing room with her sweat-dampened hair plastered to her head and a cravat gripped in each hand like a pair of venomous snakes. "Did you ring, my lord?" she growled.

Although the sunlight filtering through the window cast a Raphaelic halo around his tousled hair, Gabriel's scarred face had settled into the saturnine lines of a despot prince accustomed to having his every whim satisfied. "I was just wondering where you'd gone off to," he said, his accusing tone even more sulky than usual.

"I was sunning myself on the beach at Brighton," she replied. "I didn't think you'd miss me."

"Has there been any word from my father or his physicians yet?"

"Not since I checked ten minutes ago."

His mouth tightened, silently reproaching her. They'd both

been in an evil temper all day. Despite having enjoyed a full night's sleep, Samantha was still haunted by that elusive fragment of a dream and the possibility that he might have felt her foolish caress. What if he thought her some pathetic, dried-up old maid, starving for a man's touch?

Desperate to reestablish some semblance of propriety between them, she said stiffly, "I've been in your dressing room for half the day, my lord, sorting your cravats by fabric and length just as you ordered me to do. Surely there's no task so urgent as to take precedence over that."

"It's very hot in here." Gabriel pressed the back of his hand to his brow. "I think I might be taking a fever." He tossed back the blankets, revealing a shameless length of well-muscled thigh. Samantha could only be grateful he'd donned a pair of breeches that morning—even if they did only cover him to the knee.

Without realizing it, she dabbed at her flushed throat with one of his cravats. "The day *is* unseasonably warm. Perhaps if I open the windows . . ."

She was halfway across the room when he snapped, "Don't bother. You know the scent of lilac will only tickle my nose and make me sneeze." Collapsing against the pillows, he lifted his hand in a desultory wave. "Perhaps you could just fan me for a while."

Samantha's jaw dropped. "Shall I pop some fresh grapes into your mouth as well?"

"If you'd like." He reached for the bell. "Shall I ring for some?"

Samantha gritted her teeth. "Why don't you try some nice cool water instead? You've a little left over from your luncheon."

After tossing the cravats over the top of the cheval glass perched in the corner, Samantha poured a goblet of water from the pitcher resting on the pier table. The thick earthenware had been designed to keep the fresh springwater cool. As she approached the bed, she couldn't quite shake the sensation that if Gabriel weren't blind, he would be eyeing her as suspiciously as she was eyeing him.

"Here you go," she said, pressing the goblet into his hand.

He refused to close his fingers around it. "Why don't you do the honors? I do believe I'm too weary." He sighed. "I didn't sleep particularly well last night. I kept dreaming there was a baby bear growling in the next room. It was most distressing."

He leaned back among the pillows, parting his lips like a fledgling awaiting a feeding from its mother. Samantha stared down at him for a long, silent moment, then upended the goblet. The chill stream of water caught Gabriel full in the face. He shot to a sitting position, sputtering and cursing.

"Damnation, woman! What are you trying to do—drown me?"

Samantha backed away from the bed, slamming the goblet back down on the edge of the table. "Drowning is too good for the likes of you. You know very well it wasn't a baby bear sleeping in the next room last night. It was me! And how dare you take such scandalous liberties with my person!"

Gabriel blinked the water from his lashes, looking both outraged and perplexed. "I haven't the faintest idea what you're talking about."

"You removed my spectacles!"

A disbelieving snort of laughter escaped him. "The way you're taking on, you'd have thought I removed your clothing!"

Samantha clutched at the high-necked bodice of her homely bottle-green day dress. "How do I know you didn't?"

Silence hung between them, thicker than the heated air. Then his smoky voice dipped into low and dangerous territory. "If I had removed your clothing, Miss Wickersham, I can assure you it would have been worth waking up for." Before Samantha could decide whether that silky boast was a promise or a threat, he continued. "All I did was remove your spectacles and cover you. I was simply trying to see to your comfort."

To her amazement, a guilty flush stained his cheekbones. She wouldn't have thought him a man capable of blushing. Both lies and half-truths should have rolled right off a tongue as nimble as his.

He settled back among the blankets, his expression more imperious than ever. "Now, if you're done with my impromptu bath, you might be so kind as to fetch me a towel."

Samantha folded her arms over her chest. "Fetch it yourself."

Gabriel arched one golden brow, stretching his scar taut. "Pardon me?"

"If you want a towel, then fetch it yourself. I'm weary of waiting on you hand and foot. You may be blind, but you still have two perfectly good arms and legs."

Proving her point, he threw back the blankets and sprang to his feet, towering over her. The bell thumped to the floor with a discordant jangle, rolling halfway across the room.

Samantha had forgotten how imposing he could be when he wasn't lolling among the sheets. Especially when shirtless and wearing only a faded pair of doeskin knee breeches. Although his nearness made her breath quicken and her skin tingle with warning, she refused to retreat so much as a single step.

"Need I remind you, Miss Wickersham, that if you don't care for the working conditions here, you have only to tender your resignation?"

"Very well, my lord," she said, an icy calm washing over her. "I believe I'll do just that. I resign."

An expression of almost comical surprise crossed his face. "What do you mean, you resign?"

"I mean that I intend to collect my wages and my things and vacate your home before nightfall. If you'd like, I'll ask Beckwith to put another advertisement in the newspaper before I go. I would suggest he offer an even more extravagant wage this time, although no amount of money would be worth putting up with your ridiculous demands for more than an hour." Turning on her heel, she started for the door.

"Miss Wickersham, get back here this instant! That's an order!"

"I quit," she tossed back over her shoulder, savage glee coursing through her veins. "I'm not obliged to take your orders anymore!" Ignoring his sputtering, Samantha marched out the door, slamming it behind her with grim satisfaction.

Gabriel stood beside the bed, the slam of the door still echoing in his ears. Everything had happened so quickly that he was still struggling to absorb it. The men who had once served under his command would have never dared to question his orders, yet his stubborn slip of a nurse had brazenly defied him.

He'd won, he reminded himself grimly. Again. She had given him exactly what he had wanted—her resignation. He should be crowing with triumph.

"*Miss Wickersham!*" he bellowed, starting after her.

The hours he'd spent languishing in the bed had wreaked havoc on both his hard-won balance and his sense of direction. He'd barely taken three steps before his ankle hooked the leg of the pier table. Both he and the table began to teeter. Something slid off of its polished surface, striking the floor in an explosion of shattering glass.

It was too late to stop his forward momentum. Gabriel fell heavily, feeling a dull sting in the vicinity of his throat as he did. He lay there for a moment, fighting to catch his breath. But when he finally struggled to rise, a crippling wave of dizziness drove him back to the floor.

His hand landed in a warm, wet puddle. For a minute, he thought it was water from the shattered pitcher and goblet. But when he rubbed his fingertips together, they came away sticky.

"I'll be damned," he muttered, realizing it was his own blood.

Damned it seemed he would be, for the blood was gathering beneath him in a rapidly spreading pool.

For one dark flash of time, he was back on the heaving deck of the *Victory,* his nostrils awash in the coppery stench of blood, not all of it his own. A terrible rushing filled his ears, like the rushing of a hungry sea eager to swallow him whole.

Gabriel stretched out one arm, seeking something he could

grasp to keep himself from sliding into that yawning abyss. His groping fingers closed over a familiar shape—the wooden handle of his bell. He dragged the bell toward him, but the effort left his weighted limb too weak to lift it.

He dropped his head, bemused by both the irony and the indignity of it all. He had survived Trafalgar only to bleed to death on his own bedchamber floor, undone by a piece of furniture and an overbearing, acid-tongued nurse. He wondered if the icy-hearted Miss Wickersham would weep at his burial. Even as he felt his life's blood seeping away, the thought almost made him smile.

"Miss Wickersham?" he called out weakly. He devoted the last of his strength to wringing one last feeble tinkle out of the bell. His voice sank to a hoarse whisper. "Samantha?"

Then both the tinkling of the bell and the rushing in his ears faded to a silence as black and all-consuming as the everpresent darkness.

⤳ *Chapter 6* ⤳

My dear Miss March,

You call me both wicked and impertinent, yet I would wager those are exactly the qualities you find most irresistible in a man . . .

"Insufferable man," Samantha muttered to herself as she shoved a sateen-lined skirt into her trunk without even bothering to fold it. She balled up a threadbare petticoat and jammed it after the skirt. "I can't imagine why I was fool enough to believe I could help him."

As she stormed across her modest bedchamber, snatching up hairpins and shoes, stockings and books, she heard an all too familiar crash from the floor above her. The ceiling shuddered, raining tiny bits of plaster down on her head.

Samantha didn't even look up. "I may be a fool, but I'll not fall for that again," she said, shaking her head. "If he wants to blunder about like a bull in a china shop, then he'll have to learn to sweep up after himself, won't he?"

She was packing books into her portmanteau when she heard

it—the muffled ringing of a bell, so soft and brief she might have imagined it. Shoving a Sir Walter Scott novel after a slim volume of Shakespeare's sonnets, she snorted. Gabriel was the fool if he thought she could actually be swayed by that pathetic tinkling.

She was so preoccupied with gathering up the contents of her dressing table that several more minutes passed before she recognized what she was hearing.

Dead silence.

Mirror and hairbrush in hand, Samantha begrudged the ceiling an uncertain glance. A prickle of foreboding inched down her spine, but she quickly dismissed it. Gabriel had probably just crawled back into his bed to sulk.

She reached for her bottle of lemon verbena, only to find her hand wavering. Sinking down on the stool in front of the dressing table, she gazed at her reflection. It was an old mirror, its glass pitted and wavy, and the woman gazing back at her seemed to be little more than a stranger. Samantha drew off her homely spectacles, but still didn't recognize the pensive expression in her eyes.

Was she being courageous or cowardly? Was she standing up to Gabriel because he was a high-handed tyrant, impossible to please, or was she running away because he had dared to put his hands on her? She touched a hand to her hair, her cheek, her lips, following the path of her dream. Somehow, Gabriel's arrogance seemed far easier to bear than his tenderness. And far less dangerous to her battered heart.

Sliding her spectacles back on, she rose to tuck the bottle of lemon verbena inside her portmanteau.

It took her less than half an hour to strip the room of every sign of her brief occupancy. She was buttoning the tiny brass buttons of her traveling spencer when someone began to bang on her bedchamber door.

"Miss Wickersham! Miss Wickersham! Are you in there?"

Plucking up her bonnet, Samantha swept open the door. "Impeccable timing, Beckwith. I was just about to ring for a footman to carry my bags downstairs."

The wild-eyed butler didn't even spare her trunk and portmanteau a bewildered glance. "You have to come with me right away, Miss Wickersham! The master needs you!"

"What is it now? Does he have a pesky itch he can't reach? Or have his cravats gone limp from too little starch?" She knotted the ribbons of her bonnet beneath her chin. "Whatever silly ruse he's concocted, I can assure you that your master has no need of me. He never did." Samantha was surprised by how much it stung to hear those words coming from her own lips.

To her shock, Beckwith, the self-appointed guardian of all things proper, clutched at her arm and attempted to drag her from the room. "Please, miss," he begged. "I don't know what else to do! I'm afraid he'll die without you!"

She dug her heels into the floor, forcing Beckwith to a halt. "Oh, please! There's no need to be so overdramatic. I'm quite sure the earl will get along famously without me. He'll hardly know I'm—" Samantha blinked at the butler, really seeing him for the first time since she'd flung open her door.

Beckwith's waistcoat was rumpled and the sparse strands of hair he nursed so lovingly were no longer plastered to his head, but sticking out in all directions, revealing the shiny pink scalp beneath. Her gaze dropped to the plump fingers clutching her sleeve. Fingers streaked with rust and already leaving a vivid smear on the drab wool of her sleeve.

Her heart thudded dully in her throat.

Wrenching her arm from his grasp, Samantha shoved past him. Snatching up her skirts, she went racing down the corridor and up the stairs, taking them two at a time.

* * *

The door to Gabriel's bedchamber was still ajar.

At first the only thing Samantha saw was Gabriel sprawled face-down on the floor like some fallen giant. Her hand flew to her mouth to smother a helpless cry.

Mrs. Philpot was kneeling on the other side of him, pressing a handkerchief to the curve of his throat—a handkerchief already soaked through with bright red blood. It wasn't difficult to deduce what had happened. Jagged shards of earthenware and crystal littered the floor around them.

Samantha rushed across the room and dropped to her knees, ignoring the sharp sting as a piece of glass sliced through the folds of her skirt and into her knee. As she reached for the handkerchief, peeling it away so she could examine the ugly gash in Gabriel's throat, Mrs. Philpot settled back on her haunches, only too eager to surrender her grim duty.

The housekeeper swiped a limp strand of hair from her eyes, leaving a smudge of Gabriel's blood on her cheek. "We found him when we were bringing up his afternoon tea. I have no idea how long he's been like this." The woman's sharp gaze swept over Samantha's spencer and bonnet, missing nothing. She held up Gabriel's bell. Bloody fingerprints stained its wooden handle. "I found this right next to his hand. He must have tried to ring for help, but no one heard him."

Samantha briefly closed her eyes, remembering the faint tinkling she had so coolly dismissed. She opened them to find Beckwith standing in the doorway, wringing his pudgy hands.

"Is there a doctor in the village?" she asked.

Beckwith nodded.

"Fetch him right away. Tell him it may be a matter of life and death." When the butler just stood there, unable to tear his gaze away from his fallen master, Samantha shouted, "Go!"

As Beckwith shook off his daze and lurched into motion, Mrs. Philpot rose to retrieve one of the clean cravats draped over the cheval glass. Samantha snatched it from her hand and pressed it to

Gabriel's throat. Although the wound was still oozing, the bleeding appeared to be slowing. Samantha could only pray that it wasn't because he was dying.

Gesturing for Mrs. Philpot to mind the cravat, she grasped him by the shoulders, determined to make sure he wasn't losing blood anywhere else. It took every ounce of her strength, but with the housekeeper's help, she managed to roll him over and into her arms. Except for the errant streaks of blood and the angry slash of his scar, his face was bone-white.

"You silly, stubborn fool," she murmured brokenly. "Look what you've gone and done to yourself now."

His lashes fluttered, slowly parting to reveal those bewitching green eyes of his. As he turned his head, gazing up at her with crystalline clarity, Samantha's breath froze in her throat. Then his eyes drifted shut again, as if he'd just realized it wasn't worth the bother.

"Is that you, Miss Wickersham?" he whispered hoarsely. "I rang for you."

"I know you did." She stroked a lock of hair away from his brow. "I'm here now. I'm not going anywhere."

He scowled. "I was going to tell you to go straight to the devil."

Samantha smiled through a haze of tears. "Is that an order, my lord?"

"If it was, you wouldn't obey it," he murmured. "Impertinent wench."

As Gabriel slumped back into unconsciousness, his head lolling against her breast, Samantha decided it must have been his failing strength that made his insult sound so much like an endearment.

When Dr. Thaddeus Greenjoy emerged from Gabriel's bedchamber nearly two hours later, it was to find the earl's entire household keeping vigil in the corridor. Mrs. Philpot sat in a straight-backed chair, her lace-trimmed handkerchief pressed to her trembling lips. A miserable-looking Beckwith stood at attention beside her, while the rest of the servants huddled at the top of the stairs, whispering among themselves.

Only Samantha stood alone. Although the doctor had allowed the maids to sweep up the glass and the footmen to carry Gabriel to the bed and cut off his blood-soaked breeches, he had refused to let anyone attend him while he examined his patient, including the earl's nurse.

As he drew the door softly shut behind him, Samantha stepped forward, still wearing her rumpled, blood-streaked traveling spencer. She held her breath, waiting for him to confirm her worst fears.

The doctor's gaze swept over their somber faces. "I believe I've stopped the bleeding for now. The glass nicked his jugular. Another inch deeper and he'd have been just another name on the Fairchild family crypt." The doctor shook his head, his long, white whiskers making him look like an elderly goat. "He's a very lucky fellow, that one. Someone must have been looking out for him today."

Although a ripple of relief traveled through them all, none of the servants could meet Samantha's eyes. She knew exactly what they were thinking. She was their master's nurse. She was the one who was supposed to be looking out for him. Instead, she had left him alone, abandoned him just when he needed her the most.

Almost as if he could hear her thoughts, the doctor barked, "Are you his nurse?"

Struggling not to flinch, Samantha nodded. "I am."

He harrumphed to show her what he thought of that idea. "Young chit like you ought to be out trying to snare a husband, not shut up in some sickroom." He snapped open his bag and handed her a brown bottle. "Give him some of this so he'll sleep through the night. Keep the wound clean. And keep him in bed for at least three days." The doctor's snowy white eyebrows drew together over his jutting nose. "That won't be too daunting a task for you, will it, child?"

As a shocking image of she and Gabriel rolling naked on a field of crimson satin rose unbidden in her mind, Samantha realized to her horror that she was blushing. "Of course not, sir. I'll see to it that he abides by all of your wishes."

"You do that, miss, and that strapping young fellow will be back on his feet in no time."

The doctor snapped his bag shut and started down the stairs. The servants broke off into chattering pairs, their mood and their faces lightened.

The very soul of discretion, Beckwith waited until everyone else was out of earshot before sidling up to Samantha. "Will you still be requiring that footman to carry your bags downstairs, miss?"

She searched, but couldn't find even a hint of mockery in the butler's gentle brown eyes. "I don't believe so, Beckwith. Now, if you'll excuse me," she said, giving his arm a grateful squeeze, "I believe your master has need of me."

Samantha spent that night playing Gabriel's nurse in earnest— checking his bandage for fresh bleeding, spooning laudanum down his throat when he began to groan and toss, and tenderly checking his brow for fever. By dawn, a hint of color was beginning to steal back into his cheeks. Only then did she dare to lean her head against the back of the chair she'd dragged next to the bed and rest her exhausted eyes.

When a timid knock came on the door, she awoke with a start. Sunlight was pouring through the dormer window at the far end of the room. Her panicked gaze flew to Gabriel, only to find him sleeping soundly, his chest rising and falling with each even breath. If not for the dark smudges beneath his eyes, no one would have guessed he'd just survived such an ordeal.

Samantha swung open the door to find Peter standing there, clutching a washbasin filled with rags and a pitcher of steaming water. The young footman shot the bed a nervous glance. "Sorry to disturb you, miss. Mrs. Philpot sent me up to bathe the master."

Samantha glanced over her shoulder. Gabriel was no less imposing in sleep than in wakefulness. But she was done shirking her responsibilities. Her negligence had almost gotten him killed.

Swallowing back her trepidation, she said, "That won't be necessary, Peter."

"Phillip," he corrected.

"Phillip." Taking the basin and pitcher from his hands, she said firmly, "I'm his nurse. I'll bathe him."

"Are you sure, miss?" Blushing beneath his freckles, he lowered his voice to a whisper. "Is it proper?"

"Quite," she assured him, nudging the door shut with her foot.

Samantha rested the basin on the table beside the bed, then emptied the pitcher into it, her hands shaking so hard that water sloshed all over her skirt. There was no need for her to be so nervous, she scolded herself. Bathing Gabriel was simply another one of her duties, no different from changing a bandage or spooning medicine down his throat.

She calmed her fears by devoting all of her attention to sponging the rusty stains from his face and throat. But when the time came to draw back the sheet, she hesitated. She was supposed to be a woman of the world, a woman who wouldn't simper or swoon at the prospect of a man's nakedness. In his current state, she told herself firmly, tending to Gabriel was no different from bathing a small child.

But as she folded back the sheet, revealing his well-muscled chest and taut abdomen, it became painfully evident that he was not a child, but a man. And an extremely virile one, at that.

Dipping the cloth in the warm water, Samantha dragged it over the swells and valleys of his chest, wiping away every last trace of dried blood. Glistening drops of water caught in the golden whorls of his chest hair. As one particularly bold rivulet trickled beneath the sheet draped over his narrow hips, her helpless gaze followed, hypnotized by the lure of the forbidden.

She had assured Phillip that it was quite proper for her to be bathing him. But there was nothing proper about the sudden dryness of her mouth, the quickening of her breath, the wicked desire to lift that sheet and steal a peek beneath.

She stole a furtive glance at the door, wishing she had thought to lock it.

Nibbling on her lower lip, Samantha grasped the edge of the sheet between thumb and forefinger and tugged it upward, one tantalizing inch at a time.

"Is it just me or is there a distinct draft in here?"

As that smoky baritone, faintly slurred, but no less mocking than usual, poured over her, Samantha dropped the sheet as if it had burst into flames. "Pardon me, my lord. I was just ch-checking your—your—"

"Circulation?" he gently provided. He waved a hand in her direction. "Do carry on. Far be it from me to hinder you from satisfying your . . . curiosity. About my condition, of course."

"Just how long have you been conscious?" Samantha demanded, her suspicions growing.

He stretched, the motion sending a ripple through the taut muscles of his chest. "Oh, I'd say since just before Phillip knocked on the door."

Remembering how she had lingered so lovingly over the sculpted contours of his upper body, Samantha wanted to sink through the floorboards. "You were awake the entire time? I can't believe you were just going to let me—"

"What?" He blinked his sightless eyes, the very portrait of innocence. "Carry out your duties?"

Samantha snapped her mouth shut, knowing she couldn't argue further without incriminating herself.

She jerked the sheet up, shielding his naked chest from her

gaze. "If you're having trouble resting, I can give you some more laudanum."

He shuddered. "No, thank you. I'd rather hurt than feel nothing at all. Then at least I can be sure I'm still alive." As she checked his bandage, he offered her a rueful half-smile that squeezed at her heart. "I only hope it doesn't leave a scar. I should hate to spoil my fine looks."

Brushing aside his tousled hair, she pressed a hand to his brow. Oddly enough, it was her flesh that felt fevered. "Vanity should be the least of your concerns right now. You're lucky to be alive, you know."

"So they keep telling me." Before she could withdraw her hand, he caught her wrist and gently drew it down between them. "But what of your luck, Miss Wickersham? Weren't you supposed to be back in London by now, plying your tender mercies at the bedside of some grateful sailor who would make calf's eyes at you and propose as soon as he was back on his feet?"

"And where would be the challenge in that?" Samantha asked softly, unable to tear her gaze away from the sight of those large masculine fingers curved around her pale, delicate wrist. His thumb lay directly over her thundering pulse. "I much prefer squandering my mercies on ungrateful bullies with beastly tempers. You know, if you wanted me to stay, there was really no need to cut your throat. You could have just asked nicely."

"And ruined my reputation for beastliness? I think not. Besides, I was only ringing for you so I could have the pleasure of dismissing you myself." His thumb skated across her tingling palm in something dangerously close to a caress.

"Well, I can hardly go now," she said briskly. "My conscience would never allow me to leave until you're fully recovered from your fall."

He sighed. "Then I suppose you'll just have to stay. I should hate to sully a conscience as pristine as yours."

Discomfited by his words, Samantha tugged her wrist from his grip. His fingers left a sizzling brand on her skin.

"Of course, you're not entirely perfect," he added, nodding in the direction of the chair. "You do snore in your sleep."

"And you drool in yours," she retorted, daring to touch a finger ever so briefly to the corner of his mouth.

"Touché, Miss Wickersham! The lady's tongue is as sharp as her wit. Perhaps you should summon the doctor before I start bleeding again." He tossed the sheet back to his waist and swung his legs over the side of the bed. "Or better yet, I'll fetch him myself. Despite my little misadventure, I'm feeling amazingly spry this morning."

"Oh, no, you don't!" Samantha caught him by the shoulders and eased him back to the pillows. "Dr. Greenjoy said you're to remain in bed for at least three days." She frowned. "Although he failed to leave instructions on how I'm to keep you there."

Settling back among the pillows, Gabriel propped his hands behind his head, his sightless eyes sparkling with devilment. "Don't fret, Miss Wickersham. I'm sure you'll think of something."

Rain pattered against the mullioned windows of Gabriel's bedchamber. Instead of lulling him to sleep, its cozy rhythm only further frayed his already ragged nerves. Any hope he'd had of escaping his prison bed in the past two days had been stymied by his nurse's constant presence.

His growing restlessness seemed to magnify every sound in the room—the creak of the window seat as Miss Wickersham settled deeper into the cushions, the juicy crunch as her teeth sank through the crisp skin of an apple, the faint rustle of paper as she turned the page of her book.

By employing both memory and imagination, Gabriel could almost see her there in the spot he had so frequently occupied as a boy when this room had been his parents' bedchamber. The frosted chimney of the Argand lamp on the side table would cast a gentle oasis of light around her, keeping the shadows at bay. She probably had her feet tucked beneath her to protect them from the damp that seeped through the baseboards on a rainy day. As she took another bite of the apple, he could see her white teeth crunching through its luscious red skin, see her small pink tongue darting out to catch a droplet of juice at the corner of her mouth.

She was probably wearing one of those silly little scraps of linen and lace women fancied as caps perched atop her hair. But no matter how hard Gabriel concentrated, the face beneath it refused to come into focus.

He drummed his long fingers on the bedclothes, his frustration mounting. He cleared his throat, but the sound was greeted by nothing but the rustle of another page turning. He cleared his throat again, this time with the force of a pistol shot.

His efforts were rewarded by a long-suffering sigh. "Are you absolutely certain you don't wish me to read aloud to you, my lord?"

"I should say not," he replied with a sniff. "It would make me feel as if I were back in the nursery."

Samantha's shrug was plain in her voice. "Suit yourself. I wouldn't wish to disturb your sulking."

He gave her just enough time to settle back into the story before blurting out, "What are you reading?

"A play actually. Thomas Morton's *Speed the Plough*. It's a rather sprightly comedy of manners."

"I saw it performed at the Theatre Royal in Drury Lane once. I'm sure you'll find much in common with Mrs. Grundy," he said, referring to that bastion of prudish propriety who never actually appears onstage. "I would have thought a tragedy by Goethe would be more to your liking. Some grim morality tale where a poor wretch is doomed to eternal damnation for stealing a glimpse of stocking or some other such unforgivable transgression."

"I prefer to believe that no transgression is unforgivable."

"Then I envy you your innocence," he replied, surprised to realize he actually did.

The sound of another page turning told him she'd rather read than argue with him. He was just resigning himself to a long afternoon nap when she laughed aloud.

Gabriel scowled, the bawdy ripple stirring him in a way he hadn't anticipated. He propped up one leg, taking care to tent the bedclothes over his lap. "Was that a laugh or has your apple given you indigestion?"

"Oh, it was nothing," she said airily. "Just a particularly witty passage."

After another merry chuckle, he barked, "Well? Don't you think it's rather ill-mannered to hoard such literary brilliance for your own amusement?"

"I thought you didn't wish to be read to."

"Consider it morbid curiosity. I'm dying to know what would engage such a humorless creature as yourself."

"Very well."

As she proceeded to read an amusing exchange between two brothers who had fixed their love on the same lady, Gabriel was surprised to learn that his nurse had missed her calling. She should have taken to the stage herself. Her droll inflections brought each character to vivid life. Before he knew it, Gabriel found himself sitting up in the bed and leaning toward the sound of her voice.

At the heart of a juicy bit of banter, she stopped in midsentence. "Do forgive me. I didn't mean to ramble on and disturb your rest."

Eager to know how the scene would end, he waved away her apology. "You might as well finish now. I suppose even your infernal yammering is preferable to the sound of my own thoughts."

"I should imagine they'd grow tiresome very quickly."

It required no trick of Gabriel's imagination or memory to envision her smirk as she ducked back behind the book. But at least she did as he bade, taking up where she'd left off and reading to the end of the play. At the close of the last act, they both breathed a mutual sigh of satisfaction.

When Samantha finally spoke, her voice had lost its flinty edge. "Boredom must be the very worst of your enemies, my lord. Before the war, I'm sure you were engaged in the pursuit of many . . . *pleasures*."

Was it his imagination or did her voice seem to caress the word? "Boredom *was* the worst of my enemies. Until you arrived at Fairchild Park."

"If you'd only allow me, I could help alleviate some of your tedium. I could take you for long walks in the gardens. I could read aloud to you every afternoon. Why, I could even help you with your correspondence if you like! There must be someone who would love to hear from you. Your fellow officers? Your family? Your friends back in London?"

"Why spoil their fond memories of me?" he asked dryly. "I'm sure they'd much rather think of me as dead."

"Don't be ridiculous," she chided. "I'm sure they'd all be heartened by a brief note letting them know how you're getting along."

Gabriel was puzzled by the brisk tap of her footsteps crossing the room. Until he heard the drawer of the writing desk slide open.

Acting purely on instinct, he threw back the blankets and lunged toward the sound. This time, desperation sharpened his aim instead of dulling it. His hands closed easily over the familiar contours of the drawer, slamming it shut. He was about to breathe a sigh of relief when he realized the soft, warm object trapped between his outstretched arms was his nurse.

≈ Chapter 7 ≈

My darling Cecily,

Now that I've been bold enough to address you by your Christian name, dare I hope to imagine my own name shaped by your luscious lips?

For a dazed moment, Samantha didn't even dare to breathe. The hypnotic patter of the rain, the gentle gloom, the warmth of Gabriel's breath stirring her hair, all wove together, suspending her in a misty cocoon where time lost all of its power and meaning. Gabriel seemed to be equally mesmerized. She had insisted that he don a shirt that morning, but she hadn't insisted that he fasten it. The broad chest pressed to her back barely seemed to be stirring. His palms were still flat against the desk drawer, his muscled forearms rigid with strain.

Although their awkward stance wasn't quite an embrace, Samantha couldn't help but think how easy it would be for him to wrap his arms around her, to draw her into the raw heat of his body until she had no choice but to melt against him.

She stiffened. She wasn't some weak-kneed, starry-eyed debutante, ripe for seduction at the hands of the first gentleman who crooked a finger at her.

"Forgive me, my lord," she said, breaking the dangerous spell that bound them. "I didn't mean to pry. I was just searching for some stationery and ink."

Gabriel lowered his arms, but it was Samantha who quickly moved away, seeking to put some distance between them. Without his warmth surrounding her, the damp she'd barely noticed before seemed to sink deep into her bones, making them feel old and brittle. Sinking back down on the window seat, she hugged back a shiver.

Gabriel stood still and silent for a long moment, as if deep in thought. Then, instead of reproaching her for meddling as she expected, he tugged open the drawer. His hands didn't fumble at all as they unerringly located the contents of the drawer. As he turned and tossed the thick bundle in her direction, Samantha was so startled it almost slipped through her grasp.

"If you want something to read for your amusement, you might try these." Although scorn darkened Gabriel's face, Samantha sensed that it wasn't for her. "I think you'll find they contain all of the elements one usually enjoys in a farce—witty banter, a secret courtship, a pathetic fool so drunk on love he's willing to risk everything to win his lady's heart, even his life."

She gazed down at the ribbon-bound packet of letters. The linen stationery was worn, yet perfectly preserved, as if the letters had been handled often, but with great care. As Samantha turned them over, a woman's perfume drifted to her nose, as evocative and sweet as the first gardenias of the season.

Gabriel dragged the chair out from under the knee well of the desk, turned it around, and straddled it. "Go on," he commanded, nodding in her direction. "If you read them aloud, we can both enjoy a fine laugh."

Samantha toyed with the ends of the silk ribbon, a ribbon that had once been wound through a woman's lustrous hair. "I hardly think it would be proper for me to read your private correspondence."

He shrugged. "Suit yourself. Some plays are better performed than read anyway. Why don't I start with the first act?" He folded his arms over the back of the chair, his face hard.

"The curtain rose over three years ago when we met at a house party at Lord Langley's country estate during the Season. She was so very different from the other girls I'd known. Most of them didn't have a thought in their pretty heads beyond snaring a wealthy husband before the Season was done. But she was warm and bright and funny and well read. She could discuss poetry and politics with equal ease. We shared a single dance, and without even surrendering so much as a kiss, she stole my heart."

"And did you steal hers as well?"

His lips curved in a rueful half-smile. "I made a valiant effort. But unfortunately, my rakish reputation had preceded me. Since I was an earl and she the daughter of a humble baronet, she couldn't bring herself to believe that I would do more than trifle with her heart."

Samantha didn't know if she could blame the girl. The man in the portrait on the landing had probably won—and broken—more than his fair share of hearts. "I would have thought both she and her family would have been thrilled to catch the eye of such an esteemed—and wealthy—nobleman."

"That's just what I thought," Gabriel admitted. "But it seems her older sister was involved in some unfortunate scandal involving a viscount, a moonlight rendezvous, and the viscount's enraged wife. Her father's fondest wish was that his youngest daughter make a match with some stolid gentleman farmer or perhaps even a clergyman."

A fleeting image of Gabriel in a curate's collar nearly made Samantha laugh aloud. "I can see why you might have been something of a disappointment to him."

"Precisely. Since I couldn't sway her with my title, my wealth, or my charms, I set about trying to win her with my words. For several months, we exchanged long, bantering letters."

"Secretly, of course."

He nodded. "Had it become known that she was corresponding with a gentleman, especially one of my reputation, her good name would have been destroyed."

"Yet it was a risk she was willing to take," Samantha pointed out.

"In truth, I think we both enjoyed the thrill of the game. We would come face to face at some ball or soiree, murmur a few polite words, then pretend indifference. No one knew that I was aching to drag her away to the nearest moonlit garden or deserted alcove and kiss her insensible."

The husky note in his voice sent a dark shiver dancing over Samantha's flesh. Although she tried to fight the temptation, she saw Gabriel running a hand through his golden hair as he paced some shadowy alcove. Saw the anticipation that brightened his eyes as he scented the rich gardenia of his lady's perfume. She felt the strength in his arms as he reached out to draw her through the curtain. Heard him groaning deep in his throat as their lips and bodies brushed, consumed with the irresistible hunger of the forbidden.

"One would have thought I'd grow bored with such an innocent dalliance. But her letters enchanted me." He shook his head, looking genuinely bemused. "I had never dreamed a woman's mind could be so layered or so fascinating. My mother and sisters were rarely engaged by anything more stimulating than the latest snippet of gossip from Almack's or the most recent fashion plates smuggled from Paris."

Samantha bit back a smile. "It must have been quite a shock for you to learn that a woman could possess a mind as keen and discerning as your own."

"Indeed it was," he confessed, his silky tone informing her that he wasn't completely oblivious to her sarcasm. "After several months of this delicious torture, I wrote and tried to persuade her to elope to Gretna Green with me. She refused, but she wasn't so cruel as to leave me completely without hope. She vowed that if I could prove I had some interest in this world that extended beyond my next winning hand of faro at Brook's, some passion that didn't involve horses, hounds, or pretty young opera dancers, she would consent to become my bride, even if that meant defying her father's wishes."

"How very magnanimous," Samantha murmured.

Gabriel frowned. "She still didn't entirely trust my affections. No matter how passionately I pledged my love, there was a part of her only too willing to believe I was still an irresponsible rakehell who had inherited everything of import—my title, my wealth, my social standing." He arched a self-mocking eyebrow, stretching his scar taut. "Even my good looks."

Samantha's stomach was starting to churn. "So you set out to prove her wrong."

He nodded. "I joined the Royal Navy."

"Why the Navy? Your father could have purchased you a prestigious commission in the Army."

"And what would that have proved? That she was right about me? That I was incapable of achieving anything on my own merit, my own skills? If that were my intent, I could have joined the militia and simply played the part of hero. There's nothing like starched broadcloth and a bit of shiny braid on a man's shoulders to turn a lady's head."

Samantha saw him striding into some crowded ballroom, his cocked hat tucked beneath his arm, his tawny hair gleaming beneath the glow of the chandeliers. His dashing figure would have set all of the unmarried ladies to blushing and simpering behind their fans.

"But you knew your lady's head would not be so easily turned," she ventured.

"Nor her heart so easily won. So I signed on under Nelson's command, confident that when I returned from sea, she would be ready to become my wife. Knowing that we were to be parted for several months, I sent her one last letter, entreating her to wait for me. Promising her that I was determined to become the man—and the hero—that she deserved." He attempted a crooked smile. "So ends Act One. There's really no point in continuing, is there? You already know the ending."

"Did you ever see her again?"

"No," he replied without a trace of irony. "But she saw me. After I was brought back to London, she came to the hospital. I don't know how long I'd been there. The days and nights were equally endless and equally indistinguishable." He touched a finger to his scar. "I must have looked quite the monster with my sightless eyes and my ruin of a face. I doubt she even knew I was conscious. I didn't yet have the strength to speak. Yet I could smell her perfume, like a breath of heaven amidst the hellish stench of camphor and rotting limbs."

"What did she do?" Samantha whispered.

Gabriel clapped a hand over his heart. "Had a more sentimental playwright crafted the story, she would have no doubt thrown herself upon my chest, pledging her eternal love. As it was, she simply fled. It wasn't necessary, you know. Under the circumstances, I never would have expected her to honor her obligation to me."

"Obligation?" Samantha echoed, struggling to hide her outrage. "I thought a betrothal was supposed to be a commitment between two people who love each other."

He laughed without humor. "Then you're more naïve than I was. Since ours was a secret engagement, at least she was spared the humiliation and scandal of a public estrangement."

"How very fortunate for her."

Gabriel's eyes took on a hazy look, as if the past were somehow more visible to them than the present. "Sometimes I wonder if I ever really knew her at all. Perhaps she was just a figment of my imagination. Someone I fashioned from a clever turn of phrase and the fantasy of a stolen kiss—my dream of the perfect woman."

"She was beautiful, I suppose?" Samantha asked, already knowing the answer.

Although Gabriel's jaw hardened, his voice softened. "Exquisite. Her hair was a warm honey-gold, her eyes the color of the ocean beneath a summer sky, her skin the softest—"

Examining her own chapped hands, Samantha cleared her throat. She was hardly in the mood to sit and listen to him wax poetic over charms she did not possess. "So what became of this paragon?"

"I assume she returned to the bosom of her family in Middlesex, where she'll probably marry the local squire and retire to a country estate to raise a passel of practical, pudding-fed brats."

But none of them would have the face of one of Raphael's angels or sea-foam-green eyes framed by gilded lashes. For that, Samantha could almost pity her. Almost.

"She was a fool."

"Pardon me?" Gabriel arched an eyebrow, obviously taken aback by her matter-of-fact pronouncement.

"The girl was a fool," Samantha repeated with even more conviction. "And you're an even greater fool for wasting your time mooning over some frivolous creature who probably cared more for her pretty ball gowns and her phaeton rides in the park than she did for you." Rising, Samantha crossed to him and slapped the letters against the back of his hand. "If you don't want anyone else stumbling across your sentimental treasures, I suggest you sleep with them beneath your pillow."

Gabriel made no move to take the letters. He simply stared straight ahead, his jaw taut. His nostrils flared, but she couldn't tell if it was in anger or to drink in the cloud of rich, floral scent that wafted up from the perfumed stationery. She was beginning to wonder if she'd gone too far when he abruptly pushed the letters away.

"Perhaps you're right, Miss Wickersham. After all, letters are of little enough use to a blind man. Why don't you take them?"

Samantha recoiled. "*Me?* What on earth am I supposed to do with them?"

Gabriel rose, towering over her. "Why should I care? Toss them in the dustbin or burn them if you like. Just get them"—a rueful smile curled one corner of his mouth before he finished gently—"out of my sight."

Samantha sat on the edge of her bed in her faded cotton night-dress, gazing down at the packet of letters in her hands. Outside her window, the night had gone dark as pitch. Rain lashed at the windowpanes, as if driven by the wind to punish everyone who defied its reach. Despite the cozy fire crackling on her hearth, Samantha still felt chilled to the bone.

Her fingers toyed with the frayed ends of the ribbon binding the letters. Gabriel had trusted her to dispose of them. It would be wrong of her to betray that trust.

She gave the ribbon a tug. The silk unfurled, spilling the letters into her lap. Drawing off her spectacles, she unfolded the one on top, her hands trembling. A woman's practiced script flowed across the linen stationery. The letter was dated September 20, 1804, nearly one year before Trafalgar. Despite its flowery elegance, there was a no-nonsense slant to the words.

My dearest Lord Sheffield,

In your last rather impertinent missive, you claimed to love me for my "luscious lips" and "smoky blue eyes." Yet I am driven to ask, "Will you still love me when those lips are puckered not in passion, but with age? Will you love me when my eyes are faded, but my affections for you undimmed?"

I can almost hear you chuckling as you stride about your town house, ordering your servants about in that high-handed

*manner I find both so insufferable and irresistible. No doubt you
will waste your evening fashioning some witty response designed to both charm and disarm me.*

*Keep this letter close to your heart, my lord, as you are ever
close to mine.*

Yours,
Miss Cecily March

Cecily was unable to resist signing her name with a flourish
that betrayed her youth. Samantha crumpled the letter in her fist.
She felt no pity for the girl, only contempt. Her teasing promises
came at too high a price. She was no better than some medieval
damsel who tied her silken favor around a knight's arm before
sending him into battle to face certain death.

Gathering up the letters, Samantha rose and strode to the
hearth. She wanted nothing more than to burn them to ash as they
deserved, to pretend that callow, arrogant girl had never existed.
But as she prepared to feed them to the leaping flames, something
stayed her hand.

She thought of the long months Gabriel had hoarded them, the
passion with which he had guarded them against her prying eyes,
the helpless hunger in his expression when he had inhaled their
fragrance. It was almost as if destroying them would cheapen the
sacrifice he had made to win their author's heart.

She turned to peruse the small chamber. She'd never completely unpacked her trunk after Gabriel's accident, finding it easier to live out of it than return everything to the towering armoire
in the corner. Kneeling beside the leather-banded chest, she bundled the letters back into the ribbon and secured them with a careless knot. She shoved them into the trunk, burying them so deep
that there would be no chance of anyone stumbling across them
again.

≈ Chapter 8 ≈

My darling Cecily,

I find it difficult to believe that your mother did not address your father by his Christian name until after she'd borne him five children . . .

When Samantha entered Gabriel's bedchamber the next morning, she found him sitting at the dressing table, holding a straight razor to his throat.

Her heart leapt in her own throat. "Don't do it, my lord. I'll let you out of the bed today. I promise I will."

Gabriel swiveled toward the sound of her voice, still brandishing the razor. "Do you know one of the chief advantages of being blind?" he asked cheerfully. "You no longer require a mirror for shaving."

He might not require a mirror, but that didn't stop the polished surface above the dressing table from lingering lovingly over his reflection. As usual, he hadn't bothered to fasten the studs of his shirt. The ivory linen hung open, revealing a generous slice of gilt-dusted chest and well-muscled abdomen.

Samantha marched across the room and closed her small hand over his large one, stilling the razor before he could lift it back to his jaw. "Give me that before you cut your throat. Again."

He refused to relinquish his grip. "And why should I believe you'd be any less inclined to do the honors for me?"

"If I cut your throat, your father might cut my wages."

"Or he might double them."

She tugged until Gabriel reluctantly surrendered the pearl-handled razor into her grip.

Gently skirting his bandage, Samantha used a matching brush to dab juniper-scented shaving soap over his three-day growth of beard. Under her practiced touch, the blade glided easily through the golden stubble, revealing the rugged jaw beneath. His skin was smooth yet firm, so utterly different from her own. To reach the hollow beneath his ear, she was forced to lean over him. Her breast brushed his shoulder.

"Why this sudden interest in grooming?" she asked, keeping her voice light to hide her sudden breathlessness. "Have you a secret ambition to become the next Beau Brummell?"

"Beckwith just brought word from my father. The team of physicians he hired has returned from Europe. They want to meet with me this afternoon."

His expressive face had gone utterly still. In an effort to help him hide his hope, Samantha plucked up a towel and swiped the stray daubs of shaving soap from his face. "If you can't win them over with your good looks, perhaps you can charm them as you did me with your hospitality and fine manners."

"Give me that!" Gabriel sputtered as she briskly scrubbed at his mouth and nose. "What are you trying to do? Smother me?"

Just as she leaned forward, he reached over his shoulder. But instead of grabbing the towel, his hand closed neatly over the softness of her breast.

Hearing Samantha's breath hitch in a startled squeak, Gabriel froze. But the surge of raw heat coursing from his heart to his groin quickly thawed him. Although he would have thought it impossible, he could feel a schoolboy blush creeping up his jaw.

He'd caressed much more generous breasts in his day, but none that fit his hand so perfectly. His fingers curled around its plush softness as if they'd been molded there. Although he didn't dare move even one of those fingers, he felt her nipple stiffen against his palm through the ruched fabric of her bodice.

"Oh, my," he said softly. "That's not the towel, is it?"

She swallowed audibly, her husky voice suddenly very close to his ear. "No, my lord. I fear it's not."

He had no idea how long they might have remained that way had Beckwith not come bumbling through the door. "I wasn't sure which shirt you wanted, my lord," he said, his voice muffled by what Gabriel assumed was a towering pile of shirts, "so I had Meg launder them all."

As the butler's brisk footsteps crossed the floor, heading toward the dressing room, Gabriel and Samantha sprang apart as if they'd been caught *in flagrante delicto.*

"Very good, Beckwith," Gabriel said, knocking several jangling items to the floor as he leapt to his feet.

He would have given a decade off his life to see his nurse's expression in that moment. Had he finally succeeded in ruffling her composure? Was the color high in those downy cheeks of hers? And if so, was it the result of embarrassment . . . or desire?

He could hear her moving away from him, backing toward the door. "If you'll excuse me, my lord, there are some things I really must attend to . . . downstairs, you know . . . so I'll leave you to your undressing . . . I mean, your dressing!" There was a faint thump as if someone had run into a door, a muffled "Ow!," then the sound of that same door opening and closing.

By that time, Beckwith had emerged from the dressing room. "How very odd," the butler murmured.

"What is it?"

"It's most peculiar, my lord. I've never seen Miss Wickersham

look quite so flushed or flustered. Do you think she could be taking a fever?"

"I certainly hope not," Gabriel replied grimly. "Given how
much time I've been spending in her company, I fear I might fall
prey to the very same malady."

An innocent mistake.

That was all it had been. At least that's what Samantha kept
telling herself as she paced the foyer, waiting for Gabriel to make
his appearance. The physicians had arrived from London nearly
half an hour ago and were waiting in the library to meet with him.
Samantha hadn't been able to gather a single clue about the news
they'd come to deliver from their polite nods and guarded expres-
sions.

An innocent mistake, she repeated to herself, stopping just
short of trampling the mirrored hall tree. But there had been nothing innocent about the way both her breath and her body had
quickened beneath Gabriel's touch. Nothing innocent about the
tension that had thickened between them, as if the air had suddenly become charged with summer lightning.

Hearing a footstep behind her, she turned. Gabriel was descending the stairs, one hand gliding firmly over the gleaming mahogany banister. If she hadn't known he was blind, she might
never have guessed. His step was confident and his head held
high. Beckwith descended behind him, beaming proudly.

Samantha's heart seemed to turn over in her chest. The raging
savage Gabriel had been when she had arrived at Fairchild Park
had been replaced by an older, more world-weary twin to the man
in the portrait. The somber black of his trousers and tailcoat perfectly offset the snowy white of his shirt, cravat, and cuffs. He'd
even bound the unruly strands of his hair with a velvet queue. If not
for the unforgiving slash down his left cheek, he could have been
any country gentleman descending the steps to greet his lady.

In some strange way, the scar only accentuated his masculine beauty, giving it depth where before it had only skimmed the surface of the man.

When Samantha heard a startled gasp behind her, she realized she wasn't the only one who had witnessed his transformation. Several of the other servants were peeping out of alcoves and doorways, hoping to steal a look at their master. Young Phillip had even gone so far as to hang over the gallery on the third floor. Peter gave the tail of his twin's coat a yank before he could go toppling over the banister onto Gabriel's head.

Without quite knowing how she got there, Samantha was waiting for him when he reached the foot of the stairs.

With that uncanny awareness of her presence, he stopped exactly a foot short of charging right over her and sketched her a formal bow. "Good afternoon, Miss Wickersham. I hope my attire meets with your approval."

"You look quite the proper gentleman. Brummell himself would swoon with envy." She reached up to gently tweak a crooked fold of his cravat before realizing how wifely the gesture was. She hastily lowered her hand. It was not her place. Or her right. Stepping away from him, she said with stilted formality, "Your guests have already arrived, my lord. They're waiting for you in the library."

Gabriel turned in a half circle, betraying his first hint of uncertainty. Beckwith caught him by the elbow and angled him toward the library door.

To Samantha, he looked terribly alone, marching into the unknown with nothing but his hope to guide him. She started after him, only to have Beckwith's hand come down, gently but firmly, on her shoulder. "However dark, Miss Wickersham," he murmured as Gabriel disappeared into the library, "there are some paths a man must travel alone."

Time crept by, measured by the brass hands of the long-case clock on the landing. Their graceful sweep around the full moon of its face seemed to have slowed to fitful jerks, suitable only for ticking off decades instead of minutes.

Every time Samantha came up with a new excuse to pass through the foyer, she found half a dozen servants already there ahead of her. When she was on her way to the kitchens for a glass of milk, she found Elsie and Hannah waxing the balusters of the staircase as if their lives depended on it, while Millie stood on a tall stepladder, dusting each crystal teardrop of the chandelier with a feather duster. When she was returning the empty glass to the kitchens, she found Peter and Phillip down on hands and knees, polishing the marble floor. It seemed the servants had been hiding their hope from Gabriel just as diligently as he'd been hiding his hope from them. Although they were all craning their necks and ears toward the library, not so much as a muffled murmur escaped its thick mahogany doors.

By late afternoon, there wasn't a speck of dust to be found anywhere in the foyer. The marble floor gleamed, so slick from its repeated polishings that Meg, the stout, red-faced laundress, nearly slipped and broke her neck. The woman had made so many trips through the foyer, her basket heaped with garments, that Samantha suspected her of dragging clean clothes out of the armoires to wash.

The next time Samantha came wandering through, ostensibly to return a book to the study, Mrs. Philpot herself made an appearance. Betsy had been polishing the wainscoting adjacent to the library for nearly an hour, rubbing so hard that some of the bare oak was starting to show through the gilt finish.

"What on earth do you think you're doing?" the housekeeper snapped.

Samantha winced. But instead of scolding the young maid for loitering, Mrs. Philpot simply whisked the rag out of her hand and began to rub in the opposite direction. "You should always polish *with* the grain of the wood, not against it!"

Samantha couldn't help but notice that Mrs. Philpot's method put her ear very close to the keyhole in the library door.

By the time the sun began to set, Samantha and the other servants had given up all pretense of work. Samantha was sitting on the lowest step, her spectacles drooping and her chin propped on her hand, while the rest of the servants were draped over the chairs and stairs in various states of repose. Some were half dozing, while others waited in tense expectation, cracking their knuckles and exchanging the occasional whisper.

When the library door came swinging open without warning, they all jerked to attention. A half dozen dark-garbed men emerged, drawing the door shut behind them.

Samantha came to her feet, scanning their somber faces.

Although most of them took great care to avoid her eager gaze, a small man with kind blue eyes and neatly trimmed side-whiskers looked directly at her and shook his head sadly. "I'm so very sorry," he murmured.

Samantha sank back down on the step, feeling as if a cruel fist had just squeezed all the blood from her heart. She hadn't realized until that very moment just how high her own hopes had been.

As Beckwith appeared out of nowhere to show the physicians out, his jowls drooping, she stared at the impenetrable mahogany of the library door.

Mrs. Philpot was gripping the rounded ball at the top of the newel post, her long fingers pale. Her brisk confidence seemed to have evaporated, replaced with an almost touching uncertainty. "He must be hungry by now. Shouldn't we—"

"No," Samantha said firmly, remembering Beckwith's admonishment that there were some paths a man must travel alone. "We can't. Not until he's ready."

As sunset melted into dusk and dusk into the velvety dark of a warm spring night, Samantha came to regret her own forbearance. The minutes that had crept by while Gabriel consulted with the physicians now seemed to fly by on black, leathery wings. One by one the servants abandoned their vigil, drifting away to the kitchens or their basement quarters, no longer able to bear the deafening silence coming from the library. Although none of them would have admitted it, they would have much preferred to hear their master's shouted oaths followed by the crashing of breaking glass.

Samantha was the last to go, but after a hollow-eyed Beckwith bade her goodnight, even she had to admit defeat. She soon found herself wearing a restless path in her bedchamber rug. She had donned her nightdress and braided her hair, but couldn't bear the thought of climbing into her cozy bedstead of whitewashed iron while Gabriel was still barricaded in his own private hell.

She paced back and forth, working herself into a fine temper. Surely Gabriel's father must have known the outcome of his quest. Why hadn't the man accompanied his precious team of physicians? His presence might have softened the killing blow they'd come to deliver.

And what of Gabriel's mother? Surely her negligence was even more unforgivable. What sort of woman would abandon her only son to the care of servants and strangers?

Samantha's gaze fell on the trunk in the corner where she had tucked away his former fiancée's letters. In some small secret corner of his heart, had Gabriel believed that his lost love might be restored to him along with his lost sight? Was he mourning the death of that dream as well?

The clock on the landing below began to chime the hour. Samantha leaned against the door, counting the mournful bongs one by one until she reached twelve.

What if Beckwith had been wrong? What if there were some paths so dark and dangerous they couldn't be traversed without a hand to hold? Even if it was only the hand of a stranger.

Her own hand trembling, Samantha took up her pewter candlestick and slipped out of the room. She was halfway down the stairs before she realized she had forgotten to don her spectacles. Her candle cast flickering shadows on the wall as she crept through the foyer. The silence was even more oppressive than the dark. This wasn't the cozy silence of a house at rest. It was the smothering silence of a house holding its breath in tense expectation. It wasn't so much the absence of sound as the presence of fear.

The door to the library was still closed. Samantha closed her hand around the handle, half expecting it to be locked. But the door swung open easily beneath her touch.

Her mind was assailed by a dizzying array of half-formed impressions: the desultory crackling of the waning fire on the hearth; the empty glass next to the nearly empty bottle of scotch whisky sitting on the corner of the desk; the papers scattered across the floor as if someone had knocked them away in a fit of pique.

But all of those impressions were vanquished by the sight of Gabriel sprawled in the chair behind the desk with a pistol in his hand.

≈ Chapter 9 ≈

My darling Cecily,

*I doubt it will take me a decade to coax my name from your lips.
Ten minutes alone with you in the moonlight should suffice . . .*

"I used to boast to all my friends that I could load a pistol with my eyes closed. I guess I was right," Gabriel drawled as he tipped a leather pouch over the muzzle of the weapon. Although the bottle of scotch at his elbow had less than three fingers of liquor left in it, his hands were so steady he didn't spill so much as a speck of gunpowder.

As he used a slender iron rod to tamp down the charge, Samantha found herself transfixed by those hands—by their grace, their skill, their economy of motion. A helpless shiver of awareness rippled through her as she imagined them moving against a woman's skin. *Her* skin.

Shaking off their seductive spell, she moved to stand directly in front of the desk. "I hesitate to mention this, my lord, but don't you think a loaded pistol in the hands of a blind man might be just a wee bit dangerous?"

"That is the point, isn't it?" He leaned back in the chair, his thumb toying with the twin hammers of the loaded and primed pistol.

Despite his lax posture and laconic tone, Samantha could sense the tension coiled in his every muscle. He no longer looked the part of the perfect gentleman. His coat was draped carelessly over a nearby bust, while his cravat hung loose around the broad column of his throat. Strands of dark gold hair had escaped his queue. A feverish glitter lit his sightless eyes.

"I gather the news you received wasn't to your liking?" she ventured, gingerly sinking down in the nearest chair.

He turned his head to follow her motion, keeping the barrel of the pistol carefully averted from her. "Let's just say it wasn't quite what I was hoping for."

She struggled to keep her tone carefully conversational. "When you receive bad news, isn't it customary to shoot the messenger, not yourself?"

"I only had one pistol ball on hand. I couldn't decide which doctor to shoot."

"They offered you no hope at all?"

He shook his head. "Not even a crumb. Oh, one of them—a Dr. Gilby, I believe—put forth some balderdash about blood building up behind the eyes after a blow such as the one that I sustained. It seems there was a case in Germany where vision returned after the blood was absorbed. But once his companions shouted him down for the fool he was, even he had to admit that there had never been a spontaneous healing recorded after six months."

Samantha strongly suspected that this Gilby had been the kind-eyed physician who had offered her his sorrowful condolences. "I'm so very sorry," she said softly.

"I have no need of your pity, Miss Wickersham."

At his harsh tone, she stiffened. "You're right, of course. I suppose you have quite enough of your own."

For an elusive instant, the corner of Gabriel's mouth twitched as if he would have liked to smile. He gently rested the pistol on the leather desk blotter. Although she eyed it longingly, Samantha didn't dare make a grab for it. Even half drunk and without benefit of sight, his reflexes were probably still twice as nimble as hers.

He groped for the bottle of scotch, emptying what was left of it into the glass, then hefted the glass in a mocking toast. "To Fate, a fickle mistress whose sense of justice is exceeded only by her sense of humor."

"Justice?" Samantha echoed, utterly bewildered. "Surely you can't believe that you deserved to lose your sight. For what? Proving yourself to be a hero?"

Gabriel slammed the glass down on the table, sloshing scotch over its rim. "I'm no bloody hero!"

"Of course you are!" It took little effort for Samantha to recite what she knew of the events leading up to his injury from the accounts repeated with such relish by *The Times* and the *Gazette*. "You were the first to spot the sniper in the mizzentop of the *Redoubtable*. When you saw he had Nelson in his sights, you cried out a warning, then started across the deck toward the admiral at tremendous peril to your own life."

"But I didn't make it, did I?" Gabriel tipped the glass to his mouth, downing the scotch in a single swallow. "And neither did he."

"Only because you were downed by a piece of flying shrapnel before you could reach him."

Gabriel was silent for a long moment. Then he asked softly, "Do you know the last thing I saw as I was lying there on that deck, choking on the stench of my own blood? I saw that ball tear through the admiral's shoulder. I saw the bewilderment on his face as he crumpled to the deck in agony. Then everything went red, then black."

"It wasn't as if you pulled the trigger that killed him." Samantha leaned forward in the chair, her voice low and passionate. "And you won the battle. Because of Nelson's courage and the sacrifices of men just like you, the French were defeated. They might still try to lay claim to our land, but you taught them who would forever be master of the sea."

"Then I suppose I should thank God for being allowed to make such a sacrifice. Just think how lucky Nelson was. He'd already given an arm and an eye for the good of king and country, yet still was able to enjoy the privilege of forfeiting his life." Gabriel threw back his head with a hoot of boyish laughter, looking so much like the man in the portrait that Samantha's heart skipped a beat. "You astonish me anew, Miss Wickersham! Who would have thought the heart of a romantic beat beneath that stony breast of yours?"

She bit her lip, tempted to remind him that he hadn't seemed to find her breast the least bit stony when his fingers had been curved possessively around its softness. "You dare to accuse *me* of sentimentality? I wasn't the one hoarding old love letters in my dressing table drawer, was I?"

"Touché," he murmured, his mirth subsiding. His hand closed over the pistol again, exploring its sleek contours with a lover's caress. When he spoke again, his voice was low and devoid of mockery. "What would you have me do? You know as well as I that a blind man has no place in our society unless it's begging on some street corner or locked away in a lunatic asylum. I'll never be anything more than a burden and an object of pity to my family and anyone else unfortunate enough to love me."

Samantha leaned back in the chair, a strange calm creeping over her. "Then why don't you just shoot yourself and have done with it? When you're finished, I'll ring for Mrs. Philpot to clean up the mess."

Both Gabriel's jaw and his grip on the pistol tightened.

"Go on. Finish it," she demanded, her voice gaining in both strength and passion. "But I can promise you that the only one who pities you is yourself. Some men still haven't come home from this war. And some men never will. Others lost both arms and legs. They sit begging in the gutters, their uniforms and their pride in tatters. They're jeered at, stepped on, and the only hope they have left is that some stranger with an ounce of Christian charity in his soul might drop a halfpenny in their tin cups. In the meantime, you sit here sulking in the lap of luxury, your every whim catered to by servants who still look at you as if you hung the moon." Samantha stood, thankful he couldn't see the tears shining in her eyes. "You were right, my lord. Those men are the heroes, not you. You're nothing but a craven—a miserable coward who's afraid to die, but even more afraid to go on living!"

She half expected him to pick up the pistol and shoot her. She did not expect him to rise and start around the desk. Although his steps were as steady as his hands had been, the liquor added an extra measure of swagger to his gait. She had believed the predator she had encountered her first day at Fairchild Park had been vanquished, but now she realized he had only been slumbering behind Gabriel's heavy-lidded eyes, biding his time until he could catch the scent of his prey again.

His nostrils flared as he reached for her. Although she could have easily eluded him, something in his face stopped her. He captured her shoulders and drew her toward him, his grip rough.

"You haven't been entirely honest with me, have you, my dear Miss Wickersham?" Her heart nearly stopped before he continued. "You didn't choose this vocation because of your overwhelming compassion for your fellow man. You lost someone in the war, didn't you? Who was it? Your father? Your brother?" As he lowered his head, the scotch-flavored warmth of his breath fanned across her face, making her feel as drunk and reckless as him. "Your *lover*?" Coming from his beautifully sculpted lips, the word was both taunt and endearment.

"Let's just say that you're not the only one atoning for your sins."

His laughter mocked them both. "What would a paragon of virtue such as yourself know of sin?"

"More than you realize," she whispered, turning her face away.

His nose grazed the softness of her cheek, although she could not have said whether it was by accident or design. Without her spectacles to shield her, she felt painfully vulnerable.

"You seek to goad me into continuing to live, yet you don't offer me a single reason why I should." He gave her a shake, his grip as harsh as his voice. "Can you do that, Miss Wickersham? Can you give me a reason to live?"

Samantha didn't know if she could or not. But when she turned her head to reply, their mouths collided. Then he was kissing her, slanting his mouth over hers, sweeping the honeyed heat of his tongue over her lips until they parted with a small broken sound that was half moan and half gasp. Only too eager to accept her surrender, he drew her hard against him, tasting of scotch and desire and danger.

Her eyes fluttered shut, putting them on equal footing. In the seductive embrace of the darkness, she had only his arms to hold her, only the heat of his mouth to warm her, only the hoarse music of his groan to make her senses dance. As his tongue roughly plundered the softness of her mouth, Samantha's pulse raged in her ears, ticking off each beat of her heart, each moment, each regret. His arms slid from her shoulders to her back, drawing her against him until her breasts were crushed to the unyielding wall of his chest. She curled one arm around his neck, struggling to answer the desperate demand of his mouth on hers.

How could she save him when she couldn't even save herself?

She could feel herself descending into the darkness with him, only too eager to surrender both her will and her soul. He might claim to court death, but it was life surging between them. Life in the ancient mating dance of their tongues. Life in the irresistible tug of her womb and the delicious ache between her thighs. Life pulsing against the softness of her belly through the worn cotton of her nightdress.

"Sweet Christ!" he swore, tearing himself from her arms.

Deprived of his support, Samantha had to brace her hands

against the desk behind her to keep from falling. As her eyes drifted open, she fought the urge to shield them with her hand. After being lost in the delicious shadows of Gabriel's kiss, even the waning firelight suddenly seemed too harsh.

Struggling to catch her breath, she turned to watch Gabriel grope his way around the desk. His hands were no longer steady. They knocked over an ink bottle and sent a brass-handled letter opener skittering into the floor before finally closing over the pistol. As he swept up the weapon, his expression as resolute as she had ever seen it, a strangled cry caught in the back of Samantha's throat.

But he simply reached across the desk toward her. Fumbling for her hand, he pressed the pistol into it. "Go," he commanded through gritted teeth, folding her fingers tight around the weapon. When she hesitated, he gave her a shove toward the door, his voice rising to a shout. "Go now! Leave me!"

Casting one last stricken glance over her shoulder, Samantha tucked the pistol in the skirt of her nightdress and fled.

⇜ Chapter 10 ⇝

My darling Cecily,

Have you decided yet which of my virtues intrigues you the most—my bashfulness or my humility . . .

When Samantha heard a muffled bang, she sat straight up in her bed, terrified it was the distant report of a pistol.

"Miss Wickersham? Are you awake?"

As Beckwith resumed his knocking, she clapped a hand to her chest, seeking to steady her pounding heart. Glancing at the trunk in the corner, she remembered that Gabriel's pistol was now buried deep inside of it, next to his bundle of letters.

She tossed back the blankets and climbed out of the bed, sliding her spectacles over her bleary eyes. After Gabriel had sent her away, she had spent the rest of the night huddled in a miserable knot, convinced she had been a fool to leave him in that state. She had finally drifted into a dreamless sleep near dawn, the victim of sheer exhaustion.

Slipping into her dressing gown, she opened the door a crack.

Although Beckwith looked as if he, too, had spent a restless night, his bloodshot eyes were twinkling with good humor. "Forgive me for disturbing you, miss, but the master wishes to see you in the library. At your convenience, of course."

Samantha arched a skeptical eyebrow. Her convenience certainly wasn't something Gabriel had ever troubled himself about before. "Very well, Beckwith. Tell him I'll be down shortly."

She washed and dressed with more care than usual, pawing through her limited wardrobe for something that wasn't gray, black, or brown. She was finally forced to settle for a high-waisted morning gown cut from somber blue velvet. She painstakingly wove a matching ribbon through the tight coil of her chignon. It wasn't until she caught herself leaning over to peer into the dressing table mirror so she could spit-curl a loose tendril of hair around her finger that she realized how ridiculous she was being. After all, it wasn't as if Gabriel could appreciate her efforts.

Shaking her head at her reflection, she hurried to the door. Only to rush back to the dressing table five seconds later to dab some lemon verbena behind each ear and in the hollow of her throat.

Samantha hesitated outside the library door, her stomach beset by a most curious fluttering. It took her a minute to identify the foreign emotion as shyness. She was being ridiculous, she told herself. She and Gabriel had shared a drunken kiss, nothing more. It wasn't as if every time she looked at his mouth, she would be remembering the way it had felt on hers—the commanding way his lips had molded hers beneath them, the smoky heat of his tongue plundering . . .

The clock on the landing began to chime ten o'clock, jerking her out of her reverie. Smoothing her skirt, Samantha gave the door a forceful knock.

"Enter."

Obeying the curt command, she opened the door to find Gabriel sitting behind the desk, just as he had been the night before. But this time, there was no empty glass, no bottle of scotch, and mercifully, no weapon more lethal than a letter opener.

"Good morning, my lord," she said, slipping into the room. "I'm gratified to see that you're still among the living."

Gabriel rubbed his brow with the heel of his hand. "I wish to God that I wasn't. Then at least this infernal pounding in my head would cease."

Closer inspection revealed that he hadn't escaped the events of the night unscathed. Although he'd changed into fresh garments, dark gold stubble shaded his jaw. The skin around his scar looked pinched and white and the shadows beneath his eyes deeper than usual.

His laconic grace of last night had vanished, leaving in its place a rigid posture, which seemed to owe less to formality than to the obvious discomfort he was suffering every time he moved his head.

"Please sit." As she seated herself, he said, "I'm sorry to have summoned you so abruptly. I realize I must have interrupted your packing."

Puzzled, she opened her mouth, but before she could get anything out, he continued, his long fingers toying with the brass handle of the letter opener. "I can't blame you for leaving, of course. My behavior last night was reprehensible. I'd like to blame it on the liquor, but I'm afraid my ill temper and bad judgement must bear equal responsibility. However it might have appeared, I can assure you that I'm not in the habit of forcing my attentions on the female servants of my household."

Samantha felt a curious pang in the vicinity of her heart. She had almost allowed herself to forget that was all she was to him—a servant. "Are you entirely certain about that, my lord? I do believe I've heard Mrs. Philpot mention an incident with a certain young chambermaid on the back stairs . . ."

Gabriel whipped his head toward her, wincing as he did so. "I was barely fourteen when that happened! And as I recall, Musette was the one who cornered me . . ." He trailed off, his eyes narrowing as he realized she had deliberately provoked him.

"You can put your conscience at ease, my lord," she assured him, adjusting her spectacles. "I'm not some love-starved spinster who believes every man she meets is out to ravish her. Nor am I some moonstruck debutante swooning over a stolen kiss."

Although Gabriel's expression sharpened, he held his tongue.

"As far as I'm concerned," she said with an airiness she was far from feeling, "we can both pretend your little indiscretion never happened. Now, if you'll excuse me," she said, rising from the chair. "Unless you've found some other reason to send me packing, I have several—"

"I want you to stay," he blurted out.

"Pardon me?"

"I want you to stay," he repeated. "You claim you used to be a governess. Well, I want you to teach me."

"Teach you what, my lord? Although your manners might lack a certain polish, as far as I can tell, you're quite proficient in your letters and your numbers."

"I want you to teach me how to go on living like this." He lifted both hands, palms upward, revealing their faint tremble. "I want you to teach me how to be blind."

Samantha sank back down in the chair. Gabriel Fairchild was not a man to beg. Yet he'd just bared both his pride and his soul to her. For a long moment, she couldn't speak at all.

Mistaking her hesitation for skepticism, he said, "I can't promise to be the most agreeable of students, but I'll strive to be the most able." His hands curled into fists. "Given my recent conduct, I realize I have no right to ask this of you, but—"

"I'll do it," she said softly.

"You will?"

"I will. But I should warn you that I can be a very stern taskmaster. If you don't cooperate, you can expect a sound scolding."

A ghost of a smile skirted his lips. "What, no caning?"

"Only if you're impertinent." She rose again. "Now, if you'll excuse me, I have some lessons to plan."

She was almost to the door when Gabriel spoke again, his voice gruff. "About last night?"

She turned, almost grateful that he couldn't see the spark of hope in her eyes. "Yes?"

His ravaged countenance was as devoid of mockery as she had ever seen it. "I promise you such a regrettable lapse in judgment will never happen again."

Although Samantha felt her treacherous stomach dive toward her shoes, she struggled to inject a lighthearted smile into her voice. "Very good, my lord. I'm sure Mrs. Philpot and all of the maids will sleep more soundly in their beds tonight."

That afternoon it was Samantha's turn to summon Gabriel. She deliberately chose the sunny drawing room for their first lesson, believing its spacious open areas would best suit her plans. A beaming Beckwith ushered Gabriel into the room, then backed toward the door, bowing all the way. As he drew the doors closed, Samantha would have almost sworn the butler winked at her, although she knew that if pressed, he would swear he simply had a speck of soot in his eye.

"Good afternoon, my lord. I thought we'd begin our lessons with this." Stepping forward, Samantha pressed the object she was holding into Gabriel's hand.

"What is it?" He held the object gingerly between two fingers, as if she just might be inclined to hand him a garden snake.

"It's one of your old walking sticks. And a very elegant one, I should say."

As Gabriel's graceful fingers explored the handsome lion's head carved into the cane's ivory handle, his suspicious scowl deepened. "What good is a walking stick when I can't see where I'm walking?"

"That's precisely my point. It has occurred to me that if you ever hope to stop blundering about the house like a waltzing bear, you need to know what's in front of you *before* you crash into it."

His expression growing more thoughtful, Gabriel lifted the cane and swept it in a wide arc. Samantha ducked as it whistled past her ear. "Not like that! This isn't a sword fight!"

"If it was, I might stand a sporting chance."

"Only if your opponent was also blind." Sighing with exasperation, Samantha moved behind him. Reaching around, she closed her fingers over his until they were both firmly gripping the cane's carved head. She lowered its tip to floor level, then began to guide his arm into a gentle arc. "That's it. Just swing it slowly. Back and forth. To and fro."

Lulled by her hypnotic, singsong tone, their bodies swayed in time as if to the rhythm of some primitive dance. Samantha was seized by an absurd notion to press her cheek to the back of his shirt. He smelled so warm and deliciously male, like a glade of sun-warmed pines on a lazy summer afternoon.

"Um . . . Miss Wickersham?"

"Hmmmm?" she responded, still lost in her dreamy reverie.

Gabriel's voice shook with barely suppressed amusement. "If this is a walking stick, shouldn't we be walking?"

"Oh! Of course we should!" Jerking away from him, she smoothed a strand of hair away from her burning cheek. "I mean, of course *you* should. If you'll step right over here to the corner, I've devised a set of paths and obstacles where you can practice your skills."

Without thinking, she seized him by the forearm. Gabriel stiffened, resistance coiled in every muscle. She tugged, but his boots showed no sign of budging. Samantha realized it was the first time she'd ever tried to lead him anywhere. Even when Beckwith escorted him around the house, the butler never actually dared to touch him unless it was to briefly point him toward his desired direction.

She waited for him to shake away her hand, to bark that he wouldn't tolerate being led about like some sort of helpless child. But after a moment, she felt the tension begin to melt away beneath her firm, but gentle, grip. Although his reluctance was still palpable, when she moved, he moved with her.

With Peter and Phillip's help, she had arranged a pair of Grecian sofas, three chairs, and two ottomans into a grouping that closely approximated a cluttered parlor. Interspersed throughout that grouping were two or three occasional tables and twin Doric pedestals bearing the marble likenesses of Athena, the goddess of wisdom, and Diana, the goddess of the hunt. Samantha had even arranged a few china figurines and other breakables on the tables, believing that Gabriel needed to learn to navigate his way around small obstacles as well as large ones.

She positioned him at the mouth of her design. "This is really quite simple. All you have to do is use the walking stick to make your way to the other side of the drawing room."

He scowled straight ahead. "If I don't succeed, are you going to cane me with it?"

"Only if you don't keep a civil tongue in your head."

Although Samantha forced herself to step away from him, she could not stop her hands from making helpless little fluttering motions around his shoulders.

Instead of sweeping, Gabriel thrust the walking stick forward in more of a poking motion. As the cane glanced off the first pedestal, the smirking bust atop it began to teeter. Samantha rushed forward, catching Diana before she could go crashing to the floor.

Staggering beneath the bust's weight, she said, "That was a fine first effort! But you might try just a tad bit more subtlety. Try to think of it as one of the topiary mazes at Vauxhall," she urged, referring to the legendary pleasure gardens in London. "You wouldn't just go stabbing your way through one of those, would you?"

"Usually when a gentleman is successful in navigating a maze, there's some sort of reward waiting for him at its center."

Samantha laughed. "Theseus found only the Minotaur waiting for him."

"Ah, but the young warrior's boldness and courage in defeating the beast won Princess Ariadne's heart."

"He never would have dared to be so bold if the clever girl hadn't given him an enchanted sword and a ball of thread he could follow to the exit," she reminded him. "If you were Theseus, just what sort of reward would you fancy?"

A kiss.

The answer rose unbidden to Gabriel's lips, setting his nerves even more on edge. He was already beginning to regret the noble promise he had made that morning. If only his nurse's husky courtesan's laugh wasn't so at odds with her prim demeanor . . .

Perhaps it was just as well he couldn't see. If he could see her lips, he would constantly be thinking of how sweet they had tasted beneath his.

He had already wasted an inordinate amount of his morning wondering what color they were. Were they a tender pink, like the inside of some delicate seashell half buried in the sugary sand? Were they the dusky rose of a bloom growing wild on a windswept moor? Or were they the lush coral of some exotic island fruit that made your tongue and your senses sing with pleasure? And what difference did their hue make when he already knew they were deliciously plump—perfectly fashioned for the pleasures of kissing?

"I know what your reward will be!" she exclaimed when he made no reply. "If you practice with enough diligence, you'll soon be so proficient you'll no longer have any need of me."

Although Gabriel acknowledged her jest with a grudging smile, he was beginning to wonder if that day would ever come.

Samantha came to him in the night. He no longer required light or color, only sensation: the lemony sweetness of her fragrance, the sleek tumble of her unbound hair gliding like raw silk over his naked chest, her throaty whimper as she nestled the softness of her body against him.

He groaned as she nuzzled his ear, boldly touched her tongue to his lips, the curve of his jaw . . . the tip of his nose. Her warm breath tickled his face, smelling of musty earth, overripe beef, and moldy stockings hung over a fire to dry.

"What the—" Springing awake, Gabriel shoved the furry muzzle away from his face.

He sat up, scrubbing desperately at his lips with the back of his hand. It took his desire-and-sleep-fogged brain several seconds to absorb the fact that it wasn't night, but morning, and the exuberant creature frolicking in his bed was most definitely not his nurse.

"Why, look at that!" Samantha exclaimed from somewhere near the foot of the bed, her voice brimming with pride. "The two of you have barely been introduced and he's already taken a liking to you!"

"What in the devil is it?" Gabriel demanded, trying to get a grip on the thing. "A kangaroo?" He let out a muffled *oomph* as the interloper bounced across his aching groin.

Samantha laughed. "Don't be silly! He's a charming little collie. I was walking past your gamekeeper's cottage yesterday evening when he came trotting out to greet me. I decided he'd be just perfect."

"For what?" Gabriel said darkly, struggling to keep the squirming creature at arm's length. "Sunday luncheon?"

"I should say not!" Samantha whisked the beast away from him. From the crooning that ensued, he gathered that she was actually cuddling the little monster in her arms. "Him is no wuncheon, is he? Not our pwecious wittle fewwow."

Collapsing against the pillows, Gabriel shook his head in disbelief. Who would have thought his nurse's acid-tipped tongue was capable of spouting such drivel? At least he didn't have to watch her stroke the creature's squirming belly or, worse yet, rub noses with it. The emotion seething through him was so foreign it took him a minute to identify it. He was jealous! Jealous of some mangy mongrel with coarse fur and the breath of a three-day-old corpse.

"Careful there," Gabriel warned as the clucking and kissing noises continued. "He might give you fleas. Or the French pox," he muttered under his breath.

"You needn't worry about fleas. I had Peter and Phillip bathe him in one of Meg's old washtubs out in the yard."

"Which is where he should have stayed, as far as I'm concerned."

"But then you would have been deprived of his company. When I was a little girl, we once lived next door to an old gentleman who had lost his sight. He kept this small terrier who was his constant companion. When his footmen escorted him on a stroll, the terrier would always trot ahead on his jeweled leash and lead him around the uneven bricks and the mud puddles. If a hot coal tumbled out of the hearth and onto the rug, the dog would bark to alert the servants." As if on cue, the pup in her arms let out a shrill bark.

Gabriel winced. "How devilishly clever. Although I think burning to death in one's bed might have been preferable. Did the poor gent end up deaf as well as blind?"

"I'll have you know that dog was a loyal friend to him, a boon companion until the day the old man died. His underfootman told our upstairs maid that after they interred the old fellow, the poor dog spent days sitting outside of the family crypt, waiting for his beloved master to return." Her voice was muffled for a minute, as if she'd buried that luscious mouth of hers in the dog's fur. "Isn't that the most touching story you've ever heard?"

Gabriel was more intrigued by the fact that Samantha's family had been wealthy enough to engage the services of an upstairs maid. But when he heard her sniff and fumble in the pocket of her skirt for a handkerchief, he knew he was lost. He had absolutely no defenses whenever his sensible nurse waxed sentimental.

He sighed. "If you insist that I have a dog, can't it at least be a real one? An Irish wolfhound or a mastiff, perhaps?"

"Too unwieldy. This little fellow can follow you anywhere. And everywhere," she added, proving her point by dumping the creature back into Gabriel's lap.

He sniffed at the lemony sweetness of its fur, confirming his suspicion that the footmen had bathed the dog in Samantha's favorite fragrance. The animal wriggled free and bounded to the foot of the bed. Growling deep in its throat, it began to gnaw on Gabriel's toes through the eiderdown quilt. Gabriel bared his teeth, growling back at him.

"What would you like to call him?" Samantha asked.

"Nothing that can be repeated in front of a lady," he said, wresting his big toe from the dog's mouth.

"He is quite a tenacious little lad," she observed as the dog thumped to the floor. Feeling the quilt going with him, Gabriel made a frantic grab for it. A few more inches and Miss Wickersham would discover the shocking effect both his dream and her husky crooning had had on him.

"He is rather stubborn and intractable," Gabriel agreed. "Hard-headed. Utterly impossible to reason with or please. Set upon having his own way even if it means trampling over the needs and desires of everyone in his path. I believe I should like to call him . . ." Gabriel's lips curved into a smile as he relished her expectant silence, "*Sam*."

In the days that followed, Gabriel would have occasion to call the dog everything *but* his name. Instead of trotting along in front of him to ferret out obstacles and potential dangers, the infernal creature seemed to delight in bounding around him in circles, weaving in and out through his legs, and knocking his walking stick out from under him. Had she possessed any motive beyond perpetual exasperation, he would have suspected his nurse of trying to arrange a fatal fall.

At least no one could accuse her of exaggerating. The dog was certainly a *constant* companion. No matter where Gabriel went in the house, its eager panting and the steady click-click of little toenails on the parquet and marble floors followed. The footmen no longer had to worry about sweeping the dining room after Gabriel ate. Sam would sit directly beneath his master's chair, catching every spilled morsel in his gaping mouth before it could strike the floor. When Gabriel went to lay his head down on his pillow at night, he would find it already occupied by a warm, furry ball.

If the dog wasn't panting down his neck, it was snoring in his ear. When Gabriel could no longer bear its huffing and wheezing, he would drag the quilt off the bed and stumble into the sitting room to sleep.

He awoke one morning to discover that the dog had vanished. Unfortunately, so had half of his finest pair of Hessians.

Gabriel made his way down the stairs, using the walking stick to navigate each tread. In truth, he was rather proud of the progress he was making with it and eager to show off his growing mastery to Samantha. But the elegant cane did nothing to prevent him from stepping right into the warm puddle at the foot of the stairs.

He lifted his stockinged foot, struggling to absorb what had just happened to him in more ways than one. Throwing back his head, he bellowed, "*Sam!*" at the top of his lungs.

Both the dog and his nurse answered his summons. The dog scampered around him three times, then plopped down soundly on his dry foot, while Samantha exclaimed, "Oh, dear! I'm ever so sorry! Phillip was supposed to take him for a walk in the garden this morning. Or was it Peter?"

Shaking the dog off of his foot, Gabriel advanced toward the sound of her voice, his wet stocking squelching with each step. "I don't care if the archbishop himself was supposed to come down from London and toilet the little beast. I don't want him underfoot for another minute. Especially not under *my* feet!" He flung a finger in what he hoped was the direction of the door, although he feared it was only the hall tree. "I want him out of my house!"

"Oh, come, now. It's not really the little fellow's fault. You should know better than to wander about the house in your stockings."

"I might have been wearing the boots Beckwith had laid out for me," he explained with exaggerated patience, "if I could have found both of them. But when I awoke, the right one had mysteriously gone missing."

A masculine voice, cracking with excitement, came from the direction of the door. "You won't believe this. Look what the gardener just dug up!"

Chapter 11

My darling Cecily,

Perhaps my bashfulness has prevented me from speaking as boldly as I should—I mean to have you for my own . . .

"What is it?" Gabriel demanded, his sense of foreboding growing.

"Oh, nothing," Samantha replied hastily. "It's just Peter going on about some nonsense."

"It's not Peter, it's Phillip," Gabriel pointed out.

"How can you tell?" She sounded genuinely amazed that he could distinguish one twin from the other.

"Peter favors only a touch of rose water in his daily toilette while Phillip douses himself in the stuff in the hopes that young Elsie will take notice of him. And I don't need my sight to tell me he's probably as pink as a peony right now. What have you got there, lad?" he asked, addressing the boy directly.

"Nothing of any concern to you, my lord," Samantha assured him. "Just a particularly lovely . . . carrot. Why don't you carry it off to the kitchens, Phillip, and tell Étienne to start a nice stew for supper?"

The footman's confusion was evident in his voice. "Looks more like somebody's old boot to me. Wonder how it got all chewed up and buried in the garden."

Remembering how beautifully the Corinthian leather had hugged his calves, Gabriel barely resisted the urge to groan.

When he spoke again, his voice was soft and carefully controlled. "I'm going to make this very simple for you, Miss Wickersham. Either the dog goes"—he leaned close enough to smell the mint-flavored warmth of her breath—"or you do."

She sniffed. "Well, if you're going to put it that way. Phillip, would you please escort Sam out to the garden?"

"Certainly, miss. But what am I do with this?"

"We must return it to its rightful owner."

Before Gabriel realized what she was going to do, the muddy, drool-encrusted boot smacked him in the chest.

"Thank you," he said stiffly, removing it to arm's length.

Sweeping the walking stick ahead of him, he turned and strode back toward the stairs. But his dignified exit was spoiled when he reached their foot a step sooner than he anticipated. He froze, realizing with a sinking sensation that his right stocking was now as wet as his left.

Feeling Miss Wickersham's amused gaze on his back, he went marching up the stairs, squelching all the way.

Gabriel dragged his pillow over his ears, but not even the luxuriant layers of down could muffle the despondent howling that came drifting up through the window of his bedchamber. It had started the moment his head had hit the pillow and showed no sign of stopping before dawn. The dog sounded as if his little heart had been broken clean in two.

Throwing himself to his back, Gabriel hurled the pillow in the direction of the window. A reproachful silence hung over the rest of the house. Miss Wickersham was probably curled up in her bed, sleeping the blissful sleep of the virtuous. He could almost see her there, the silky strands of her unbound hair spilling across the pillow, those petal-soft lips of her parted by each breath. But even in his imagination, shadows veiled her delicate features.

She had probably washed the lemon verbena from her skin while preparing for bed, leaving only the essential sweetness of her scent. It was richer and more intoxicating than any bought fragrance could ever be, promising a garden of earthly delights no man could resist.

Gabriel groaned, his body aching with frustration and longing. If the dog didn't settle down soon, he'd be howling right along with it.

Tossing back the quilt, he rose and padded toward the window. He fumbled with the latch, then jerked up the sash, earning a splinter in his thumb for his efforts.

"Hush!" he hissed down into the void beneath his window. *"For pity's sake, can't you please just hush!"*

The dog's howling abruptly ceased. There was a hopeful whimper, then silence. Breathing a sigh of relief, Gabriel turned back toward the bed.

The howling resumed, twice as heart-wrenching as before.

Gabriel slammed down the window, then strode back to the bed and groped for the dressing gown draped over the bedpost. He charged out of the room without even bothering to retrieve his walking stick.

"Serve them all right if I took a tumble down the stairs and broke my neck," he muttered as he felt his way down the steps, creeping along an inch at a time. "Instead of crying over my grave, the dog would probably take a piss on it. Ought to order the gamekeeper to shoot the damn thing."

After stumbling over an ottoman and barking his shins on the clawed foot of a bombé chest, he managed to get one of the French windows in the library unlatched.

As he swung open the window, the cool night air caressed his skin. He hesitated, reluctant to expose his ravaged face to the dispassionate light of the moon.

But that mournful howling continued, calling to something deep inside of him. For all he knew, there was no moon.

He picked his way across the flagstone terrace, the loose stones jabbing the soles of his bare feet, then stepped into the dew-soaked grass, following the sound. He was almost on top of it when the night went quiet. So quiet he could hear the distant croak of a pond toad and the ragged whisper of his own breathing.

Dropping to his knees, he patted the ground around him with both hands. "Oh, for heaven's sake, where are you, you little mongrel? If I didn't want to find you, you'd be slobbering all over me."

A nearby bush rustled and a solid bundle of fur came shooting into his arms as if it had been launched from a cannon. Whimpering joyfully, the little collie stood up on his hind legs and began to bathe Gabriel's face in warm, wet kisses.

"There, there," he murmured, gathering the trembling animal into his arms. "There's no need to go all sentimental on me. All I want is a decent night's rest."

Still holding the dog, Gabriel staggered to his feet and began to make the long trek back to his chamber. He had to admit that with that small, warm body tucked beneath his chin, the night didn't seem quite so dark or the trek so long.

Not even Samantha dared comment the next morning when Gabriel made his way downstairs with Sam trotting cheerfully at his heels. Although he still grumbled about the dog being constantly underfoot, whenever he thought no one was looking, she would catch him stroking the pup's silky ears or dropping a particularly choice morsel of meat beneath the table.

By the end of that week, Gabriel was able to negotiate the maze of furniture without gouging any of the table legs or sending a single marble goddess or china shepherdess toppling to her doom.

Pleased with his progress, Samantha decided it was time for their next lesson.

That evening Gabriel found himself pacing back and forth in front of the dining room doors, his growling belly making him feel more like a caged animal with each step. He had arrived at his customary supper hour, only to be informed by a stammering Beckwith that dinner would be delayed and he was to wait outside the doors until he was summoned.

Gripping his walking stick, Gabriel pressed one ear to the door, intrigued by the mysterious rustling and clinking coming from within. Both his curiosity and his foreboding increased when he recognized his nurse's soft, yet commanding, murmur.

Gabriel was so intent on trying to make out her words that he didn't hear Beckwith approach the door. When the butler swept it open, he nearly fell headfirst into the room.

"Good evening, my lord," Samantha said from somewhere to his left, amusement ripe in her voice. "I hope you'll forgive the delay. I appreciate your patience."

Scowling, Gabriel planted the tip of the walking stick on the floor, struggling to regain both his footing and his dignity. "I was beginning to wonder if this was going to be a midnight supper. Or perhaps an early breakfast." He cocked his head, but didn't hear the familiar panting that usually accompanied his every meal. "Just what have you done with Sam? Is it too much to hope that he's dressed out on a silver platter with an apple in his mouth?"

"Sam will be dining in the servants' hall tonight. But don't fret on his behalf. Peter and Phillip have promised to drop an ample amount of food beneath their chairs. I hope you'll forgive me for banishing him, but I thought it was time you grew accustomed to being surrounded by the trappings of civilization again." A smile warmed her voice. "So to that end, the table is draped with a cloth of snowy white linen. There are three branched silver candlesticks along its length, each holding four slender wax tapers and casting a hospitable glow over the finest china, crystal, and silver plate Mrs. Philpot could provide."

It didn't require much imagination for Gabriel to envision the charming picture Samantha painted. There was only one problem. Even with his walking stick in hand, he was afraid to take so much as a single step toward the table for fear of bumbling over something breakable or catching himself on fire.

Sensing his hesitation, Samantha gently claimed his elbow. "If you'll allow me, I'll escort you to your chair. I took the liberty of seating you at the head of the table where you belong."

"Does that mean you'll be dining in the servants' hall where *you* belong?" he asked as she guided him around the table.

She patted his arm. "Don't be ridiculous. I wouldn't dream of depriving you of my company."

At her urging, he slid into his chair. As he heard her take a seat to his immediate right, he awkwardly folded his hands in his lap. He'd forgotten what he was supposed to do with them when they weren't snatching for food. They suddenly seemed too large and awkward for his wrists.

To his keen relief, one of the servants immediately arrived with the first course.

"Roast turkey breast with wild mushrooms," Samantha offered as the footman ladled a portion onto his plate.

The succulent aroma drifted to Gabriel's nose, making his mouth water. He waited until he heard the footman leave before reaching for his plate. Samantha cleared her throat sharply.

He jerked his hand back, duly chastened.

"Your fork is to your left, my lord. Your knife to the right."

Sighing, Gabriel patted the tablecloth next to his plate until he located his fork. Its weight felt foreign and clumsy in his hand. On his first stab toward the plate, he missed the food entirely. The silver clinked loudly against the fine bone china, making him wince. It took three more tries to locate a lone mushroom. After chasing the vexatious thing around the plate for nearly a minute, he finally managed to skewer it with the fork and bring it to his mouth.

Savoring its musky flavor, he asked, "What are you wearing, Miss Wickersham?"

"Pardon?" she asked, plainly taken aback by the question.

"You described everything else in the dining room. Why not yourself? For all I know, you could be sitting there in your chemise and stockings." Spearing another mushroom, Gabriel ducked his head to hide a smile at the deliciously wicked image.

"I hardly think my attire is pertinent to the enjoyment of our meal," Samantha replied, her voice dripping frost. "Perhaps we should have begun our evening with a lesson in civilized discourse."

Gabriel would have preferred to swipe the dishes off the table and give her a lesson in uncivilized inter—

He swallowed the mushroom, halting that dangerous line of thought. "Humor me, why don't you? How am I to engage in civilized discourse with a lady when I can't even picture her in my mind?"

"Very well," she said stiffly. "Tonight I happen to be wearing a dinner gown fashioned from black bombazine. It has a rather high ruff in the Elizabethan style and a woolen shawl to shield me from any drafts."

He shuddered. "Sounds like something one's maiden aunt might wear to a burial. Especially her own. Have you always favored such grim colors?"

"Not always," Samantha replied softly.

"What about your hair?"

"If you must know," she replied, exasperation evident in her voice, "I have it wound into a knot and tucked into a black lace net at my nape. It's a style I find to be quite serviceable."

Gabriel spent a moment in thought before shaking his head. "I'm sorry. That simply won't do at all."

"*I beg your pardon?*"

"I can't bear to picture you draped in widow's weeds. It's spoiling my appetite. At least I was spared a description of your shoes, which I'm sure are the very height of sensibility."

He heard a faint rustling, as if Samantha had lifted the table-cloth to peer underneath it, but she offered no defense.

He leaned back in his chair, stroking the stubble on his chin. "I believe you're wearing something in the scandalous new French style—a cream muslin, perhaps, with a high waist and a low, square-cut bodice, its fabric designed to gently embrace the feminine form in all of its glory." He narrowed his eyes. "And I don't see you wearing a shawl, but a cashmere stole as soft as angel's wings draped right above that deliciously kissable dimple in the crook of your elbow. Your hem grazes your ankles, just high enough to offer a teasing glimpse of a blush-colored silk stocking with every step you take."

He expected her to interrupt his shocking recitation with an outraged protest, but it was almost as if she'd been hypnotized by the smoky timbre of his voice.

"On your feet, you're wearing a pair of pink silk slippers, utterly frivolous, unsuited for anything but sashaying into a ball-room and dancing the night away. A matching ribbon has been twined through your topknot of artfully disheveled curls, a few of which have been allowed to tumble around your cheeks, almost as if you had just emerged from your bath."

For a long moment, there was no sound at all. When Samantha finally did speak, there was a breathless quality to her voice that made Gabriel want to grin. "Certainly no one can accuse you of lacking imagination, my lord. Or a rather shocking familiarity with women's garments."

He lifted one shoulder in a sheepish shrug. "A consequence of spending too much of my youth attempting to remove them."

Her swallow was audible. "Perhaps we'd best eat before you feel compelled to describe my imaginary undergarments."

"That won't be necessary," he replied in a tone as smooth as silk. "You're not wearing any."

Samantha's sharp intake of breath and the violent clink of silver against china warned him that she had filled her mouth to keep from having to endure any more of his impertinence.

Wishing he could do the same, Gabriel made another stab at his plate. He managed to spear a slab of the meat, but he could tell by its weight that it was still far too large to bring to his lips without earning a reprimand. Gritting his teeth, he sighed. The turkey could have been no more elusive if it had been running up and down the table, squawking and flapping its wings. If he didn't wish to starve before morning, it seemed he would have no choice but to engage the services of his knife.

He groped to the right of his plate, but before he could locate the knife's handle, its blade sliced neatly into the pad of his thumb.

"Damn it all!" he swore, tucking the throbbing appendage between his lips.

"Oh, dear!" Samantha cried in genuine dismay. "Are you hurt?" He heard the scrape of her chair as she rose.

"Don't!" he snapped, brandishing the fork in her direction as if it were a saber. "I don't need your sympathy. What I need is some food in my stomach, because if I get any hungrier I just might eat you."

He heard her sink back into her chair. "I wasn't thinking," she said softly. "Won't you at least allow me to cut up your meat?"

"No, thank you. Unless you're planning on following me around for the rest of my life, cutting up my meat and wiping my chin, I'd best learn to do it myself."

Tossing down the fork, Gabriel reached for his goblet, hoping a generous mouthful of wine might dull his embarrassment at being such a clumsy lout. But his awkward swipe only succeeded in overturning the goblet. He didn't need his sight, only Samantha's startled gasp, to know that the wine had gone spilling over the snowy white tablecloth and into her lap.

He surged to his feet, shame, hunger, and frustration finally getting the best of him. "This is madness! I'd be better off begging on some street corner than pretending I still have a hope in hell of passing myself off as a gentleman!" He slammed one fist down on the table, rattling the china. "Did you know that ladies used to compete for the privilege of sitting next to me at supper? That they would vie for my attentions as if they were some rare and delectable sweetmeat? What woman is going to want my company now? She'd have nothing to look forward to but a few surly growls and a lapful of claret. That is, if I didn't inadvertently set her curls on fire before supper was even served!"

Fisting his hands in the tablecloth, he gave it a hard yank, sending all of the china, all of the crystal, all of Samantha's fine efforts tumbling to the floor with a resounding crash.

Gabriel felt a draft at his back as someone came rushing in.

"It's all right, Beckwith," Samantha said quietly. The butler must have hesitated, for she added in a voice that brooked no argument, "I'll see to it."

Then Beckwith and the draft were gone, leaving them alone again. Gabriel stood there at the head of the table, flushed and breathing hard. He wanted Samantha to rage at him, to tell him what a monster he'd become. He wanted her to tell him that there was no help for him, no hope. Maybe then he could stop trying, stop fighting . . .

Instead, he felt her shoulder brush his thigh as she knelt at his feet. "Once I get these things cleared away," she said softly over the muted clinking of broken glass and shattered china, "I'll send for a fresh plate."

Her sedate calm, her refusal to let him ruffle her composure, only made him angrier. Groping for her wrist, Gabriel snatched her up and against his heaving chest. "You seem quite capable of working yourself into a fine temper when you're defending the naïve fools who serve your king and country, yet you won't defend yourself. Have you no heart?" he bit off. "No feelings at all?"

"Oh, I have feelings!" she shot back. "I feel every barbed lash of your tongue, every cutting remark. If I had no feelings, I certainly wouldn't have wasted my entire day trying to make supper a pleasant experience for you. I wouldn't have risen at dawn to quiz your cook about your favorite dishes. I wouldn't have spent all morning combing the woods for some particularly succulent mushrooms. And I certainly wouldn't have spent half the afternoon trying to decide which china should grace your table—the Worcester or the Wedgwood." Gabriel could feel her slender body trembling with emotion. "Yes, I have feelings. And I have a heart as well, my lord. I just have no intention of letting you break it!"

As she jerked out of his grip, something hot and wet splashed on Gabriel's hand. He heard her fleeing footsteps crunch across the broken glass, then the slam of a door.

Knowing he was well and truly alone, Gabriel touched his tongue to the back of his hand, tasting salt.

Sinking heavily into his chair, he buried his head in his hands. "She was right about one thing, you stupid oaf," he muttered to himself. "You could certainly use a lesson in civilized discourse at the supper table."

It was a long time before Gabriel felt a warm hand settle on his shoulder. "My lord? May I help you?" Beckwith's voice quavered slightly, as if he were already steeling himself for a brusque rejection.

Gabriel slowly lifted his head. "You know, Beckwith," he said, reaching around to pat the devoted manservant's hand, "I believe you just might."

≈ *Chapter 12* ≈

My darling Cecily,

I can't tell you how relieved I am that you claim to admire bold-ness in a man . . .

Samantha was sulking.

She wasn't particularly adept at it. Even as a small child, she'd rarely had to resort to petulance to win her way. Usually a sweet smile and a logical argument was all it took to wheedle what she wanted from her mama and papa. But now she had no hope of ever getting what she wanted.

For three days she barely left her bedchamber unless it was to dine with the servants in their basement hall. She carried a book with her at all times. If anyone even looked as if they were think-ing of approaching her, she would bury her nose in it until they went away, taking their sidelong glances and worried sighs with them.

She knew that she was being childish, that by not fulfilling her duties she was giving Gabriel ample cause to have Beckwith send a message to his father and have her dismissed. But she could no longer bring herself to care.

It didn't improve her mood to realize he was avoiding her just as studiously as she was avoiding him. Apparently, the mere thought of encountering her by chance was so repugnant to him that he'd ordered that the drawing room doors be kept closed and locked whenever he sought refuge there. Samantha would march right past the doors, determined to ignore the succession of odd thumps and the occasional excited bark that drifted to her ears.

Beckwith and Mrs. Philpot seemed equally indifferent to her misery. Twice, she found them huddled in some secluded corner, muttering to each other in a most distracted manner. The minute they spotted her, they would snap their mouths shut with a guilty start and go rushing off, mumbling about some pressing task such as polishing the soup ladle or making sure Meg put adequate starch in the table linens. Samantha assumed they were discussing the kindest way to inform her that she should start looking for another position.

She found sleep to be as elusive as peace. On the third night after her quarrel with Gabriel, she was lying in bed, scowling up at the ceiling, when her stomach began to growl. Since she'd already wasted half the night flinging herself this way and that beneath the bedclothes, she decided to creep downstairs and pilfer a cold pasty pie from the deserted kitchens.

She was passing by the drawing room when a muffled strain of song drifted to her ears. Thinking how odd it was that the doors would be closed when it was well after midnight, she pressed an ear to one of their gilded panels.

She wasn't losing her wits. The sound she'd heard *had* been music. Of a sort. A man was humming while a woman accompanied him in a warbling soprano.

Before she could identify the words of the song, the man began to chant a staccato, "One, two, three, four . . . one, two, three, four . . ."

A tremendous crash sounded. After a lengthy and mysterious silence, brisk footsteps hastened toward the door.

Samantha darted across the foyer, barely managing to duck behind a life-sized marble statue of Apollo before one of the doors came swinging open.

Beckwith emerged from the darkened room, huffing slightly, his sparse strands of hair ruffled as if by a woman's fingers. Samantha's mouth fell open in shock as Mrs. Philpot followed, smoothing her apron and tucking a loose strand of hair behind her ear.

The housekeeper tilted her patrician nose in the air. "Goodnight, Mr. Beckwith."

"Sleep well, Mrs. Philpot," he replied, sketching her a formal bow.

As they went marching off in separate directions, Samantha emerged from behind the statue, her mouth still hanging open. She wouldn't have been surprised had Elsie and Phillip come spilling out of the drawing room, flushed and giggling, but she never would have suspected the staid butler and stern housekeeper of indulging in a midnight rendezvous. It seemed the senior domestic staff of Fairchild Park was luckier in love than she was. Shaking her head, she went creeping back up the stairs, her appetite spoiled.

By the next afternoon, Samantha's morose mood was beginning to wear on her own nerves. Snatching up her shawl, she decided to go for a long walk on the grounds of the park, hoping the chasing clouds and blustery April wind would drive all thoughts of Gabriel from her head.

She returned to find a large rectangular wooden box resting on her bed.

Tossing her shawl over the nearest chair, she approached the box warily. Perhaps Beckwith had ordered it sent up to help hold her belongings when she was turned out on her ear.

She gingerly eased the lid off the box. A gasp rose unbidden to her lips. Nestled within its sandalwood-scented confines was a lady's gown, the delicate muslin a rich buttercream hue. Unable to resist the temptation, Samantha lifted the dress and smoothed it against her chest.

She hadn't seen anything so exquisite in a *very* long time. The gown's short puffed sleeves were trimmed with a piping of blond lace, while a broad satin ribbon gathered the fabric just below the softness of her breasts. The square bodice was cut just low enough to entice a man's eye. Because the fabric was so light as to be nearly sheer, only the most delicate and feminine of undergarments could be worn beneath its classically draped skirt.

From its gauzy shoulders to the graceful train flowing from its scalloped hemline, the gown couldn't have fit Samantha more perfectly had it been tailored especially for her by one of the most fashionable modistes in Paris.

I believe you're wearing something in the scandalous new French style.

As Gabriel's smoky baritone caressed her senses, she spotted the vellum card that had been dislodged from the gown's folds.

Still hugging the dress, she plucked the card from the box, recognizing Beckwith's precise script. "'Lord Sheffield requests the pleasure of your company for supper tonight at eight o'clock,'" she murmured.

As the card fluttered from her fingers, she slowly lowered the dress to the bed, realizing how ridiculous it must look against her sensible brown worsted.

She had no choice but to decline Gabriel's gift and his invitation. She wasn't one of his former mistresses, to be coaxed out of her sulk with expensive gifts and honeyed words. Her wistful gaze was drawn back to the box. She'd been so besotted with the dress that she hadn't finished unearthing its treasures.

She reached back into the box, only to find her fingertips caressing . . .

. . . a cashmere stole as soft as angel's wings draped right above that deliciously kissable dimple in the crook of your elbow.

Samantha snatched back her hand. How could a blind man know about that dimple? Because every woman had one, she reminded herself sternly. Gabriel had probably kissed an abundance of them before losing his sight.

She swept up the lid, determined to secure this particular Pandora's box before another, even more beguiling temptation could fly up into her face.

On your feet, you're wearing a pair of pink silk slippers, utterly frivolous, unsuited for anything but sashaying into a ballroom and dancing the night away.

"Not the shoes," Samantha whispered, her fingers curling around the lid of the box. "Surely he wouldn't be so diabolical."

Lowering the lid to the bed, she cautiously nudged the stole aside. A helpless moan escaped her lips. The slippers tucked into the bottom of the box were the soft rose of a woman's blush, so lovely and ethereal they appeared more suited to fairy feet than mortal.

Samantha's gaze dropped to her sturdy leather half-boots. They were even more scuffed and dusty than usual from tromping across the park's grounds in such a fine snit. She glanced back at the slippers, biting her lip. Surely there wouldn't be any harm in just trying them on. After all, what were the odds that they might actually fit? Snatching up a buttonhook, Samantha plopped down on the rug and began to unfasten her boots.

Samantha had grown accustomed to clomping around the mansion in her practical boots. With the delicate, low-heeled slippers laced around her ankles, she felt as if she were floating down the long curving staircase. She stole a glance at her reflection in the mirrored hall tree as she passed through the foyer. She wouldn't have been surprised to find a pair of gossamer wings sprouting from the creamy shoulders half bared by the elegant dress.

With its graceful skirt billowing about her ankles, she didn't feel like Gabriel's sensible nurse, but like a foolish young girl with a heart full of hope. Only she knew how dangerous that hope could be. As she turned toward the dining room, Samantha drew her homely spectacles from the pocket of the dress and defiantly slipped them on.

Although there was not a servant in sight, she could not shake the sensation of being watched, of doors softly opening and shutting behind her. As she passed the drawing room, she would have sworn she heard a wistful sigh, then Elsie's delighted giggle, hastily muffled. She whirled around to find the drawing room doors standing ajar. The darkened room appeared to be deserted.

She arrived at the dining room just as the clock on the landing began to chime eight o'clock. The imposing mahogany doors were closed. Samantha hesitated, unsure of her welcome. Gabriel must have felt like a beggar at his own feast as he awaited her summons a few nights ago.

Mustering her nerve, she straightened her stole, then knocked firmly on the door.

"Come in."

Samantha accepted the husky invitation, only to find the young prince from the portrait standing at the head of the table in a flickering pool of candlelight.

❧ *Chapter 13* ❧

My darling Cecily,

I should warn you that you encourage my boldness at your own risk . . .

The man standing at the head of the long table could have comfortably graced any dining or drawing room in London. From the glittering diamond stickpin securing the immaculate folds of his snowy white cravat to the sprightly leather tassels on his second finest pair of Hessians, he was a sight to make any valet beam with pride. His ruffled shirtfront and cuffs were perfectly accented by a deep blue cutaway tailcoat and a pair of buff-colored pantaloons that hugged his lean hips like a second skin.

His unfashionably long hair had been smoothed back into a black velvet queue, baring the strong line of his jaw and the striking planes of his face. The candle glow softened the harsh edges of his scar, cloaked the emptiness of his gaze.

Samantha's throat tightened with a yearning she could not afford to feel.

"I hope I didn't keep you waiting, my lord," she said, bobbing a curtsy he could not see. "I had planned to dine in the servants' hall. Where I belong."

The right corner of his mouth twitched. "That won't be necessary. You're not my nurse tonight. You're my guest."

With painstaking care, Gabriel moved to the chair at his right elbow and drew it out, arching one tawny eyebrow in invitation. Samantha hesitated, knowing she would be far safer if she remained at the foot of the table, well out of his reach. But Gabriel's expression was so boyishly hopeful that she found herself sweeping around the table to join him. As he leaned over to guide her chair effortlessly beneath the table, she was acutely aware of the strength in his muscular arms, the heat radiating from his broad chest.

He sank into his own chair. "I hope you don't mind the Worcester china. I'm afraid the Wedgwood met with an unfortunate accident."

Samantha's own lips twitched. "How very tragic." Peering around, she realized that the sideboard was empty and the linen-draped table was set with a variety of dishes, all within easy reach. She eyed a luscious platter of fresh strawberries. "I don't see anyone to attend us. Have you given the rest of the servants the night off as well?"

"I thought they deserved a respite from their duties. They've been very diligent this week."

"I should say so. It must have taken hours of work just to make this dress."

"Fortunately, there's so little fabric involved in the new styles that Meg was able to whip up the gown while suffering only one or two sleepless nights."

"And just how many sleepless nights did you suffer, my lord?"

Instead of answering, Gabriel reached for the bottle of claret that rested between them. Samantha snatched up her napkin, preparing for the worst, but his hand closed neatly around the graceful neck of the bottle. She watched in openmouthed surprise as he poured a healthy splash of the ruby liquid into both of their goblets without spilling a single drop on the pristine tablecloth.

"I can see the servants aren't the only ones who have been diligent this week," she observed softly, taking a sip of the rich red wine.

"May I serve you?" he asked, reaching for the spoon in a silver chafing dish of chicken fricassee.

"Certainly," she murmured, watching in fascination as he doled a precise portion onto both of their plates.

Disdaining fork and knife, he picked up his own spoon and began to eat. "So am I to assume the gown meets with your satisfaction?"

Samantha smoothed her skirt. "It's nearly as lovely as it is impractical. How did Meg manage to size it so perfectly?"

"She has a good eye for such things. She said you weren't much taller than my youngest sister, Honoria." A smile flirted with his lips. "Of course, had I gone by Beckwith's measurements, you could have worn the garment as a tent."

"What of the slippers? Am I to assume you have an equally gifted blacksmith?"

"There are advantages to living so close to London, you know. It does Beckwith's heart good to make the occasional trip to the shops on Oxford Street. And it wasn't difficult for Mrs. Philpot to sneak into your room and trace one of your boots while you were dining downstairs."

"The servants at Fairchild Park are a crafty lot, just like their master. You must know that I can't possibly keep these lovely things. It wouldn't be proper."

"Oh, come, now. I didn't flaunt convention that badly. You'll notice that I didn't include a single undergarment."

"That's just as well," Samantha replied sweetly, tucking a tasty morsel of chicken between her lips. "Since I'm not wearing any."

Gabriel's spoon clattered to the table. He took a huge gulp of the wine, but still seemed to be having difficulty swallowing. "I must say that I've never regretted my infirmity more," he finally managed to rasp out. He cleared his throat, his expression sobering. "I hope you'll accept more than my gifts. I hope you'll accept my apology for behaving so abominably the other night."

As Samantha watched his hand pat the tablecloth, patiently searching for the spoon, her smile faded. The spoon was only a few inches from his searching fingers, but it might as well have been in the next room. "I'm afraid I'm the one who should be begging your forgiveness. I hadn't realized how challenging such a simple task as eating must be for you."

He shrugged. "A knife and fork are rather tricky to manage. If I can't *feel* the food, I can't *find* the food." A thoughtful frown creased his brow. "Why don't I show you?"

Shoving his chair back, he rose, napkin in hand, and circled behind her chair. Samantha's pulse quickened as he leaned over her. His claret-warmed breath stirred the tiny hairs at her nape, making her regret sweeping her hair up into a frivolous topknot.

Before she could protest, he had reached around to draw off her spectacles. Working strictly by feel, he rolled the napkin into a band and gently draped it over her eyes, securing it behind her head with a loose knot.

Without the candlelight to guide her, Samantha had only Gabriel to rely on—his warmth, his scent, his touch. As the backs of his fingers grazed her throat, inciting a helpless shiver, she realized just how vulnerable she was to him.

"Are you to have your revenge by making me eat chicken fricassee with my fingers?" she asked.

"I wouldn't be so cruel. Not when we have the blind feeding the blind." She heard the scrape of platters as he reached around her to push one dish away and draw another one near. "Try this," he said, pressing a fork into her hand.

Feeling more than a little ridiculous, Samantha took a stab toward the dish in front of her. She wasn't sure what her target was supposed to be because it kept rolling away from her. After chasing it around the dish several times, she finally managed to impale the elusive thing. As she lifted the fork, the succulent aroma of fresh strawberry drifted to her nose. Her mouth started to water. The hard-won morsel was only an inch from her lips when it tumbled off of her fork to land with an impudent plop on the table.

"Blast it all!" she swore, waiting for Gabriel's mocking laughter to ring out.

But he simply reached around and gently removed the fork from her hand. "You see, Miss Wickersham, when one is deprived of one's sight, one is forced to rely on other senses. Such as scent . . ." As the tart fragrance of the strawberry flooded her nostrils, Samantha would have almost sworn she felt Gabriel's nose graze the side of her throat in a whisper-soft caress. "Touch . . ." His warm fingers curled possessively around her nape as he brushed the strawberry back and forth across her tingling lips, coaxing them apart. His voice deepened. "Taste . . ."

Seized by a delicious languor, she could not stop herself from opening for him. Not since the serpent approached Eve in the Garden had a woman been so tempted by forbidden fruit. Accepting her unspoken invitation, Gabriel slid the plump strawberry past her parted lips, where its sweet flesh exploded on her tongue. A low moan of satisfaction escaped her.

"More?" he offered, his smoky voice as enticing as the devil's in her ear.

Samantha wanted more. Much more. But she shook her head and pushed his hand away, afraid he might arouse a hunger that could never be satisfied. "I'm not a child," she said, deliberately mimicking him. "And I won't be fed like one."

"Very well. Suit yourself." She heard him shuffling dishes again, smacking his lips as he tasted each one in turn. "There," he finally said, returning the fork to her hand. "Try that."

Although the silky note in his voice should have warned her, Samantha boldly plunged the fork toward the dish, determined to prove she could capture whatever it contained on her first try. She gasped as her arm sank wrist-deep into a bowl of chilled goop.

"Étienne's syllabubs are quite legendary," Gabriel murmured in her ear. "He's been known to spend hours whipping the cream until he gets it to just the right consistency."

"Why, you sneaky wretch!" Samantha dragged her hand out of the sticky treat. "You did that on purpose."

She was fumbling for her napkin when Gabriel's hand closed over her wrist. "Allow me," he said, bringing her hand to his mouth.

Samantha was unprepared for the shock of her forefinger sliding between Gabriel's lips. The moist heat of his mouth was a stark contrast to the chill of the syllabub. He licked and sucked the rich cream from her finger with a sensual abandon that melted her defenses. It was only too easy to imagine him employing that same skillful tongue on other, even more vulnerable, parts of her body.

Samantha snatched back her hand, her cheeks burning beneath the blindfold. "When you invited me to sup with you, my lord, I wasn't aware that I was to be the main course."

"On the contrary, Miss Wickersham. You'd make a much more delectable dessert."

"Because of my sweet nature?" she could not resist asking in her most withering tone.

He laughed aloud. Unable to resist witnessing that rare occurrence, Samantha dragged off the makeshift blindfold. Gabriel was sprawled back in his chair, a crooked grin deepening the beguiling crinkles around his eyes.

For the rest of the evening, he was the ideal dinner companion, giving her a glimpse of the legendary charm that had tempted so many women to vie for his affections. After they'd finished off the rest of the syllabub, using their spoons instead of their fingers, he rose and offered her his hand.

Samantha dabbed at her lips with her napkin, afraid that she might follow wherever he would lead. "It's getting rather late, my lord. I really should retire."

"Don't go yet. I've something to show you."

Unable to resist that earnest plea, Samantha rose and slipped her hand into his, her wariness increasing. Using his walking stick to guide them, he escorted her from the dining room and down a long, shadowy corridor to a pair of gilded doors she had never noticed before.

Groping for the brass handles, he threw open both doors at once.

"Oh, my!" Samantha breathed, gazing upon a vision straight out of her imagination.

It was the ballroom she had discovered during her very first exploration of the mansion. But instead of looking down upon it from the gallery, she was poised at the very heart of its splendor. Every candle in the brass chandeliers had been lit, casting a shimmering glow over the blue-veined Venetian tiles. A row of French windows crowned with the graceful arches of glazed fanlights overlooked the moonlit garden.

Gabriel propped his walking stick against the wall. He would have no need of it here. There were no cumbersome pieces of furniture to fall over, no delicate figurines to shatter.

"May I have the pleasure of this dance, my lady?" he asked, offering her his arm.

"You've been practicing, haven't you?" Samantha said in an accusing tone, remembering the mysterious strains of music and the puzzling thumps she'd heard coming from the drawing room. "I thought Beckwith and Mrs. Philpot were having a midnight rendezvous."

Gabriel laughed as he led her to the center of the gleaming floor. "I doubt I left them with the necessary stamina. Beckwith and I knocked heads more times than I care to recount and Mrs. Philpot's poor toes never would have recovered if I hadn't been wearing stockings instead of boots. It didn't take us long to discover that I'm a miserable failure at both minuets and country dances."

"If you can't *feel* your partner," she began, remembering his earlier words.

". . . I can't *find* my partner. Which is why I spent most of last night waltzing with Beckwith." He sighed. "It's such a pity Mrs. Philpot doesn't waltz."

"Waltzing?" Samantha echoed, unable to hide her shock. "Why, the archbishop himself has denounced it as the height of debauchery!"

Gabriel's eyes sparkled with merriment. "Just imagine what he would have thought if he'd have seen me waltzing with my butler."

"Even the Prince of Wales claims it's utterly indecent for a man to hold a woman so close. That such proximity between partners can only lead to all manner of improprieties."

"Indeed?" Gabriel murmured, sounding far more intrigued than scandalized. He laced his fingers through hers, drawing her even closer.

Samantha's breath grew short, as if she'd already taken several turns around the ballroom. "Such a progressive dance might be acceptable in Vienna or Paris, my lord, but it's been banned in every ballroom in London."

"We're not in London," Gabriel reminded her, taking her into his arms.

He nodded toward the gallery. As a lone harpsichord manned by an unseen servant began to play, Gabriel splayed one hand at the small of her back and swept her into motion, accompanied by the tender strains of "Barbara Allen." The wistful ballad, with its tale of squandered opportunities and lost love, had always been one of Samantha's favorites. She'd never before heard it played as a waltz, but it lent itself perfectly to the gliding cadence of the dance.

As his body settled into the irresistible rhythm, Gabriel felt his natural grace returning. He closed his eyes, other, even more delicious sensations coming back to him as well—the thrill of holding a warm, female body against his, the silken whisper of her skirts, the trust with which she gave herself over to his lead. For the first time since Trafalgar, Gabriel did not mourn the loss of his sight. Whirling about the deserted ballroom with Samantha in his arms, he felt whole again.

Throwing his head back with an exultant laugh, Gabriel swept her into several swirling turns around the ballroom.

By the time the last strains of "Barbara Allen" had faded, they were both breathless with laughter. As the harpsichord launched into "Come Live with Me," a winsome tune more suited to an allemande than a waltz, their steps slowed to a halt. Gabriel held fast to Samantha, reluctant to surrender both her and the moment.

"If you're trying to convince me how civilized you are, you're failing miserably," she pointed out.

"Perhaps beneath our polished manners and fancy silks, we're all just barbarians at heart." Bringing her hand to his mouth, he pressed a kiss to the very center of her palm, allowing his lips to linger against her silky skin. "Even you, my prim and proper Miss Wickersham."

There was no mistaking the husky tremor that ran through her voice. "If I were possessed of a more cynical nature, my lord, I might suspect you of setting this stage not for an apology, but for a seduction."

"Which would you prefer?" No longer able to resist the temptation, Gabriel lowered his head, seeking his answer directly from her lips.

Samantha closed her eyes, as if by doing so she could deny any culpability in what was about to happen. But there was no denying the shudder of longing that went through her as Gabriel's lips brushed hers in a feathery caress. This was nothing like the kiss they had shared in the library. That had been a passionate assault on her senses. This was a lover's kiss—a leisurely sample of all the pleasures he had to offer, even more tempting and dangerous to her lonely heart.

He caressed the plump curves of her lips beneath his own, coaxing them to part, to accept the honeyed persuasion of his tongue. As its velvety heat swept through her mouth, delving deeper with each stroke, Samantha felt herself melting against him, felt the last of her resistance being scorched away. Suddenly she was the beggar at the feast—a feast of the senses her body had been denied for far too long. She wanted to gorge herself on him, sate her every craving with the fulsome delight of his kiss.

As her tongue joined the primal dance, savoring the claret-sweetened taste of him, he groaned deep in his throat. He didn't require his sight to slip his hand into her bodice and find the softness of her breast through her silk chemise, to flick his thumb lightly across her distended nipple until she moaned into his mouth, awash in a pleasure as intense as it was forbidden.

Shamed by that helpless moan and afraid of where his greedy fingers might venture next, Gabriel tore both his hand and his mouth from Samantha.

Fighting to steady the hoarse rasp of his breathing, he rested his brow against hers. "You haven't been entirely truthful with me, have you, Miss Wickersham?"

"Why would you say such a thing?"

Assuming the note of panic in her voice was the result of his indiscretion, he nuzzled his way to the delicate shell of her ear and whispered, "Because, much to my dismay, you are most definitely wearing undergarments."

The song came to a close in that moment, the abrupt silence reminding them that there was an audience in the gallery.

"Shall I play another tune, my lord?" Beckwith's cheerful voice came floating over the gilded railing, assuring them that the butler was still oblivious to the drama being played out on the ballroom floor.

It was Samantha who summoned the fortitude to disengage herself from his arms, Samantha who called out, "No, thank you, Beckwith. Lord Sheffield requires his rest. He'll be resuming his lessons tomorrow promptly at two o'clock." Her voice was no less crisp when she turned back to Gabriel and said, "Thank you for dinner, my lord."

Amused by her transformation back into his stern nurse, he sketched her a formal bow. "And thank you, Miss Wickersham . . . for the dance."

He cocked his head to listen to her fleeing footsteps, wondering, not for the first time, what other secrets his nurse might be hiding.

Beckwith returned to the servants' hall to find Mrs. Philpot sitting all alone in front of the fire, savoring a warm cup of tea.

"How did the evening go?" she asked.

"I'd say it was a smashing success. Just what they both required. But we weren't quite as discreet as we'd hoped. Apparently, Miss Wickersham overheard us in the drawing room last night." He chuckled. "She thought the two of us were having a midnight rendezvous."

"Fancy that." Mrs. Philpot lifted her teacup to her lips to hide her own smile.

Beckwith shook his head. "Who could imagine a fussy old bachelor and a sedate widow fumbling in the dark like two lovestruck children?"

"Who indeed?" Resting her teacup on the hearth, Mrs. Philpot began to tug the pins from her hair one by one.

As the skeins of black silk came tumbling around her shoulders, Beckwith reached down to sift his fingers through them. "I've always loved your hair, you know."

She caught his plump hand and pressed it to her cheek. "And I've always loved you. At least since you worked up the courage to call a lonely young widow 'Lavinia' instead of 'Mrs. Philpot.'"

"Do you realize that was almost twenty years ago?"

"It seems like only yesterday. So what songs did you play for them?"

" 'Barbara Allen' and your favorite, 'Come Live with Me.' "

" 'Come live with me and be my love,' " she said, quoting Marlowe's timeless poem.

" 'And we will all the pleasures prove,' " he finished, drawing her to her feet.

She smiled up at him, her eyes sparkling like a girl's. "Do you think the master would dismiss us if he knew?"

Beckwith shook his head before kissing her gently. "From what I witnessed tonight, I think he would envy us."

≈ *Chapter 14* ≈

My darling Cecily,

*How dare you suggest that my family would consider you be-
neath me? You are my moon and stars. I am but dust beneath
your delicate feet . . .*

Promptly at two o'clock the following afternoon, Samantha came
marching through the foyer in her sensible half-boots, her expression so resolute that the other servants scurried to get out of her
path. Her hair had been drawn into a severe knot at the nape of her
neck and her lips were pursed as if she'd been sucking on lemons
instead of perfuming herself with them. The unflattering cut of
her dark gray morning dress managed to obscure any hint of a
trim ankle or shapely curve.

She paced the drawing room as she waited for Gabriel, her old-
fashioned petticoats rustling as if they had been soaked in starch.
It hardly improved her temper to know that all of her efforts to ap-
pear respectable would be wasted on Gabriel. For all he knew, she
could be waiting for him wearing nothing but her stockings and
silk chemise. She fanned herself with her hand, her wicked imagi-

nation supplying a dizzying array of images of what he might do to her if she was.

He finally came sauntering into the drawing room at half past two, sweeping his walking stick in a jaunty arc in front of him. Sam trotted at his heels, clutching a battered boot in his mouth.

Tapping her foot, Samantha glared at the clock on the mantel. "I suppose you have no inkling of how late you are."

"Not a clue. I can't see the clock," he gently reminded her.

"Oh," she said, momentarily nonplussed. "I suppose we'd best get started, then." Reluctant to touch him, she seized the sleeve of his shirt and tugged him to the mouth of her makeshift maze.

He groaned. "Not the furniture again. I've already done it a hundred times."

"And you'll do it a hundred more until navigating with the walking stick becomes second nature to you."

"I'd much rather practice my dancing," he said, the silky note in his voice unmistakable.

"Why practice a skill you already excel at?" Samantha retorted, giving him a light shove toward an overstuffed sofa.

When Gabriel reached the end of the maze, grumbling something about a Minotaur beneath his breath, his walking stick met only air.

Frowning, he waved the cane in a wider arc. "Where in the devil did the davenport go? I could have sworn it was here just a few days ago."

In reply, Samantha stepped in front of him and threw open a pair of floor-to-ceiling French windows, clearing the path to the terrace. Barking shrilly, Sam dropped the boot and went scampering past them, taking off like a shot after some imaginary hare. A soft breeze, scented with lilac, drifted into the room.

"Since you seem to have mastered both the drawing room and the ballroom," she explained, "I thought we'd take a walk around the grounds this afternoon."

"No, thank you," he said flatly.

Taken aback, she asked, "And why not? You said you were bored with the drawing room. I should think you'd be eager to enjoy a new diversion and a little fresh air."

"I have all the air I need right here in the house."

Puzzled, Samantha glanced down. He was gripping the walking stick as if it were a lifeline, his knuckles white with strain. His expressive face was set and stiff, the left corner of his mouth drawn downward. The effortless charm of last night had vanished, leaving in its place a forbidding mask.

Her breath caught on an odd little hitch as she realized that Gabriel wasn't angry. He was afraid. Thinking back, she also realized that she hadn't seen him brave the sunlight even once since her arrival at Fairchild Park.

Reaching down, she gently pried the walking stick from his grip and propped it against the wall. She boldly rested her hand atop his rigid forearm. "Your lungs might not require fresh air, my lord, but mine do. And you can hardly expect a lady to take a stroll on such a glorious spring afternoon without a gentleman to escort her."

Samantha knew she was taking a risk, appealing to a gallantry he no longer possessed. But to her surprise, he reluctantly cupped his fingers over hers and inclined his head in a mocking bow. "Never let it be said that Gabriel Fairchild could deny a lady anything."

He took one step forward, then another. Sunlight poured over his face like molten gold. As they stepped over the threshold, he tugged her to a halt. She feared he was going to balk, but it seemed he had only paused to draw a breath deep into his lungs. Samantha did the same, drinking in the smell of newly turned earth and the intoxicating perfume of the plump wisteria blooms twining around a nearby trellis.

As Gabriel's eyes drifted shut, she was tempted to close hers as well, to focus her senses entirely on the caress of the sun-warmed breeze and the twitter of the robin scolding its mate as the two of them built a nest in the bough of a nearby hawthorn. But if she had, she would have missed the look of raw sensual pleasure that crossed Gabriel's face.

Her spirits soaring, she urged him into motion, guiding him toward the emerald-green swath of lawn that sloped down to a crumbling stone folly at the edge of a rambling wood. Every detail of the park's meticulous landscaping, from its fresh-hewn rocks to its meandering brooks, had been artfully designed to mimic an encroaching wilderness.

His fingers still resting lightly over hers, Gabriel easily kept pace, gaining confidence and grace with each long stride. "We really shouldn't venture too far from the house. What if someone from the village sees me? I wouldn't wish to frighten the little children back to their beds."

Despite his dry tone, Samantha knew his words were spoken only half in jest. "Children only fear the unknown, my lord. The longer you remain in seclusion at Fairchild Park, the more fearsome your reputation will grow."

"We certainly wouldn't want them to believe I'm some sort of misshapen monster lurching about in the dark, now, would we?"

Samantha glanced up at him, but it was impossible to tell if he was mocking her or himself. His eyes may have lost their sight, but not their droll twinkle. They were even more spectacular in the sunlight, their gold-fringed depths as clear and bright as a crystal sea. The shimmering air burnished his hair to the color of a newly minted guinea.

"There's really no need for you to remain a prisoner in your own home when you have these beautiful grounds at your disposal. I gather you were once very active. There must still be some outdoor pursuits you could enjoy."

"How about archery?" he quipped. Sam came bounding out of the woods, forcing them to slow as he capered around their feet. "Or there's always the hunt. At least no one could blame me if I mistook a pup for a fox."

"You should be ashamed of yourself," she chided. "Sam may very well be the saving of you someday. He's quite intelligent, you know."

Hearing his name, the collie dropped to the grass and writhed around on his back, his eyes rolling back in his head and his tongue lolling out. Samantha lifted her skirts and stepped over him, hoping her companion wouldn't notice.

But Gabriel seemed to be preoccupied with other matters. "Perhaps you're right, Miss Wickersham." Samantha glanced up at him, startled by his easy capitulation. "Perhaps there is some outdoor pursuit I could still enjoy. Something that might *even the odds*, as it were."

Gabriel won every single round of blind man's bluff.

There was simply no besting him. Not only could he catch even the most agile of servants before they could dart out of his reach, he could identify them with little more than a perfunctory sniff of their hair or clothing. His reflexes were still so keen that he could also elude anyone wearing the blindfold, slipping from their outstretched fingers an instant before they tightened into a snare.

When Samantha had first summoned the staff to join them in their game, they had been shocked to discover their master reclining on one elbow on the sun-drenched hillside, his hair falling loose from its velvet queue and a blade of grass tucked between his lips. They'd been even more shocked when his nurse had explained what was required of them. While the other servants lined up in rigid formation, as if to greet a visiting dignitary, Beckwith "tsked" and "tutted" his disapproval and Mrs. Philpot declared that she had never before witnessed such a disgraceful exhibit.

Peter and Phillip were the first to break out of formation. Delighted to escape their duties on such a spectacular spring day, the twins eschewed the subtleties of the game, preferring to tackle and pummel one another with their freckled fists at every opportunity. Whenever he managed to straddle his howling brother, Phillip would steal shy glances at Elsie to make sure the pretty young maid was watching.

Seduced by the balmy breeze and their master's good humor, the other servants slowly lost their reticence. When it was his turn to wear the blindfold, Willie, the wiry Scottish gamekeeper, ended up chasing Meg the laundress, his knobby hands stretched into claws. Squealing like a schoolgirl, Meg lifted her skirts and went barreling down the slope, her stout legs windmilling wildly and Sam barking at her heels. When she dodged left instead of right, Willie shot right past her, tripping over his own boots and rolling the rest of the way down the hill and into the brook.

"Since Willie couldn't catch Meg, it's Master's turn again!" Hannah cried, clapping her hands in anticipation.

While Meg dragged the dripping, cursing gamekeeper out of the creek by his ear, Beckwith gently directed Gabriel to the top of the hillside. Even Mrs. Philpot had begun to get into the spirit of the game. Without being asked, she stepped forward to give her employer three brisk spins, then danced well out of his reach with a sprightly grace that set the keys at her waist to jingling.

As Gabriel got his bearings, the rest of the servants stood frozen into place on the sunny hillside. None of them was allowed to stir so much as an inch unless Gabriel drew near enough to touch them. Only then were they allowed to flee. Samantha deliberately placed herself at the outer edge of their circle, just as she had on every one of Gabriel's turns. She was determined not to give him any excuse to lay his hands on her.

Gabriel slowly pivoted, his hands resting on his lean hips. It wasn't until the wind ruffled Samantha's hair, teasing a wayward strand from her chignon, that she realized she had made the mistake of positioning herself upwind of him. His nostrils flared. His eyes narrowed in a look she knew only too well.

He turned and started straight for her, his masterful strides eating up the ground between them. As he brushed past Elsie and

Hannah without slowing, the maids cupped a hand over their mouths, struggling to suppress their giggles.

Samantha's feet seemed to be rooted to the earth. She couldn't have run if Gabriel had been some charging beast, intent upon devouring her. She was keenly aware of the other servants' intent gazes, the trickle of sweat easing its way between her breasts, the way her blood seemed to thicken like honey in her veins.

As always, Gabriel stopped a mere heartbeat before running right over her. As his hand brushed her sleeve, Peter and Phillip groaned at her lack of resistance. It was too late to flee. All he had to do now was name her and the round would be done.

"Name! Name!" the girls began to chant.

Gabriel held up his other hand, begging their silence. He had identified the other servants by nothing more than a whiff of wood smoke or laundry soap. But it was also well within his rights to identify his captive by touch.

As the corner of his mouth curled into a lazy half-smile, Samantha stood frozen into place, helpless to stop the approach of his hand. It was as if the others had vanished, leaving them all alone on that breezy hillside.

Her eyes fluttered shut as Gabriel's fingers brushed her hair, then played lightly over her face. He gently skirted around the edge of her spectacles, tracing every curve and hollow as if to memorize her features. Despite the warmth of the afternoon, his touch sent delicious ripples of gooseflesh dancing over her skin. How could his hands be so rough and masculine, and yet so tender all at the same time? As his fingertips grazed the softness of her lips, her dread melted away to something else, something even more perilous. She found herself wanting to lean into him, to tilt her head back and offer up some sweet sacrifice solely to please him. She swayed, so swept away by this scandalous yearning that it took her a moment to realize he had stopped touching her.

Her eyes flew open. Although Gabriel's head was lowered, the uneven rise and fall of his chest warned her that he was not unaffected by their brief contact.

"I'm not entirely sure," he called out in a voice strong enough to carry across the hillside, "but judging by the softness of the skin and the delicate perfume, I believe I might have captured . . ." He paused, deliberately heightening the anticipation. "Warton, the stable boy!"

The servants exploded in raucous laughter. One of the grooms-men cuffed a sputtering young Warton on the shoulder.

"Only two more chances, my lord," Millie reminded him.

Gabriel tapped his bottom lip with his forefinger. "Well, if it's not Warton," he drawled, his voice softening, "then it must be my dear . . . my dutiful . . . my devoted . . ."

As he clapped a hand to his heart, eliciting fresh titters from the maids, Samantha held her breath, wondering just what exactly he was about to reveal.

". . . Miss Wickersham."

The servants burst into hearty applause; Gabriel swept one arm toward Samantha in a graceful bow.

She smiled and dropped a mocking curtsy, speaking through her gritted teeth. "At least you didn't identify me as one of your carriage horses."

"Don't be absurd," he whispered. "Your mane is far silkier."

A beaming Beckwith tapped him on the shoulder, then draped a linen kerchief over his hand. "The blindfold, my lord."

Gabriel turned back to Samantha, one of his eyebrows cocked at a devilish angle.

"Oh, no, you don't!" She backed away as he advanced on her, twirling the blindfold in a most menacing manner. "I've had quite enough of your ridiculous games. All of them," she added, knowing the emphasis wouldn't be lost on him.

"Come, now, Miss Wickersham," he chided. "You wouldn't make a blind man chase you, would you?"

"Oh, wouldn't I?" Snatching up her skirts, Samantha took off across the hill, shrieking with helpless laughter when she heard Gabriel's footsteps closing in behind her.

The mood inside the marquess of Thornwood's lumbering town coach ranged from glum to dour. Only seventeen-year-old Honoria dared to betray any sign of hope, sitting up to peer out the window at the passing hedgerows as the vehicle swayed its way down the broad lane toward Fairchild Park.

Her two older sisters were practicing the air of sophisticated ennui so essential to young ladies of a certain age, beauty, and quality. Eighteen-year-old Eugenia was enjoying loving communion with the hand mirror she'd pulled out of her satin reticule, while nineteen-year-old Valerie punctuated every bump and jolt with a long-suffering sigh. Valerie had been particularly unbearable since becoming engaged to the youngest son of a duke at the end of last year's Season. No matter what turn the conversation took, she managed to preface every other sentence with, "Once Anthony and I are wed . . ."

Seated across from them, their father mopped his florid brow with a lace-trimmed handkerchief.

Eyeing his flushed face, his wife murmured, "Are you quite certain this was a wise idea, Teddy? If we had warned him we were coming—"

"If we had warned him we were coming, he'd have ordered the servants to turn us away at the door." Since it was not his habit to speak sharply to his wife, Theodore Fairchild softened his rebuke by reaching over to pat her gloved hand.

"As far as I'm concerned, that would have been a blessing." Eugenia reluctantly dragged her gaze away from her reflection. "Then at least he wouldn't have the chance to snap and growl at us like some sort of rabid wolf."

Valerie nodded. "The beastly way he behaved at our last visit, one would have thought he'd gone mad as well as blind. 'Tis fortunate that Anthony and I are not yet wed. Why, if he had heard the disgraceful way Gabriel dared to address me—"

"You two should be ashamed of yourselves, speaking of your brother so!" Honoria jerked her gaze away from the window to glare at them, her sherry-brown eyes burning with passion beneath the fluted brim of her bonnet.

Unaccustomed to receiving such a stern set-down from their good-natured little sister, Valerie and Eugenia exchanged a startled glance.

As the coach passed through a pair of ornate iron gates and began to climb the steep hill leading to the carriage drive, Honoria continued. "Who pulled you out of the freezing water, Genie, when you fell through the ice at Tillman's Pond even though you'd been warned it was too thin for skating? And who defended your honor, Val, when that nasty boy at Lady Marbeth's fete claimed you had allowed him to steal a kiss? Gabriel has been the finest big brother any girl could want, and yet there the two of you sit, mocking and insulting him like a pair of ungrateful cows!"

Valerie reached over and squeezed Eugenia's hand, her light green eyes sparkling with tears. "That's not fair, Honoria. We miss Gabriel just as badly as you do. But that ill-tempered brute who railed and swore at us the last time we came here was *not* our brother. We want *our* Gabriel back!"

"Now, now, girls," their father murmured. "There's no need to make a difficult situation worse by quarreling amongst yourselves." While Honoria returned her sullen gaze to the window, he attempted a ghost of his jolly smile. "Perhaps when your brother sees what we've brought for him, 'twill soften him toward us."

"But that's the problem," Lady Thornwood blurted out. "According to your precious physicians, he won't be seeing anything, will he? Not today and not ever." Her plump face crumpled, tears streaking through her face powder. She took the handkerchief her husband proffered and dabbed at her streaming eyes. "Perhaps

Valerie and Eugenia are right. Perhaps we shouldn't have come at all. I just don't know if I can bear seeing my darling lad locked away in that dark house like some sort of animal."

"Mama?" Honoria rubbed at the mottled glass of the coach's window, a note of wonder softening her voice.

"Don't trouble Mama right now," Eugenia snapped. "Can't you see that she's distraught?"

Valerie drew a vial of hartshorn from her reticule and held it out to her mother. "Here, Mama. Use this if you start to feel a fit of the vapors coming on."

Lady Thornwood waved it away, her attention captured by the dazed expression on her youngest daughter's face. "What is it, Honoria? You look as if you've seen a ghost."

"Perhaps I have. I think you'd best take a look."

As Honoria pushed open the window, Lady Thornwood climbed over her husband's knees, trodding heavily on his toes as she joined her daughter. Their curiosity piqued, Valerie and Eugenia crowded behind them.

There appeared to be some sort of diversion in progress. The participants were scattered all over the grassy hillside overlooking the mansion, their laughter and shouts ringing like music through the air. They were too preoccupied with their merriment to even notice the approaching coach.

Craning his neck to see over the wall of bonnets, the marquess's mouth fell open. "What on earth are the servants doing wasting their time on such nonsense when they're supposed to be working? What do they think this is—Christmas Day? Why, I should order Beckwith to sack the lot of them!"

"You'll have to catch him first," Valerie pointed out as the butler went barreling across the hillside, chasing a shrieking Mrs. Philpot.

Eugenia clapped a hand over her mouth to muffle a scandalized giggle. "Just look at that, Val! Who would have thought the stuffy old goat had it in him?"

The marchioness was turning to rebuke her daughter for having such a saucy tongue when her gaze fell on the man skirting his way around the edges of the revelry. She went so pale that it appeared she might have need of that hartshorn after all.

As he paused at the crest of the hill, his commanding figure framed by the dazzling blue sky, she touched a hand to her heart, believing for one jubilant moment that her son had returned to her. He stood tall and straight, his shoulders thrown back, his golden hair gleaming in the sunlight.

But then he turned and she saw the jagged scar spoiling his fine looks—the grim reminder that the Gabriel she had known and loved was gone forever.

Samantha knew she couldn't elude Gabriel forever. But she could lead him on a merry chase and that she did, circling around behind the other servants as they resumed the game. He might lack sight, but he was as sure of foot as a mountain lion, which was why it shocked her when he stumbled over a thick tuft of grass and went down like a stone.

"*Gabriel!*" she cried, using his Christian name without realizing it.

Lifting her skirts, she went racing back to his side. She dropped to her knees beside him in the grass, already envisioning the worst. What if he'd shattered an ankle? Or struck his head on a rock?

Haunted by the memory of his blood-stained body sprawled on his bedchamber floor, she gathered his head into her lap and tenderly smoothed the hair from his brow. "Can you hear me, Gabriel? Are you all right?"

"I am now." Before Samantha could react to that smoky murmur, he had wrapped his arms around her waist and rolled her into the grass, knocking her spectacles askew.

She never expected him to be so bold, to tumble her to the ground right there in front of the servants and God, as if he were a shepherd boy and she a dairy maid, ripe for the ravishing. But tumble her he did, his legs tangling in her skirts as they both exploded with breathless laughter.

The next thing she knew, she was on her back with Gabriel's big, warm body covering hers. His grip gentled; their laughter faded.

Too late, Samantha realized that everyone else had fallen silent as well.

She glanced over Gabriel's shoulder, blinking through her crooked spectacles. A stranger was standing over them—a stout, barrel-chested man, garbed in gold-and-green-striped stockings and a rather old-fashioned pair of knee breeches. The faded gold of his hair was lightly powdered, making it difficult to determine his age. Cuffs of exquisite Valencian lace framed his thick wrists. As he extended a hand to her, the enormous ruby signet ring crowning his middle finger glinted like a drop of fresh blood in the sunlight.

"M-m-my lord," Beckwith stammered. His blindfold hung askew over one eye, giving him the look of a plump, pasty pirate. "We received no word. We weren't expecting you."

"That much is evident," the man snapped in an imperious tone Samantha recognized all too well.

Only then did she realize that she was gazing up into the stern visage of Theodore Fairchild, the marquess of Thornwood, Gabriel's father—and her employer.

Chapter 15

My darling Cecily,

I can assure you that my family will adore you as much as I do . . .

Ignoring the marquess's outstretched hand, Samantha shoved Gabriel off of her and scrambled to her feet. Gabriel wasted no time in climbing to his own feet, his posture stiff and his expression guarded. The rest of the servants stood around in awkward clusters, looking as if they'd much rather be emptying chamber pots or mucking out the stables.

Straightening her spectacles, Samantha dropped into a low curtsy. "I'm pleased to make your acquaintance, my lord. I'm Samantha Wickersham, your son's nurse."

"I can certainly see why he's made such a marked improvement since our last visit." Although his voice was gruff, she would have almost sworn she saw a glint of humor in the marquess's eyes.

She could only imagine what a scandalous picture she must present. With her skirt wrinkled and stained with grass, the color high in her cheeks, and her hair tumbling out of its knot to hang halfway down her back, she probably looked more like the village strumpet than a respectable woman one would hire to look after their son.

Four exquisitely dressed women were huddled on the hillside behind the marquess, their every curl in place beneath their elaborate bonnets, their every bow, ribbon, and lace ruffle starched to perfection. Samantha felt her mouth tighten. She knew their kind only too well.

Although they made her feel like even more of a hoyden, she lifted her chin, refusing to humble herself before them. If Gabriel's family hadn't abdicated their responsibility for him, it wouldn't have been necessary to hire her. And if his father dismissed her now, there would be no one to look after him.

"You may find my methods of treatment rather unconventional, Lord Thornwood," she said. "But I believe that copious amounts of sunshine and fresh air have the power to improve both body and disposition."

"Heaven knows I've ample room for improvement in both of those areas," Gabriel murmured.

As the marquess turned to his son, his arrogance seemed to melt away. He couldn't quite bring himself to look directly into Gabriel's face. "Hello, lad. It's good to see you looking so well."

"Father," Gabriel said stiffly. "I wish I could say the same."

One of the women came sweeping across the grass toward them, her satin petticoats rustling. Although her skin was as pale and soft as antique lace, age had robbed her of little of her plump prettiness.

Gabriel stood stiffly, his face a wary mask, as she rose up on tiptoe and brushed a kiss against his unmarked cheek. "I do hope you'll forgive us for barging in on you like this. It was such a spectacular day—just perfect for a long drive in the country."

"Don't be silly, Mother. How could I expect you to do any less than your Christian duty? Perhaps on the way home you can stop by the orphanage or the workhouse and spread some more good cheer among the unfortunates."

Although Samantha winced, Gabriel's mother only sighed, as if his acerbic welcome were no more than she had expected. "Come along, girls," she called out, crooking a gloved finger at her daughters, "and give your brother a proper greeting."

The two willowy, golden-haired girls hung back as if fearing Gabriel might bite, but the sturdy little brunette came rushing forward to fling her arms around his neck, nearly knocking him off balance. "Oh, Gabe, I couldn't bear to spend another moment away from you! I've missed you so!"

Showing his first sign of thawing, he patted her awkwardly on the shoulder. "Hullo there, Little Bit. Or should I address you as Lady Honoria? Unless you're wearing Valerie's heels, I do believe you've grown two inches since your last visit."

"Would you believe I'm to be presented at court in a fortnight? I haven't forgotten your promise, you know." Linking her arm through Gabriel's as if she were afraid he was going to bolt, she turned her grin on Samantha. One of her front teeth was slightly crooked, only adding to her winsome charm. "Ever since I was a little girl in the nursery, my brother has been promising me that he would dance the first dance with me at my coming-out ball."

"How very gallant of him," Samantha said softly, catching the brief spasm of pain that flickered across Gabriel's face.

The marquess cleared his throat. "Don't hog all of your brother's attention, Honoria. Have you forgotten that we have a surprise for him?"

As Honoria reluctantly disengaged herself from Gabriel and rejoined her sisters, their father turned and beckoned toward the liveried footmen manning the imposing town coach parked on the drive. They leapt down from their perches and began to loosen the ropes on something large and draped with canvas that was tied to the boot of the coach.

As the two of them carried their cumbersome burden up the

hill, struggling beneath its weight, Gabriel's father rubbed his hands together in anticipation. By the time the footmen had deposited it on the grass in front of Gabriel, Samantha was as curious as the rest of the servants.

"The minute your mother and I laid eyes on it, we knew it was just the thing." Beaming at his wife, the marquess stepped forward and whisked away the canvas with a majestic flourish.

Samantha narrowed her eyes, struggling to bring the unfamiliar object into focus. When she finally succeeded, she almost wished she hadn't.

"What is it?" she heard Elsie whisper to Phillip. "Some sort of torture device?"

Mrs. Philpot gazed off at the distant horizon while Beckwith edged nearer to her, taking a sudden interest in the tops of his shoes.

Warned by the servants' awkward silence, Gabriel snapped, "Well, what in the devil is it?"

When no one answered, he dropped to one knee and began to run his hands over the thing. As his seeking fingers traced the contours of an iron wheel, realization slowly dawned across his face.

He straightened, the motion unnaturally stiff. "An invalid's chair. You've brought me an invalid's chair." His voice was just low and dangerous enough to make the hair on Samantha's nape rise.

His father was still beaming. "Deucedly clever, isn't it? This way, you'll no longer have to worry about stumbling or crashing into things. You can just climb in, throw a blanket over your lap, and someone can push you about wherever you wish to go. Someone like Beckwith or your own Miss Wickersham here!"

Samantha tensed, waiting for the inevitable explosion. But when Gabriel finally spoke, his carefully modulated voice was more damning than any shout. "Perhaps it has escaped your notice, Father, but I still have two perfectly good legs. Now, if you'll excuse me, I think I'll make use of them."

Sketching a curt bow, he turned on his heel and went stalking off in the opposite direction of the house. Although he didn't even have his walking stick to guide him, Samantha could not bring herself to humiliate him further by following him or ordering one of the servants to do so. Even Sam did not dare to chase after him. The little collie plopped down next to Samantha, his morose gaze following Gabriel as he disappeared into the woods.

As Beckwith had warned her, there were some paths a man had to travel alone.

Samantha sat in the small breakfast parlor where Beckwith had first interviewed her, listening to the French gilt clock on the mantel tick away the minutes of her life. Gabriel's disappearance had left her with no choice but to serve as impromptu hostess for his family. She had excused herself just long enough to repair her hair and don a fresh gown—a somber affair of deep maroon bombazine with nary a frill or furbelow to soften its severe lines.

The marchioness perched on the very edge of her wing chair, her lips pursed in disapproval and her gloved hands folded in her lap, while the marquess slumped in his, his ample belly straining the buttons of his paisley waistcoat. Valerie and Eugenia huddled together on a Grecian sofa, looking so miserable Samantha almost felt sorry for them. Honoria perched on an ottoman at their feet, hugging her knees to her chest and looking more seven than seventeen. The hulking invalid's chair sat in the corner, its sinister shadow reproaching them all.

As the golden light slowly faded, there was nothing but the occasional sigh and the muffled clink of a teacup to break the painful silence.

Samantha lifted her own cup to her lips, grimacing when she realized the tea had long since cooled.

She lowered the cup to find Gabriel's mother openly glaring at her. "Just what sort of nurse are you, Miss Wickersham? I can't believe you just let him wander off like that without even dispatching a servant to tend to him. What if he's tumbled into a ravine and broken his neck?"

Samantha rested the cup on its saucer, trying to pretend the woman wasn't echoing her own fears. "I can assure you that there's no need to fret, my lady. Your son is far more self-sufficient than you would guess."

"But it's been nearly three hours. Why hasn't he returned?"

"Because we're still here." At her husband's glum pronouncement, the marchioness turned her glare on him. He slumped deeper into his chair.

"Then why can't we go home?" Valerie and Eugenia said almost in unison.

"Oh, please, Papa," Valerie begged. "We're so bored!"

Eugenia wadded her lace handkerchief into a ball, her expression hopeful. "Val's right, Mama. If Gabriel doesn't want us here, then why don't we honor his wishes and just go away? Miss Wickersham will still be here to look after him."

"I don't see why he needs a nurse," Honoria blurted out, shooting Samantha an apologetic look. "You could just leave me here and I could take care of him!"

"What about your presentation at court?" her father gently reminded her. "And your coming-out ball?"

Honoria ducked her head, allowing a fall of soft brown curls to veil her pensive profile. She might be more devoted to her brother than her sisters were, but she was still seventeen. "Gabriel needs me more than I need any silly coming-out ball."

"I have no doubt that you would take excellent care of your brother," Samantha said, choosing her words with care, "but I'm sure it would give him far greater comfort to know that you'd made your debut and had a chance to find a husband who will adore you as much as he does."

While Honoria gave her a grateful glance, Gabriel's mother

rose and paced to the French window that had been left cracked open to invite a breeze into the stuffy parlor.

She stood gazing out into the deepening dusk, her eyes haunted by shadows. "I don't know how he can bear to go on living like this. Sometimes I think it would have been a blessing if he'd have just—"

"Clarissa!" the marquess barked, sitting up and thumping his walking stick on the floor.

Lady Thornwood whirled around, a hysterical note sharpening her voice. "Oh, why not just say it, Theodore? We all think it, don't we, every time we look at him."

Samantha rose to her feet. "Think what?"

Gabriel's mother turned to face her, her expression fierce. "That it would have been a blessing if my son had died on the deck of that ship. A blessing for his life to have ended cleanly and quickly. Then he wouldn't have had to go on suffering. He wouldn't have to go on living this—this miserable half-life as half a man!"

"And how convenient that would have been for you!" A bitter smile touched Samantha's lips. "After all, your son would have died a hero. Instead of being forced to confront a surly stranger on this beautiful spring afternoon, you could have driven out here to place flowers on his crypt. You could all weep prettily, mourn his tragic loss, and still have your grieving done in time for the first ball of the Season. Tell me, Lady Thornwood—is it Gabriel's suffering you wish to end? Or your own?"

The marchioness paled as if Samantha had slapped her. "How dare you speak to me so, you presumptuous creature!"

Samantha refused to be cowed. "You can barely stand to look him in the face, can you? Because he's no longer the golden boy you adored. He can't play the role of perfect son to your doting mother. So you're ready to bring the curtain down on his head. Why do you think he's not here right now?" She swept her accusing gaze around the room before returning it to Gabriel's mother. "It's because he knows *exactly* what you're all thinking every time you look at him. Your son may be blind, my lady, but he's not stupid."

As Samantha stood there, her trembling hands clenched into fists, she slowly became aware that Valerie and Eugenia were gaping at her in openmouthed horror. Honoria's bottom lip trembled as if she were one sharp word away from bursting into tears.

Shame washed over Samantha. Even so, she couldn't bring herself to regret her words, only the loss of what they had cost her.

She turned to the marquess, lifting her chin to meet his gaze squarely. "Forgive me for my impertinence, my lord. I'll have my things packed and be ready to travel by morning."

As she started for the door, the marquess rose to block her path, his bushy eyebrows drawn into a stern line. "Hold on just a minute there, girl. I haven't dismissed you yet."

Samantha bowed her head, waiting for him to give her the setdown she deserved for speaking so disrespectfully to his wife.

"Nor will I," he said. "Judging from the impressive display of temper I just witnessed, you might be exactly what that hardheaded son of mine needs." Retrieving his walking stick, he brushed past Samantha and headed for the door, leaving her standing in mute shock. "Come, Clarissa, girls. We're going home."

Lady Thornwood gasped. "Surely you can't expect me to go off and just leave Gabriel all alone here." She shot Samantha a venomous look. "With *her*."

"The girls are right. He won't return as long as we're here." The marquess's lips curved in a wry smile, reminding Samantha so much of Gabriel that her heart skipped a beat. "I can't honestly say that I blame the lad. Who wants a flock of vultures hovering about when you're fighting for your life? Come, girls. If we hurry, we might just make our beds before midnight."

Valerie and Eugenia scrambled to obey their father, snatching up reticules, fans, shawls, and bonnets as they went. Giving Samantha one last smoldering look that warned her she would not forget—or forgive—her insolence, the marchioness went sweeping past, her ample bosom jutting out like the prow of a warship. Honoria hesitated in the doorway just long enough to give Samantha a wistful little wave.

As the wheels of their town coach went clattering away down the drive, Samantha was left all alone with only the invalid's chair for company. She glared at the hateful thing, wanting nothing more than to claw the stuffing out of its horsehair cushions with her bare hands.

Instead, she lit an Argand lamp and rested it on the table beside the window. She had been standing there for several minutes, her troubled gaze searching the shadows, before she realized what she'd done. It wasn't as if she could depend upon the lamp's glow to guide Gabriel home.

Perhaps his mother was right. Perhaps she should send someone out to search for him. But it hardly seemed fair to send the servants out to drag him home as if he were a recalcitrant child who had run away over some petty slight.

What if he didn't want to be found? What if he was weary to death of everyone trying to impose their expectations on him? His family had made it clear that they only wanted *their* Gabriel back—the man who had strode through life with unswerving confidence, charming his way into every heart he encountered.

Despite her passionate denouncement, was she truly any better than them? She had come to this place believing she wanted only to help him. But she was beginning to question her own motives, to wonder if her selfless devotion was hiding a very selfish heart.

Samantha gazed down at the lamp's flame. Its flickering light couldn't guide Gabriel home.

But she could.

Taking up the lamp, she slipped out the French window and into the night.

* * *

Samantha struck out for the woods, since that was where Gabriel had disappeared. The lamp, which had seemed so bright in the house, cast a pale glow around her, barely bright enough to hold the shadows at bay. Its flame was dwarfed by the velvety blackness of the moonless night sky, the tangle of branches above her head as she slipped into the woods. She couldn't imagine what it must be like to live in such darkness night and day.

As the canopy of branches thickened, blocking out every trace of the sky, her steps slowed. Nightfall had transformed Fairchild Park from an artfully designed landscape into an uncharted wilderness, fraught with perils and terrors. She picked her way over the trunk of a fallen tree, unsettled by the mysterious rustling and the eerie cries of unseen night creatures. She was beginning to yearn for Gabriel's big, strong body in more ways than one.

"Gabriel?" she called out softly, not wanting to risk the servants back at the house hearing her.

The only answer was a renewed rustling in the underbrush coming from somewhere behind her. Samantha stopped. So did the rustling. She took one tentative step, then another. The rustling resumed. Hoping and praying that it was only her starched petticoats, she held them off the ground and took another step. The rustling grew even louder. She stopped again, her fingers freezing into icy claws around the handle of the lamp. The rustling ceased, only to be replaced by a feral panting, so near Samantha would have sworn she could almost feel the hot breath of some invisible predator on the back of her neck.

There could be no doubt about it.

Someone . . . or something . . . was following her.

Mustering all of her courage, she whirled around, swinging the lamp in front of her. "Show yourself!"

A pair of moist brown eyes emerged from the shadows, followed by a wriggling body and a wagging tail.

"Sam!" Samantha breathed, dropping to her knees. "Shame on

you, you bad dog!" Despite her rebuke, she scooped the dog into her arms, cradling him to her pounding heart. "I shouldn't scold, should I?" She straightened, stroking his silky ears. "I suppose you just want to find him, too."

As she ventured deeper into the woods, calling Gabriel's name at ever more frequent intervals, she clung to the small collie, reluctant to surrender his comforting warmth. She had been walking for a long time before she realized that there was no way to retrace her steps. She was beginning to believe that Gabriel was probably going to have to send the servants out to look for her when a large structure loomed out of the darkness. Half wood and half stone, it appeared to be some sort of barn or stable, long deserted and long forgotten.

Perhaps it was a place Gabriel had known when he roamed these woods as a boy. A place where he might seek shelter if he stumbled upon it.

Still clutching both the lamp and the dog, Samantha nudged open the door hanging half off its hinges, wincing at its piercing creak.

She held up the lamp, scattering a wan circle of lamplight across ancient oak beams, moldering piles of hay, rotting bridles, and rusty bits hanging on splintered wooden pegs.

No longer able to ignore his wiggling, Samantha put Sam down so he could run around and sniff everything in sight. Except for the mice rustling in the hay, they seemed to be the only living creatures in attendance.

"Gabriel?" she called out, reluctant to disturb the unnatural hush. "Are you here?"

She wandered deeper into the gloom. Near the center of the stable, a rickety wooden ladder disappeared into the darkness above.

Samantha sighed. She had no desire to risk her neck exploring some rotting loft, but there was no point in coming this far and not investigating every possibility. Gabriel might not be here now, but perhaps she would discover some sign that he had been.

Looping her long skirts over her arm and balancing the lamp carefully in one hand, she began the long, awkward ascent up the ladder. Menacing shadows danced ahead of her, fleeing the lamp's flickering glow. When she finally reached the top and hauled herself onto the dusty planks, she breathed a sign of relief.

The loft appeared to be as deserted as the rest of the stable. There was no sign that anyone had taken shelter there in the past twenty years. The night sky was visible through the square of the open loft door, moonless, but not completely devoid of light. A milky sprinkling of stars had been flung across its inky canopy.

Samantha turned, narrowing her eyes to scan the shadows beneath the beams. Was it her imagination or had she detected a hint of motion? What if Gabriel had sought shelter here after all? What if he had somehow hurt himself and was unable to answer her call? She pressed deeper into the loft, shuddering when a thick veil of cobwebs brushed the top of her head.

"Is anyone here?" she whispered, swinging the lamp ahead of her.

The shadows exploded into motion. Samantha went stumbling backward, surrounded by the frantic whir of leathery wings and high-pitched squeaks. As the startled bats abandoned their roost and went darting toward the open loft door, she instinctively threw up her arms to shield her hair and eyes from their thrashing wings.

The lamp flew from her hand and went sailing over the edge of the loft, landing on the dirt floor below in an explosion of glass. The last of the bats vanished into the night. Spurred on by Sam's startled yelp and the acrid stench of smoldering lamp oil, Samantha lunged for the ladder, thinking only to extinguish the blaze before it could ignite the hay and engulf the entire stable.

She was a third of the way down the ladder when her foot plunged right through a rotting rung, shattering her balance as well as the wood. She teetered precariously for what seemed like an eternity, poised between despair and hope, then went plummeting backward off the ladder into empty air.

She heard her head strike the floor with a dull thud, heard Sam whimpering as he licked her cheek and nudged her ear with his cold, wet nose, heard the hungry crackling as the flames began to lick at the hay.

"Gabriel?" she whispered, seeing him smiling down at her in the sunlight in the instant before her own world dissolved into darkness.

~ *Chapter 16* ~

My darling Cecily,

You call me both persistent and persuasive yet you resist my charms at every turn . . .

Gabriel sat just inside the door of the folly, listening to the brook gurgle its way over the rocks. The roofless structure had been constructed to resemble the crumbling turret of some ancient castle. As a lad, he had spent many thrilling hours waving a wooden sword to rescue it from barbarian hordes who bore a marked resemblance to his baby sisters.

He sat on a stone bench with his back to the wall, his long legs sprawled in front of him. The night breeze ruffled his hair. It had fallen half out of its leather queue, veiling the jagged evidence of his scar. He bore other signs of the day's misadventures as well. His boots were scuffed, the sleeve of his shirt shredded by brambles. There was a fresh scrape on the back of his hand and a painful knot on his knee.

But the deepest wound he bore had been done to his heart

when he had overheard the exchange between his mother and
Samantha.

After wandering aimlessly in the woods for hours, using a
branch as a makeshift walking stick, he had finally blundered his
way back to the house. Thinking to slip in undetected, he had felt
his way around the walls until he found an open window. But his
plans were thwarted when his mother's voice came drifting
through that window.

*. . . it would have been a blessing if my son had died on the deck of
that ship. A blessing for his life to have ended cleanly and quickly. Then
he wouldn't have had to go on suffering. He wouldn't have to go on living
this—this miserable half-life as half a man!*

Gabriel had slumped against the wall, shaking his head. His
mother's words did not possess the power to wound him. They
only confirmed what he had long suspected.

And how convenient that would have been for you!

He was turning away from the window when Samantha's
voice rang out, freezing him in his tracks. He cocked his head to
the side, seduced by both the fury and the passion of her words.
He would have given almost anything to see his mother's face in
that moment. He doubted that anyone had ever dared speak to
Clarissa Fairchild, the marchioness of Thornwood, with such un-
repentant cheek.

*It's because he knows exactly what you're all thinking every time
you look at him. Your son may be blind, my lady, but he's not stupid.*

When Samantha was done, it was all he could do not to step
into that room and shout, *Bravo!* while giving her a hearty round of
applause.

"That's my girl," he had whispered, realizing with his next
breath that it was true.

That was the blow that had left his heart reeling. The blow that
had sent him staggering away from the house to seek refuge in the
cool seclusion of the folly.

Gabriel turned his face toward a sky he could not see, the

merry babbling of the brook mocking him. It seemed he had squandered most of his youth worshiping at the altar of beauty, only to fall in love with a woman he had never seen.

He didn't even care what Samantha looked like, he realized with a shock. Her beauty had nothing to do with creamy skin, a dimpled cheek, or long, luxuriant hair the color of warm honey. She might be as homely as a troll, but she would still be irresistible to him. Her beauty radiated from within—from her intelligence, her passion, her stubborn insistence on making him a better man than he ever believed he could be.

He was no longer willing to settle for anything less. Even his beloved Cecily had turned out to be nothing more than a beautiful dream that had faded in the harsh light of dawn. He might not be able to see her, but he knew in his heart that Samantha would be there every time he reached for her.

Gabriel fumbled for his makeshift walking stick. He might as well return to the house and take his scolding. Samantha would no doubt consider his eavesdropping to be the very height of ill manners. But perhaps it would soften her temper when he confessed that he adored her more than life itself. As he rose, a grin touched his lips. He wished he could see his mother's face when he informed her that he had every intention of marrying his nurse.

Gabriel was halfway to the house when he heard a familiar barking coming from the direction of the woods.

"What in the devil—?" he managed to get out before something small and sturdy came barreling into his legs, nearly knocking him over.

Not even Sam's clumsy exuberance could spoil Gabriel's good humor. "You're going to be the death of me one of these days," he chided, using the branch to steady himself.

As he continued toward the house, he could hear the dog dancing in circles around him, barking frantically and making every step a potential hazard. "What are you trying to do, Sam? Wake the dead?"

In reply, the dog grabbed the end of the branch, nearly yanking it out of Gabriel's grip. Although Gabriel tugged back, the dog was not to be dissuaded. He sank his teeth deep into the wood, growling low in his throat.

With an exasperated oath, Gabriel knelt in the dew-soaked grass. Instead of leaping into his arms as he expected, the collie caught Gabriel's already mangled sleeve between his teeth and began to tug at it, alternating between growling and whimpering.

"For God's sake, what is it?" Gabriel tried to gather the dog in his arms, but Sam fought to escape him, quivering and bucking like some sort of wild thing.

Gabriel frowned. The little collie hated to be outside after dark. By this time of night, he was usually curled up on Gabriel's pillow, snoring contentedly. Why would he suddenly choose to brave the woods all alone after dark?

He wouldn't.

That still, small voice in Gabriel's head contained the ring of absolute truth. Sam would only brave the woods by night if he were accompanying someone. Someone who might be out looking for Gabriel. Someone like Samantha.

Ignoring his frantic wriggling, Gabriel sniffed at the dog's fur. Sure enough, the unmistakable fragrance of lemon verbena clung to his silky coat. But its crisp sweetness was nearly eclipsed by another odor, bitter and dark.

Smoke.

Gabriel stood abruptly, sniffing at the air. Anyone else might have attributed the hint of ash in the air to a wisp of wood smoke curling its way up a chimney. But it flooded Gabriel's lungs like a dark mist of dread.

The dog slipped from his arms. Still barking frantically, Sam raced a few feet toward the woods, then darted back to Gabriel's feet, as if urging him to follow.

Gabriel stood there, torn between the house and the woods. He needed help, but Samantha needed him, and there was no way of knowing how much time he had lost trying to interpret the dog's signals.

He finally turned in what he hoped was the direction of the house and bellowed, *"Fire! Fire!!!"* at the top of his lungs. He would have almost sworn he heard a door opening and a startled female voice, but he didn't have time to linger and make sure.

"Take me to her, Sam! *Go!*" he commanded, following the sound of the dog's frantic yips.

Needing no other encouragement, Sam took off into the woods. Gabriel went crashing after him, swinging his branch like a sword.

Ignoring the bite of the brambles and the sting of the branches slapping at his face, Gabriel charged through the woods like some sort of wild beast. He fell more than once, stumbling over rotting tree trunks and exposed roots. But he dragged himself to his feet and kept going, stopping every few paces to listen for Sam's ringing bark.

If he lagged too far behind, the dog would come bounding back to his side, as if to make sure he was still following. With each step Gabriel took, the smell of smoke grew stronger.

After a grueling plunge through the underbrush, he stumbled to a halt in some sort of clearing. He cocked his head to listen, hearing nothing but the peaceful night sounds of the forest. Fighting panic, he concentrated harder, finally catching Sam's bark— distant, but still audible. Gabriel took off in that direction, hell-bent on reaching Samantha before the dog had to retrace his steps again.

The smoke was no longer a smell, but a palpable presence, thick and choking. As Gabriel rushed blindly through it, his branch struck something immovable, snapping in two. He hurled it away. Clawing back a curtain of ivy, he flattened one palm against the rough-hewn surface. The stone wall was hot enough to make him snatch back his hand.

He must have arrived at the old stable at the very edge of the Fairchild property. The structure had been abandoned long before he was born.

"Samantha!" he shouted, feeling frantically for some sort of opening.

Sam was barking wildly now, near hysteria. Gabriel followed the sound to an open door. The dog rushed inside the stable and Gabriel knew he had no choice but to follow. He couldn't afford to wait for someone from the house to find them. He was Samantha's only hope.

Taking a deep breath, he dashed after the dog. He could hear the crackling flames licking at the ancient timber beams above him. The roiling smoke curled deep into his lungs, seeking to crowd out all of the air.

"*Samantha!*" he shouted hoarsely, praying that she could still hear him.

He had taken only a few steps when he heard a loud crack. Before he could throw up a hand, something heavy struck him sharply on the temple.

Gabriel began to fall in the barn, but when he landed, he was back on the heaving deck of the *Victory* with shrapnel whistling overhead and the acrid stench of cannon fire singeing his nostrils. Blood trickled down his face, into his eyes and mouth, and when he lifted his aching head, he saw Nelson crumpling to the deck in slow motion, his face a mask of bewilderment.

Gabriel's hands clenched into fists. Nelson had died on his watch. Samantha would not.

Summoning every last ounce of his will, he staggered to his feet, throwing a hand up to shield his face from the burning embers raining down from the loft. Sam's bark had shifted to a high-pitched whimpering that sounded almost eerily human.

Half lunging, half crawling, Gabriel fought his way across the floor to the sound. Something crunched beneath his boot. When he reached down and felt the twisted frames of Samantha's spectacles, his heart nearly stopped.

But then his searching hands closed over something warm and soft. He drew Samantha's limp body up and into his arms, shuddering with relief when he felt the whisper of her breath against his face.

"Hold on, angel," he whispered, pressing a fervent kiss to her brow. "Just hold on to me and everything will be all right."

Carrying her like a child, he went lunging back toward the direction he had come, trusting that Sam would follow. As he stumbled out of the door, the stable collapsed behind them in a roaring inferno, the blast of heat nearly knocking Gabriel off his feet.

He didn't slow his long strides until they were well away from the choking cloud of smoke and ash. As Samantha sucked in her first breath of the crisp night air, she began to cough—a hoarse, agonizing sound torn from deep in her chest. Dropping to his knees in a bed of damp leaves, Gabriel cradled her across his lap. Her cheek was warm beneath his hand, but there was no way for him to determine its color. Dying a little with each of her tortured breaths, he waited for the bitter spasm to pass.

Something cold and wet nudged his arm. Gabriel's seeking hand closed in Sam's fur. He gently kneaded the collie's body, trying to soothe its violent trembling. "You're the best dog in the world, Sam," he said, his own teeth chattering with reaction. "As soon as we get back to the house, I'm giving you every last one of my boots. Hell, I'll even buy you your own pair if you want."

When Samantha's eyes fluttered open, she found Gabriel hovering over her, his face taut with worry. Even scarred and streaked with soot, it was the most beautiful sight she had ever seen.

"I saw you," she croaked, reaching up to tenderly swipe a smudge of soot from his cheek. "Smiling down at me in the sunlight right before everything went dark."

He tried to smile then, but some other emotion contorted his mouth. He buried his face in her hair, holding her as if he'd never let her go. Samantha moaned softly at how right it felt to be in his arms again.

"Are you hurt?" He lowered her back to his lap, frantically running his hands over her arms and legs. "Did you break anything? Are you burned anywhere?"

"Don't think so." She shook her head, then winced as the motion sent a stabbing pain shooting down her neck. "But my head aches."

"Mine, too," he admitted with a rueful laugh.

For the first time, Samantha noticed the bloody gash on his left temple. "Oh!" she rasped, hot tears filling her eyes as she realized how close she had come to losing him. "Looking for you. Bats st-startled me. Dropped the lamp. My fault."

His eyes sparkled down at her from the dappled shadows. "I suppose we'll just have to take the cost of the stable out of your wages, then, won't we? It'll probably take you several years of service to pay off your debt to me."

"How did you find me?" she asked, both her breath and her words beginning to come easier.

"I had a little help."

Following his nod, Samantha lifted her head to find Sam curled up in a nest of leaves a few feet away, still sniffing nervously at the air. His coat was matted with soot and scorched black in places.

"You told me he might be the saving of me someday," Gabriel said. "You were right."

"He could have been the death of you!" Balling up her fist, Samantha hit him weakly on the shoulder. "Hasn't anyone ever told you that the blind are not to go rushing into burning buildings?"

"I suppose now you're going to scold me for being such an idiot."

She shook her head fiercely, ignoring the resulting pain. "Not an idiot. A hero." The tears spilled from her eyes as she reached up to stroke his cheek, the jagged length of his scar. "*My* hero."

Swallowing hard, he captured her hand in his, bringing her fingertips to his lips. "Ah, but you're the hero, my dear. With a captain half as fierce as you beneath his command, Nelson could have driven Napoleon all the way back to Paris."

"Why would you say such a silly thing? I was defeated by a rotten ladder and a roost of bats."

"I was speaking of a more formidable opponent. My mother."

Samantha blinked up at him, realization slowly dawning. "You heard?"

"Every magnificent word. It was all I could do not to demand an encore."

Something about Gabriel's expression was stealing Samantha's breath away in an entirely different manner. She'd seen him look mocking and sarcastic and irritated and amused at her expense, but she'd never seen him look quite so . . . resolved.

"It's very ill-mannered to lurk outside of windows and eavesdrop, you know," she pointed out. "Even when you're blind."

He shook his head. "I knew I couldn't avoid that scold forever. Have I ever told you how very much I admire you, Miss Wickersham?"

A nervous laugh escaped her. "I should say not. Nor is it necessary. I'm quite content with my own regard. I have no need or desire to be admired."

His hand brushed her hair. "What about adored? Would you care to be adored?"

Her heart was beginning to thunder in her chest. Perhaps she had spoken too soon. Perhaps she was mortally wounded after all. "Most certainly not! Only foolish young girls with their empty heads stuffed with all sorts of romantic notions yearn for that sort of attention."

"Just what do *you* yearn for . . . Samantha?" Before she could rebuke him for using her Christian name, his warm palm found the curve of her cheek. "Isn't there something you want so badly that it makes you ache?" His thumb grazed the fullness of her lips, lips that were aching for his kiss.

"You," she whispered helplessly, curling her hand around his nape and drawing his mouth down to hers.

Despite the mingled taste of soot and tears, it was the sweetest kiss Samantha had ever known. Gabriel held nothing back. As he wrapped his arms around her, his tongue swept through her mouth, igniting a fire even more consuming than the one they had just escaped. To taste its flames, Samantha would willingly risk being scorched to cinders.

He laid her back on the bed of leaves, moving over her like the shadow of a dream. She closed her eyes, only too eager to join him in the darkness.

Dragging his mouth away from hers, he kissed and nuzzled his way down the sensitive column of her throat, inhaling deeply as if she smelled of the most potent perfume instead of lemons and smoke. "I can't believe I almost lost you," he said hoarsely, flowering his lips against the pulse that beat at the side of her throat.

She clung to his broad shoulders, adrift in a delicious sea of sensation. "I'm sure Beckwith could have hired another nurse. Perhaps he could have even persuaded the widow Hawkins to come back and look after you."

Gabriel shuddered against her throat, but she couldn't tell if it was from laughter or horror. "Bite your tongue, woman." He lifted his head, a devilish sparkle lighting his eyes. "Or better yet, let me do it."

As his mouth slanted over hers again, Samantha boldly gave him every opportunity. He dragged one honeyed kiss after another from her lips until she was breathless with longing and he was panting with need. She was hardly aware when his hips began to move against hers in a dance even more provocative than the one they had shared in the ballroom.

But there was no ignoring the waves of pleasure that began to fan out from her lower body. She gasped into his mouth as he rubbed himself against the aching mound between her legs. It was both shocking and thrilling to finally feel that part of him she'd seen so clearly outlined beneath his breeches, to know exactly what he wanted to do to her with it.

Her knees fell apart beneath her skirt. His hand cupped her there, seeking to reach her through the thick layers of wool and linen.

Samantha moaned and writhed beneath his rough petting, stunned by how shameless she'd become, how hot she burned for the caress of his fingers against her bare flesh. When he withdrew his hand, she wanted to cry out with disappointment. But then she felt it slide beneath her skirt. His fingers glided over the wool of her stocking and past her garter to the silky flesh of her inner thigh with a tender urgency she could not resist.

When she felt his fingertips graze the curls between her thighs, Samantha buried her face against his throat, seized by a sudden and unbearable shyness.

His touch was no longer rough, but exquisitely tender. His fingers licked at her swollen flesh like living flames, melting her every misgiving in a heated rush of nectar.

Gabriel groaned. "I knew if I could just get under those demure skirts of yours, I could prove you weren't made of ice. Melt for me, angel," he whispered, ravishing her ear with his tongue even as he slipped his longest finger deep into that honeyed softness.

She moaned as her body shuddered helplessly around the probing thickness of his finger, a wanton thing no longer under her control. She had always known he had the reputation of being a skilled lover, but she hadn't realized that he would know her body better than she did, that he would be capable of focusing solely on her pleasure to the exclusion of his own.

The cost of his restraint was betrayed by the ragged rasp of his breathing, the rigid length of flesh pressed against her thigh.

He added another finger to his exploration, gently stretching her, spreading her, even as the pad of his thumb brushed back and forth over the rigid nubbin of flesh at the crux of her damp curls, teasing it to throbbing delight.

His deft fingers continued to pleasure her until she was writhing and whimpering, nearly incoherent with a need she had never known she possessed. A wave of dark bliss swelled over her head. As it broke, sending a primal ecstasy spilling through her body in a relentless tide, he kissed her hard, capturing her broken cry in his mouth.

His kiss slowly gentled, as if seeking to soothe the delicious aftershocks that wracked her body.

"I'm so sorry!" she gasped when she could finally speak.

Gabriel smoothed a sweat-dampened tendril of hair from her brow. "What for?"

"I didn't mean to be so selfish."

He chuckled. "Don't be ridiculous. I enjoyed that nearly as much as you did."

"You did?"

He nodded.

Emboldened by his confession, Samantha reached between them and stroked the unabated length of his desire through the buttery doeskin of his breeches. "Then you'll probably enjoy this even more."

Gabriel sucked in a taut breath. "I'm sure I would," he said, forced to bite off each word from between his clenched teeth, "but I'm afraid I'll have to wait until later."

"Why?"

He deposited a tender kiss on her pouting lips. "Because we're about to have uninvited company."

Still half dazed with pleasure, Samantha sat up in his arms, only to hear the sound of something large and clumsy crashing through the underbrush.

Gabriel managed to jerk down her skirt just as Beckwith came bursting out of the woods, with Peter and Phillip right behind him.

"Thank heavens you're all right, my lord!" the butler exclaimed, waving his lantern over the two of them. "When we saw that the barn had collapsed, we feared the worst."

"Sweet Christ, Beckwith!" Gabriel threw up a hand, shying away. "Would you get that blasted light out of my eyes? You're blinding me!"

A dumbfounded silence fell over the clearing as they all, including Gabriel, realized what he had just said.

Chapter 17

My darling Cecily,

*If you won't allow me to seduce you, then you're leaving me with
no other choice . . .*

"Does *she* have to be here?" the marchioness of Thornwood asked,
shooting Samantha a withering glare.

Samantha would have liked nothing more than to escape the
crowded study. It was torture to sit there on the edge of her
straight-backed chair with her face so composed when her heart
was being ripped in two, torn between hope and despair.

Before she could rise and murmur her excuses, Gabriel said
firmly, "She most certainly does. She *is* my nurse, you know." Although he couldn't turn his head in her direction, the warmth in
his voice assured her that she was far more than that to him.

He was sitting in front of a baize-covered card table, his head
strapped into some sort of iron device provided by Dr. Richard
Gilby, the only physician who had dared to offer him the smallest
inkling of hope that his vision might return. The short man with
his kind eyes and neatly trimmed side-whiskers hadn't uttered one

word of complaint at being rousted from his bed in the middle of the night by the marquess of Thornwood, who had been rousted from *his* bed by a jabbering Beckwith. The physician had simply gathered up several devices that looked more like medieval torture devices than instruments of healing and set out for Fairchild Park with the rest of Gabriel's family.

Although the sun had risen several hours ago, Eugenia and Valerie still dozed at opposite ends of a brocaded sofa. A bright-eyed Honoria hovered behind the doctor, eagerly studying every instrument he drew from his bag. The marquess paced in front of the fire, walking stick in hand, while his wife sat in one of the massive wing chairs that flanked the hearth as if it were a throne, her hands plucking nervously at her handkerchief.

Samantha could not quite bring herself to meet the woman's disapproving gaze. Although she had washed the soot from her skin and hair and changed into a fresh gown, there was nothing she could do to scrub away the indelible memory of Gabriel's touch and the shattering pleasure it had brought her.

"Aha!" the doctor barked, making them all jump.

His knowing nods and cryptic harrumphs were beginning to wear on their nerves. Although he had the most at stake, only Gabriel seemed content to wait until the man had finished his examination before he started demanding answers. Sam was the only one in the room who seemed less concerned by the unusual proceedings. The collie was curled up on the hearth rug, gnawing on a shiny riding boot.

The marquess thumped his cane on the floor, his florid face shiny with sweat. "What is it, man? Have you discovered something?"

Ignoring him, Dr. Gilby whirled around and snapped his fingers toward the windows. "Close the curtains again. Immediately."

Both Beckwith and Mrs. Philpot rushed to comply, nearly tripping over each other's feet. Although the rest of the servants had been banned from the room, Samantha had seen Peter and Phillip's heads bob past the mullioned windows more than once in the past hour.

The gloom that descended with the curtains gave her a welcome respite. At least she could study Gabriel without trying to hide the yearning in her eyes. Now that she no longer had her spectacles to shield them, she felt as if her every emotion was on parade.

Dr. Gilby attached an enormous magnifying glass to the front of the iron headpiece. As he held a flickering candle in front of it, Honoria stood on tiptoe to peer over his shoulder.

"What do you see now?" he asked Gabriel.

"Moving shadows? Shapes?" Gabriel shook his head, his eyes narrowing as he struggled to concentrate. "To be honest, not much of anything."

"Excellent," the doctor pronounced, handing the candle to Honoria.

He removed the shade from the oil lamp at his elbow, then brought the lamp quickly toward Gabriel's face. Gabriel visibly flinched.

"What about now?"

Gabriel turned his head so he wouldn't have to look directly at the lamp. "A ball of flame, so bright I can hardly bear to look at it."

It was impossible to tell if Dr. Gilby's gusty sigh boded happiness or disaster. He unbuckled the device from Gabriel's head, then turned and waved his arms at the windows like a maestro who had just finished conducting the performance of his career. "You may open the curtains."

As Beckwith and Mrs. Philpot swept back the heavy drapes, sunlight flooded the drawing room. Samantha studied her folded hands, afraid to look at Gabriel.

The marquess took his wife's fluttering hand in his and squeezed it tight. Even Eugenia and Valerie stirred themselves, gazing at the doctor with hopeful green eyes that were nearly identical to their brother's.

But it was Gabriel who broke the tense silence. "Why the sudden change, Doctor? Before last night, I couldn't make any sort of distinction between light and shadow."

Tucking the iron device back in his bag, Dr. Gilby shook his head. "We may never know. I suspect the sharp blow to the head dislodged a clot of blood that could have taken months to dissolve on its own, if indeed it ever did."

Gabriel gingerly fingered the gash on his temple. "I should have ordered my butler to whack me over the head with one of my walking sticks a long time ago."

Samantha wanted to go to him, to wrap her arms around him and press a tender kiss to that wound he had earned on her behalf.

She had no right to touch him, but she could ask the one question that hung unspoken in the air. The question everyone else was too afraid to ask.

"Will he see again?"

The doctor patted Gabriel on the shoulder, his blue eyes twinkling. "It may be a few days or a few weeks before your mind is able to make out more than shadows and shapes, son, but I have every reason to believe that you're going to make a full recovery."

Samantha clapped a hand to her mouth to catch an involuntary sob.

Letting out a joyful whoop, Honoria threw her arms around Gabriel's neck. The rest of his family crowded around him—Eugenia, Valerie, and his mother smothering him in their perfumed embraces while his father clapped him heartily on the back. Even Sam jumped up to join the happy fray, adding his shrill bark to the merry burst of chatter and laughter.

Samantha glanced over to find Mrs. Philpot in Beckwith's arms, her narrow back shaking with emotion. As the butler met Samantha's gaze over the housekeeper's shoulder, she would have almost sworn she saw a glimmer of sympathy in his eyes.

She rose and slipped from the room, knowing she no longer had any place there. She mounted the stairs to the second floor, keeping her chin high and her spine straight in case any of the other servants were watching. Finally reaching the refuge of her bedchamber, she closed and bolted the door behind her.

Keeping a hand clamped over her mouth to muffle her sobs, she slid down the door, a sharp pang of mingled joy and grief bending her almost double. Even as the tears began to spill over the back of her hand, she could not have said if she was crying for Gabriel or for herself.

Samantha sat on the edge of the bed in her nightdress, methodically braiding her hair. That was all she'd been doing since barricading herself in her bedchamber that morning—going through the motions of living. When Mrs. Philpot had sent Elsie up with a supper tray, she had dutifully eaten every spoonful of the hearty kale soup, although she wanted nothing more than to pour it out the window. If she could just keep living one moment at a time, then perhaps she wouldn't have to face the future.

A future without Gabriel.

Her fingers faltered. The half-braided strand of hair slipped through her hands. She could no longer deny the truth. Her work here was done. Gabriel had no further need of her. He was back where he belonged—in the loving arms of his family.

Climbing down from the bed, she went to the armoire and dragged out her battered leather portmanteau. She propped it open beside the bed before unlatching the lid of her trunk.

She never thought she'd wax nostalgic over the ugly serges and sensible wool stockings she'd been wearing since arriving at Fairchild Park, but suddenly she wanted nothing more than to bury her face in them and weep. Gently easing them aside, she fished out a single clean chemise and petticoat and tucked them into the portmanteau along with a slim volume of Marlowe's poetry. She was about to close the trunk when a creamy corner of stationery caught her eye.

Gabriel's letters.

She had tried to bury them so deep they would never surface. Yet here they were again, as compelling and irresistible as they had been on the day they were received.

Samantha tugged the ribbon-bound bundle into her hands, letting the trunk fall shut. She moved to sit on the side of the bed, running her fingertips over paper so worn from repeated handling that it threatened to crumble beneath her touch. She could imagine Gabriel caressing the fine linen with his strong hands, weighing each word as if it were gold.

She knew she would hate herself later, but she could not resist loosening the ribbon that bound them. Just as she was unfolding the first letter and holding it up to the light of the tallow candle that burned on the table next to her bed, a knock sounded on the door.

Samantha jumped to her feet with a guilty start. She frantically scanned the room, then kicked the portmanteau under the bed. She was halfway to the door before she remembered the letters clutched in her hand.

The knock came again, its impatient edge unmistakable.

"One moment, please!" she cried out before rushing back to the bed and shoving the letters under the mattress.

She swung open the door to find Gabriel standing there, garbed only in a dressing gown of forest-green silk. Before she could utter a word, he reached for her. Cupping her face in his hands, he swept his tongue into her mouth, kissing her with a fierce tenderness that stole her breath away. By the time he dragged his lips away from hers, she was dizzy with desire.

"And a good evening to you, too, my lord," she whispered, still swaying on her feet.

Pushing her aside, Gabriel charged into the room. He slammed the door behind him and leaned against it.

"What is it?" Samantha cast the door a worried glance. "Are you being pursued by barbarian hordes?"

"Worse. It's my family." He ran a hand through his already

tousled hair. "They've settled into the mansion like a flock of pigeons. I thought I was never going to elude them. Do you know how hard it is to sneak past someone you can't see?"

Thankful that he also couldn't see her swollen eyes and the tear stains on her cheeks, she said lightly, "According to Dr. Gilby, you won't have to worry about that much longer, will you?"

He shook his head as if he still couldn't quite comprehend his good fortune. "Amazing, isn't it? But do you want to know the most astonishing thing of all?" He reached for her again, his seeking hand closing around her slender wrist. "When Dr. Gilby told me that I would make a full recovery, I realized the thing I wanted to see most in the world was your sweet face."

Samantha turned that face away from him. "I fear you might be sorely disappointed."

"That's quite impossible." All traces of humor disappeared from his voice, leaving it curiously somber. "You could never disappoint me."

Biting her lip, she tugged her wrist from his grasp and moved out of his reach. She was less afraid that he might start kissing her again than of what she might do if he did. "To what do I owe the honor of this rather unconventional visit?"

Gabriel leaned against the door and folded his arms over his chest, his convincing leer sending a delicious shiver down her spine. "Don't play the innocent with me, Miss Wickersham. I'm hardly the first lord of the manor to sneak into the bedchamber of his most irresistible servant."

"Wasn't it you, my lord, who told me you weren't in the habit of forcing your attentions on the females in your employ?"

Pushing himself away from the door, Gabriel moved toward the sound of her voice with the grace of a prowling panther. "Why would I need force when seduction is so much more effective? And so much more"—his lips caressed the word—"pleasurable."

Samantha began to back away from him, fearing this more playful Gabriel was even more of a danger to her heart. Yet at the same time, she could not resist joining in the game. "You should know by now that I'm not the sort of woman to be seduced by expensive baubles, a few flowery words, or some extravagant promises made in the heat of the moment. Neither my body nor my heart is so cheaply won."

As Gabriel's shadow fell over her, the back of her knees struck the bed. He pressed a hand to her chest, sending her tumbling back into it. Before she could protest, he followed her down, gently cupping her cheek in one of his big hands. "I haven't any baubles on me at the moment, but what if I promise to make you my wife and love you for the rest of our days?"

Chapter 18

My darling Cecily,

Every minute seems an eternity while I await your reply . . .

"Have you gone stark raving mad?" Samantha shoved at Gabriel's chest with enough force to send him tumbling clear off the bed and onto the floor.

He sat up, looking bewildered. "I never realized it was so much safer to propose by letter."

Bouncing off the bed, Samantha began to pace the small room, her frantic strides reflecting the turmoil in her heart. "Perhaps the blow to your head affected more than your vision, my lord. Perhaps it affected your memory as well. Because you seem to have forgotten that *you* are an earl—a peer of the realm—while *I* am a mere servant."

"What you are, Samantha—"

She whirled around to face him. "*Miss* Wickersham!"

A half-smile played around his beautifully chiseled lips, only infuriating her further. "What you are, *Miss* Wickersham, is the woman I adore and intend to make my wife."

She threw her hands up in the air. "There's no help for you, then, is there? You're regaining your sight only to lose your mind."

"Has it occurred to you that you have no choice but to marry me?"

"Why would you say such a thing?"

"Because I've already compromised you. Or have you forgotten?"

She could tell by the challenging set of his mouth that he knew there would be no forgetting the shameless way her body had wept beneath his hand, the shudders of pleasure that had wracked her to the core. She would carry that memory to her grave.

"I release you from any obligation. There's no reason you should spend the rest of your life paying for a . . . a foolish indiscretion."

He arched one tawny eyebrow. "Is that all last night was to you? An indiscretion?"

Unable to come up with a convincing denial, Samantha resumed her pacing. "I'm sure your mother would have been horrified had she known you proposed to that baronet's daughter. What would she say if you told her you intended to marry your nurse?"

Gabriel reached for the hem of her nightdress as she swept past him, tugging her into his lap. He wrapped his strong arms around her, making any thought of escape impossible. "Why don't you come with me right now and we'll find out?"

Her squirming only settled her deeper into his embrace. "You'll give the poor woman an apoplexy! Why, the news would probably kill her! Or me," she added grimly.

He laughed. "She really isn't the dragon she pretends to be. As a matter of fact, when we first met, I noticed a marked similarity in your—"

Samantha clapped a hand over his mouth. "Don't say it! Don't you dare say it!"

Still laughing, Gabriel tugged her hand from his lips. "I'm sure you'll grow to love her someday." Both his grip and his voice softened as the sparkle of mischief faded from his eyes, leaving them glowing with a tender light. "After all, she is going to be the grandmother of your children."

Gabriel's words slid like a knife into Samantha's heart, giving her a glimpse into a future she could never share. She blinked back a rush of tears. She might not have tomorrow, but she could have tonight.

"I was wrong," she whispered.

He frowned. "About what?"

"I *am* the sort of woman who can be seduced by flowery words and extravagant promises." Cupping his cheek in her hand, she lifted her face to his.

As Gabriel felt the softness of Samantha's lips flower beneath his, it was as if a light dawned somewhere in his soul. Curling an arm beneath her hips, he lifted her to the narrow iron bedstead, laying her back among the rumpled sheets.

He knew he should wait until after they were wed. But he'd been waiting so long for this moment—for more than a lifetime, it seemed.

"Wait," she said, nearly stopping his heart. "I just want to put the candle out."

He waited until she was back in his arms before murmuring, "I don't need the candle anyway. All I need is you."

Finding the hem of her nightdress, Gabriel gently tugged it over her head. In that moment, he felt like a bridegroom. Knowing that Samantha was naked beneath him, that he could spend all night exploring the exquisite treasures of her body, made his mouth go dry and his hands shake with longing.

It had been so long since he'd held a naked woman in his arms. Even before Trafalgar, he'd spent months of self-imposed celibacy longing for Cecily. While the other sailors aboard the *Victory* had satisfied their cruder urges with harbor prostitutes during their brief stints ashore, he had remained aboard the ship rereading Cecily's letters. Although his body had burned for release, he had been content to let it smolder while he dreamed of the day when they would be reunited. If he had known that day would never come, he still would have been willing to wait for this moment. For Samantha.

Gabriel unknotted the sash of his dressing gown and shrugged it off of his shoulders, desperate to be skin to skin with her, flesh to flesh. Kissing her as if each kiss would be their last, he glided like raw silk down her body, groaning when his chest encountered the plump softness of her breasts, when his swollen staff brushed the downy curls between her legs. He wanted to bury himself in her right then and there, to seize all the pleasure that had been denied him through those long, lonely months.

But Samantha was no harbor prostitute. She deserved more than a rough-and-tumble coupling. She clutched at his shoulders and moaned in protest when he dragged his mouth away from hers and rolled to her side. There was barely enough room for both of them in the narrow bedstead, but that suited Gabriel just fine. The cozy confines made it that much easier for him to throw one leg over her thigh, to nuzzle her throat while his hand cupped the fullness of one breast. Her nipple was already as ripe as a succulent berry begging to be taken into his mouth.

Eager to please, he did just that—tugging and teasing, suckling and soothing, with his lips and tongue and teeth, until she was arching beneath him, her hands tugging at his hair. A familiar exultation quickened in his veins. He didn't need his sight for this. Making love to a woman in the dark had always come as naturally to him as breathing.

"I can feel that," she whispered between panting breaths, sounding both disconcerted and scandalized.

"I should hope so," he replied, reluctantly lifting his head from her breast. "I wouldn't want to waste your time."

"No. I mean . . ."

Gabriel had the keen sensation that if he could see her face in that moment, it would have been tinted with an adorable blush.

". . . *down there*," she finished.

He shook his head, a helpless laugh escaping him. "I can promise you that you're going to feel a lot more than that *down there* before I'm through with you."

As if to make good on his promise, he sent his hand gliding over the satin-soft skin of her abdomen. She shivered with anticipation beneath his touch, but he prolonged both the pleasure and the torment by taking his own sweet time exploring the slight curve of her belly, the sensitive hollows just above her hipbones.

By the time his fingers grazed the softness of her nether curls, it took little more than a nudge of his thigh to coax her legs apart, to allow him unfettered access to what lay between them.

"You make me feel like such a wanton," she confessed, her every breath a sigh of delight. "As if I would do anything for you . . . with you."

Gabriel hadn't believed it possible for him to get any harder than he already was, but as a dizzying array of erotic images flashed through his mind, he realized he was wrong. "I'll be more than glad to give you a lifetime to prove that."

"What if we didn't have a lifetime?" She wrapped her arms around him in a grip that was surprisingly fierce. "What if we only had this moment?"

"Then I wouldn't squander a single opportunity to do this," he said, claiming her mouth for an achingly tender kiss. "Or this." He lowered his lips to her breast, swirling his tongue around her distended nipple. "Or this." His voice deepened to a groan as he sifted his fingers through her curls, stroking the sleek flesh beneath.

She moaned beneath his touch, a throaty song of welcome. Her body was already moistening to receive him, flowering like a bloom beneath the kiss of the sun. He used the pad of his thumb to smear its sweet dew over the secret bud nestled between those velvety petals. He wanted her to burn for him, to ache for that moment when she would take him deep inside of her and make him her own.

"Please, Gabriel . . ." She arched against his hand, her voice a ragged whisper in his ear. "I can't wait any longer."

As her thighs fell apart, she reached over to caress his throbbing length, extending to him the one invitation no man could resist.

As her fingers encircled him like velvet ribbons, he gritted his teeth against a primal frisson of ecstasy. "Well, since you asked so nicely."

He rolled on top of her. His erection nudged those damp curls, poised at the very gates of heaven.

"Gabriel, there's something I have to tell you." She clutched at his back, the note of panic in her voice unmistakable.

His fingertips found her lips, stilling them with a tender caress. "It's all right, Samantha. There's nothing more I need to know. I realize you haven't been entirely forthcoming with me. A woman like you never would have sought a post like this if you hadn't been running from your past. But I don't care. I don't care if there was another man before me. I don't care if there were a dozen men. The only thing I care about is that you're in my arms, right here, right now."

To prove that he was a man of his word, Gabriel drew back his hips and thrust himself deep inside of her. Through a fog of mindless pleasure, he heard her broken cry, felt something fragile and irreplaceable give way before his body's insistent demand.

He lay buried to the hilt in her, afraid to move, afraid to breathe. "Samantha?"

"Hmmmm?" she replied in a hoarse squeak.

Gabriel fought to hold himself still even as her body squeezed him in a vise of raw pleasure. "Just what was it you were going to tell me?"

He heard her swallow. "That I've never done this before."

He collapsed against her throat, biting off a reverent oath. "Do you want me to stop?" Even as he offered, Gabriel didn't know if he could.

She shook her head violently. "No." Tangling her fingers in his hair, she dragged his mouth back to her lips. "Never."

As their tongues tangled in a dark dance of delight, she arched against him, that simple motion gloving him in rapture. Gabriel had always prided himself on his sophistication. He was shocked to learn that he was still barbarian enough to want to beat his chest and roar with triumph, all because he was the first man to have her—the only man. He began to move, gliding in and out of her with long, deep strokes deliberately designed to melt her whimpers of pain to moans of pleasure.

With Samantha to share it with him, the darkness was no longer an enemy, but a lover. Everything was texture and sensation, friction and contrast. She was soft. He was hard. She was smooth. He was rough. She gave. He took.

Believing she deserved some extra indulgence for the pain he had caused her, something to make it all worthwhile, Gabriel reached between them. Without missing a stroke with his tongue or his cock, he gently fingered her until she convulsed around him with a husky cry that was nearly his undoing.

Drawing her arms over her head and lacing his fingers through hers until they were palm to palm, heart to heart, he whispered fiercely, "Hold on, angel. Don't ever let go."

Samantha obeyed, wrapping her slender legs around him. Then there was no more holding back, no more resisting the driving rhythm that beat like tribal drums through his blood. Gabriel rode her, hard and fast and deep, until they were both mindless with pleasure, until he felt those dark shivers of rapture begin to ripple out from her womb once again.

As exultation thundered through him, spilling out in a hot torrent, Gabriel slammed his mouth down over hers, afraid their mingled cries would rouse the entire household.

* * *

Samantha awoke in Gabriel's arms. The bedstead was so narrow that there was only room for them to lie side by side with her back nestled against his chest like two spoons in a drawer.

She glanced toward the window, grateful to discover that the night sky was still dark without a single pink streak to herald the dawn. She would have been content to lie there forever with Gabriel's muscular arm wrapped around her waist, his breath stirring her hair, her bare bottom snuggled against his hips. She could feel his heart beating against her back in the sweetest of lullabies.

Before last night, she'd had a vague idea of what transpired between a man and woman in the bedchamber. But nothing could have prepared her for the reality. For the first time, she understood why one deceptively simple act drove women to court ruin and men to risk everything. She understood why sonnets were written and duels were fought and lives were lost, all for the sake of the magic that was made when a man and woman came together, moving as one in the shadows of the night.

There was a new tenderness between her thighs, a fresh ache to match the one in her heart. Yet it was a sweet ache and a small price to pay for the miracle of holding Gabriel deep inside of her.

Almost as if he could sense the direction of her thoughts, Gabriel stirred. His arm tightened around her waist as he drew her even deeper into the cup of his body.

Something nudged the softness of her bottom. Something hard and insistent. Samantha could not resist giving her rump an experimental wiggle.

Gabriel let out a sleepy grunt before muttering, "Don't bait the dragon, angel, unless you wish to be eaten alive." He eased the tumbled strands of her hair aside, brushing his lips against her nape with a tenderness that made her shiver with yearning. "I shouldn't have been so rough and greedy with you before. You need time to recover."

Knowing that time was the one luxury she did not have, she

arched against him, pressing the softness of her bottom against the heavy weight of his arousal. "All I need is you."

Gabriel groaned in her ear. "You're not playing fair, woman. You know that's the one thing I could never deny you."

But he could deny himself while he pleasured her. One of his hands took turns gently teasing her distended nipples between thumb and forefinger, while the other slipped between her legs, soothing the swollen flesh he found there with exquisite care. Before long, Samantha felt herself melting in a breathless rush of pleasure. She had to bite the pillow to keep from crying out loud.

Only then did he fill his hands with the softness of her breasts and slide deep inside of her from behind. She wanted nothing more than to move against him, to urge him to move, but he held both her and himself utterly still until her body began to pulse around him, its insistent beat echoing the rhythm of her heart.

"Please . . ." she moaned, near to swooning in his arms. "Oh, Gabriel, *please* . . ."

Her incoherent plea was not wasted on him. She had never dreamed it was possible to be ravished so tenderly and yet so thoroughly. By the time he was through with her, she could not have said where his body ended and hers began. She only knew that her heart felt as if it were breaking and her cheeks were wet with tears.

"You're crying," he accused, gently urging her to her back.

She sniffed back a sob. "No, I'm not."

He touched a finger to her cheek, then to his lips, proving her a liar. "It's just as I always suspected," he said sternly. "You needn't try to hide the truth any longer."

Drawing in a ragged breath, Samantha blinked up at him.

He gently cupped one hand over her thundering heart. "Beneath that practical façade of yours beats the sentimental heart of a true romantic. Don't worry, Miss Wickersham. Your secret is safe with me." He leered down at her, the devilish slash of his scar only making him look like more of a libertine. "As long as you make it worth my while, of course."

"You can depend upon it, my lord." Drawing his mouth down to hers, Samantha sealed her vow with a fierce kiss.

Samantha slid the last pin into her hair, securing the heavy mass at the nape of her neck. She wore the same brown skirt and traveling spencer she had worn upon her arrival at Fairchild Park. To the casual observer, it might have appeared she was exactly the same woman. Such an observer wouldn't have noticed the rosy hue in her cheeks, the patch of beard-burn on her throat, the puffy tenderness of lips still swollen from her lover's kisses.

Drawing on her straw bonnet, she turned to face the bed.

Gabriel was sprawled on his stomach in the pearly dawn light, his imposing frame taking up most of the mattress. His head was pillowed on his arms, his right knee cocked to the side, nearly dragging the sheet off of his lean hips. A thick fall of tawny hair veiled his face.

Her golden giant.

Her hands ached to touch him one last time, but she knew she couldn't risk waking him. In a vain attempt to take the edge off of the temptation, she drew on a pair of black gloves.

She had no choice but to leave her trunk behind. She'd already eased the half-packed portmanteau out from under the bed. She had only one task left to complete.

She approached the bed, her every step measured as if it would be her last. As she knelt, only inches from his face, Gabriel stirred and mumbled something in his sleep. Samantha held her breath, believing for one shattering moment that he would open his eyes, that instead of looking through her, he would look right into the depths of her soul.

Instead, he uttered a deep sigh and rolled away from her, his big hand patting the tumbled bedclothes as if searching for something.

Sliding her hand beneath the mattress, she retrieved the stack of letters she'd shoved there so carelessly the night before. Without taking the time to secure them in their ribbon, she tucked the bundle into the portmanteau, then buckled the latches of the traveling bag.

She drew a folded piece of paper from the pocket of her skirt. Her hand trembled ever so slightly as she rested it on the pillow next to Gabriel's head.

The next thing Samantha knew, she was standing by the door, portmanteau in hand.

She allowed herself one last look at Gabriel. She had thought to atone for her sins by coming here, but it seemed she had only compounded one sin with another, even more unforgivable one. But perhaps her greatest sin of all had been falling so deeply in love with him.

Tearing her gaze away from the bed, she slipped from the room, gently drawing the door shut behind her.

≈ Chapter 19 ≈

My darling Cecily,

I carry your letters and all of my hopes for our future next to my heart . . .

"Beckwith!"

As that familiar bellow came roaring through the corridors of Fairchild Park, every servant in the mansion jerked to wild-eyed attention. Their stunned gazes snapped to the ceiling as a deafening crash sounded, followed by a string of oaths hot enough to blister the gilt off the wainscoting.

There was the sound of footsteps stampeding down the stairs, then a shrill yelp followed by another oath. "Well, if you'd stay out from under my feet, I wouldn't step on your blasted tail!"

Toenails clicked across the marble floor as Sam beat a hasty, and wise, retreat.

Beckwith exchanged an anxious look with Mrs. Philpot before calling out, "I'm in the dining room, my lord."

Gabriel came storming through the dining room door, wearing nothing but a dressing gown and a formidable scowl. He was brandishing his walking stick as if it were a weapon. "Have you seen Samantha? When I woke this morning, she was gone."

Someone let out a scandalized gasp. Gabriel slowly turned, obviously realizing too late that they were not alone.

He sniffed at the air, his nostrils flaring. "All I can smell is bacon and freshly brewed coffee. Who else is here?"

"Oh, n-n-not much of anyone, really," Beckwith stammered. "Just Mrs. Philpot. Elsie. Your mother. Your father. And, um"—he awkwardly cleared his throat—"your sisters."

"What? No Willie the gamekeeper? What's wrong? Couldn't he tear himself away from his hunting long enough to join the rest of the household for breakfast?" Gabriel shook his head. "Oh, never mind. The only person I care about is Samantha. Have you seen her?"

Beckwith frowned. "Now that you mention it, I don't believe I have. Which surprises me, because it's nearly ten o'clock and Miss Wickersham is usually very industrious. She's quite devoted to her work."

Looking Gabriel up and down from his bare feet to his uncombed mane of hair, his father chuckled. "I should say so."

Eugenia, Valerie, and Honoria burst into giggles.

"Girls!" their mother snapped, shooting them a glare. "You're excused from the table. Leave us at once."

As the crestfallen girls began to slink out of their chairs, Gabriel said, "Let them stay. They're not children anymore. It's time you stopped banishing them to the nursery every time there's some sort of family drama."

"See?" Honoria whispered, poking Valerie in the ribs as they settled back into their seats. "I told you he was the best big brother in the world."

"I'll go see if I can find Miss Wickersham, my lord," Mrs. Philpot said. "Perhaps one of the other servants has seen her."

"Thank you," Gabriel replied.

As she slipped from the room, the marquess leaned back in his chair, linking his hands over his ample belly with a wistful sigh. "I remember when I was only a few years younger than Gabriel here. There was this fetching little upstairs maid—"

"Theodore!" His wife turned her basilisk glare on him.

He reached over to pat her hand. "That was long before I met you, darling. Once I set my eyes on you, they never strayed again. All I was trying to say is that it happens to the best of men. There's certainly no shame in dallying with the help."

Gabriel rounded on his father. "I'm not dallying with Samantha! I love her and I have every intention of making her my wife."

Both his father and his mother gasped.

"Shall I fetch the hartshorn?" Eugenia whispered. "Mummy looks as if she's going to swoon."

"A commoner?" Horror rippled through Valerie's voice. "You're going to wed a commoner?"

"I can assure you that there is nothing common about Miss Wickersham," Gabriel said.

"Why, I think it's the most romantic thing I ever heard!" Honoria exclaimed, her brown eyes sparkling. "I can just see you come swooping in on your white horse to rescue her from a life of genteel poverty."

Gabriel snorted. "If anyone's done any rescuing around here, it's her."

"Now, son," his father said, "there's no need to make any hasty or rash decisions. You found out only last night that your sight was going to be restored to you. I can understand how you might have been overcome with emotion. Allowed yourself to be swept away into the arms of this . . . this . . . ."

"Yes?" Gabriel drawled, looking as dangerous as anyone had ever seen him.

"Charming girl," his father finished brightly. "But that doesn't mean you have to rush into matrimony with an unsuitable prospect. Why, once you get your sight back and return to London, you can let her a cozy flat somewhere near your town house, set her up as your mistress if you like."

Gabriel's face darkened, but before he could respond, Mrs. Philpot came bustling back into the dining room. "I'm sorry, my lord, but I can't find a trace of her anywhere. No one has seen her. But I did find this note in her room." Her voice faded to a near whisper, making them all wonder just what else she had found. "On her pillow."

"Read it," Gabriel commanded, groping for the nearest empty chair.

As he sank down, Mrs. Philpot handed the note to Beckwith.

The butler reluctantly unfolded the plain sheet of foolscap, his pudgy hands trembling ever so slightly. " 'My dear Lord Sheffield,' " he read, " 'I always told you that there would come a day when you would no longer have need of me. Although I know you are a man of honor, I would never expect you to honor promises made in the heat of . . . ' " Beckwith faltered, shooting Gabriel's family an anguished look.

"Go on," Gabriel said, his own eyes dark and flat.

" 'I would never expect you to honor promises made in the heat of passion. Those fires burn too brightly, blinding even those who should be able to see. Soon you will have your sight—and your life—back. A life I can have no part of. I beg you not to think too harshly of me. Perhaps in some small corner of your heart, you will be able to remember me fondly, as I am ever your . . . Samantha.' "

As Beckwith folded the note, Mrs. Philpot edged closer to him, her trembling fingers groping for his sleeve. Tears were trickling openly down Honoria's cheeks and even Eugenia was forced to dab at the tip of her nose with her napkin.

"You were right, weren't you?" his mother said softly, resting her teacup on the table. "She was a very uncommon girl."

His father sighed. "I'm sorry, lad, but surely you must know that it's for the best."

Without a word, Gabriel rose and strode toward the door, sweeping his walking stick ahead of him.

"Where are you going?" his father asked, plainly bewildered.

He swung around to face them all, his face taut with determination. "I'm going to find her, that's where I'm going."

His father exchanged a troubled look with his mother before asking the one question uppermost in all of their minds. "But what if she doesn't wish to be found?"

Samantha slipped into the attic bedchamber of the large Tudor cottage without bothering to close the door behind her. Although the air was musty and shadows draped the spacious room, she didn't think she could bear to draw back the curtains and throw open the mullioned windows. The morning sunshine would only hurt her eyes.

She rested the portmanteau on the bed, her shoulders slumping with weariness. After hauling the thing around through several sleepless, crowded coach rides, it felt as if it were loaded with rocks instead of a few undergarments, a packet of old letters, and one slim volume of poetry. If not for the letters, she might have been tempted to toss it into the nearest ditch during her long walk from the village that morning. The cheerful twitter of the birds nesting in the hedgerows that lined the lane had only seemed to mock her.

She still wore the same drab brown garments she had worn three days ago when she had slipped out of Fairchild Park at dawn. Dust layered the hem of her skirt and there was a dried milk stain on her bodice where some charwoman's infant had spit up on her during the particularly bumpy ride from Hornsey to South Mims.

Samantha knew she should be chafing from such indignities, but a merciful numbness had descended on her soul. Even as she wondered if she would ever feel anything again, she had to admit the numbness was preferable to the piercing grief that had stabbed her heart when she had left Gabriel sleeping in her bed.

She sank down on the stool in front of the dressing table. She had left this room a girl, but it was a woman who gazed back at her from the shadows of the mirror. From her somber expression, one would have never guessed that her eyes could sparkle with happiness or that her cheeks had once dimpled in a teasing smile.

Her arms ached with exhaustion as she lifted them and began to drag the pins from her hair, one by one. The limp mass came tumbling around her shoulders. She blinked at herself with drowsy eyes, eyes the color of the sea beneath a summer sky.

Footsteps sounded on the stairs—her mother's footsteps, so brisk and familiar that Samantha felt an unexpected rush of nostalgia for the time when her mother could have soothed any heartache, no matter how keen, with a brisk hug and a cup of warm tea.

"One would think," her mother trilled as she came trotting up the stairs, "that when one's mother had given one leave to go traveling abroad with one's wealthy friend, one might be grateful enough to at least send a post to let one's mother know that one was still alive and not languishing in some filthy French dungeon somewhere. Nor should one come sneaking into the house like a common thief instead of announcing her return. Why, I would have never known you were home if your sister hadn't—"

Samantha swiveled on the stool.

Her mother was standing in the doorway. She clapped a hand to her heart, her expression horrified. "Good Lord, Cecily! What have you gone and done to your beautiful hair?"

Chapter 20

My dearest Lord Sheffield,

You claim to be naught but dust beneath my delicate feet, yet to me you are stardust sprinkled across a night sky, forever in my dreams, but out of my reach . . .

"She can't simply have vanished into thin air. It's not possible!"

"One wouldn't think so, my lord. But that appears to be exactly what happened. Once her coach reached London that afternoon, Miss Wickersham's trail went stone cold. My men have been searching for over two months and they haven't been able to locate a single trace of her. It's almost as if she never existed."

"Oh, she existed, all right." Gabriel closed his eyes for a moment, remembering Samantha warm and soft in his arms, more real than anything he had ever touched in his life.

What if we didn't have a lifetime? What if we only had this moment?

Her cryptic question had haunted him ever since he'd been fool enough to let her slip out of his arms. And his bed.

He opened his eyes to survey the small, dapper man who sat on the other side of his desk. The mist in them faded a little more each day. Before long, he would be able to go out and comb the streets for Samantha himself. Until then, he had no choice but to put his trust in this man. Danville Steerforth was one of a half dozen Bow Street Runners of long standing. He and his fellow detectives with their showy red waistcoats and bright blue coats had come highly recommended, both for their skill and their discretion.

The man didn't even seem fazed by Gabriel's scar. He'd probably seen far worse in his line of work.

"Our door-to-door search of Chelsea yielded nothing," Steerforth informed him with a twitch of his caramel-brown mustache. "Are you certain she left no other clues as to where she might have come from? Where she might have been going?"

Running his thumb along the blade of a brass-handled letter opener, Gabriel shook his head. "I've searched every inch of the trunk she left in her bedchamber a dozen times. I found nothing but a few nondescript items of clothing and a bottle of lemon verbena."

He did not share the moment when he had opened the armoire to discover that she had left his gifts behind. Gifts he had never actually seen until that moment. As he had gently fingered the delicate muslin of the gown, the cashmere stole, the frivolous pink slippers suited only for dancing, the wistful strains of "Barbara Allen" had echoed through his memory. His dispassionate recitation also failed to reveal that the familiar fragrance of her perfume had sent him staggering from the room, aching with longing.

"What about her letters of reference? Have those turned up?"

"I'm afraid not. It seems my man returned those letters to her on the same day she was hired."

Steerforth sighed. "That's most unfortunate. Even a single name might have given us a trail to follow."

Gabriel raked his memory. There was something niggling at the back of his mind, some maddening detail he couldn't quite grasp. "During the very first meal we shared, she mentioned working for some family. Caruthers? Carmichael?" He snapped his fingers. "Carstairs! That was it! She told me that she'd served as governess for a Lord and Lady Carstairs for two years."

Steerforth came to his feet, beaming at him. "Excellent, my lord! I'll set up an interview with the family immediately."

"Wait," Gabriel commanded as the man gathered his walking stick and hat. With his vision growing a little crisper each day, he couldn't bear the thought of just sitting around the mansion and letting strangers search for Samantha. "Perhaps it would be best if I conducted this interview myself."

If Steerforth was disappointed to have his sleuthing usurped, he hid it well. "As you wish. If you dig up any leads we can follow, contact me immediately."

"You can count on it," Gabriel assured him.

Steerforth hesitated at the door, turning his felt hat over in his hands. "Forgive me if I'm speaking out of turn, Lord Sheffield, but you never have told me why you're so desperate to locate this woman. Did she rob you while she was in your employ? Steal something that was irreplaceable?"

"Yes, she did, Mr. Steerforth." A rueful smile played around Gabriel's lips as he gazed up into the man's sympathetic eyes. "My heart."

Cecily Samantha March sat on the flagstone terrace of Carstairs Hall, taking tea with her best friend and partner-in-deceit, Lord and Lady Carstairs' only daughter Estelle. The warm June sun caressed her face while a balmy breeze stirred her short cap of honey-gold curls.

She'd spent two months dousing her hair in mineral oil but, to her mother's chagrin, still hadn't managed to rid it completely of the henna-induced tint. Deciding she could no longer bear to have Samantha Wickersham staring back at her from the mirror, Cecily had finally chopped most of it off in a fit of pique. Estelle had assured her that bobbed curls were all the rage in London anyway.

Cecily thought they suited her—made her look more mature, less like the foolish girl she had once been.

Of course, her mama had cried when she saw what Cecily had done and her papa had looked near to bursting into tears himself. But neither of them had had the heart to scold her. Her mama had simply ordered one of the maids to sweep up the fallen locks and toss them in the fire. Cecily had sat and watched them burn.

"Has your family started wondering why you're spending so much time over here?" Estelle asked, helping herself to a scone from the tea tray on the table.

"I'm sure they're glad to be rid of me. I'm afraid I'm not very good company these days."

"Nonsense. You've always been marvelous company. Even when you're moping about with a broken heart." Estelle smeared clotted cream on the flaky layers of pastry and tucked it into her mouth.

At least when she was with Estelle, Cecily didn't have to pretend everything was as it should be. She didn't have to laugh at her brothers' jokes and feign interest in her sister's latest needlework project. She didn't have to reassure her mother that she was perfectly content reading in her room until the wee hours of morning or avoid her papa's bewildered eyes. She could tell by the worried glances they exchanged that she wasn't giving a particularly convincing performance. She had perfected her acting skills during all of the amateur theatricals she and her siblings had put on for their parents when she was a child, but they seemed to have deserted her on the day she abandoned the role of Gabriel's nurse.

Estelle licked a dab of cream from the corner of her mouth. "I was afraid your parents might think it odd that we've been spending so much time in each other's company when we were supposed to have spent half the spring touring Italy with my parents."

"Shhhh!" Cecily nudged Estelle under the table, reminding her that Lord and Lady Carstairs sat just inside the tall, arched windows of the drawing room, enjoying their own tea.

With her quick wit, black curls, and dancing dark eyes, Estelle was the only friend Cecily could have trusted to help her carry out such a risky scheme. But discretion had never been one of her stronger traits.

"It's just fortunate that I returned home only a few days before you and your family did," Cecily murmured, hoping Estelle would take the cue and lower her own voice.

Estelle leaned closer. "We didn't have much choice with that rascal Napoleon threatening to blockade all of England. Mama didn't want us to get stuck in Italy and miss the entire Season. She was afraid I'd catch the eye of some passionate, but penniless, Italian count instead of some stodgy English viscount who will always care more for his hounds than me."

Cecily shook her head. "That only makes me loathe the little tyrant more. What if your family had returned home *before* I did? My parents would have been frantic with worry. I'm just grateful that our families don't travel in the same social circles. I can only imagine the disaster if they tried to compare notes on our journey."

"I promised to send word to Fairchild Park the second we set foot on English soil, didn't I? That would have given you ample time to come up with some new excuse."

"Like what?" Cecily asked, taking a sip of her tea. "Perhaps I could have just sent my mother a note—'I'm terribly sorry, Mama, but I've run off to offer my services as a nurse to a blind earl who just happens to be one of the most notorious rakehells in the *ton*.'"

"*Former* rakehell," Estelle reminded her, arching one dark graceful wing of an eyebrow. "Didn't he swear off seducing women and breaking hearts the first time you met?"

"So he claimed. And if I hadn't been such a callow fool, I would have believed him. Instead, I challenged him to run off and join the Royal Navy just so he could prove himself worthy of my love." She shook her head, sickened by the naïve and selfish child she had been. "If I had eloped to Gretna Green with him when he asked, he never would have been wounded, never would have lost his sight."

"And you never would have gone to Fairchild Park."

"When I heard the rumors that he was living all alone in that house like some sort of wounded animal, I thought I could help him," Cecily said softly, watching a pair of peacocks strut across the rolling green lawn.

"Did you?"

She was spared from answering by the strident jangle of the front door pull. She frowned at Estelle. "Are your parents expecting anyone?"

"No one but you." Estelle blinked up at the midafternoon sun. "Odd time of the day for a surprise caller, isn't it?"

They both cocked their heads toward the drawing room just in time to hear the butler intone, "The earl of Sheffield."

Cecily felt all of the blood drain from her face. Although her first instinct was to duck under the table, she probably would have remained paralyzed with shock had Estelle not grabbed her by the wrist and yanked her behind the fat rhododendron bush growing through a crack in the flagstones just outside one of the windows.

"What in blazes is he doing here?" Estelle hissed.

Cecily shook her head wildly, feeling as if her heart were going to pound right out of her chest. "I don't know!"

They crouched behind the bush, hardly daring to breathe as introductions were made and pleasantries exchanged.

"I do hope you'll forgive the intrusion." Gabriel's deep, smoky voice drifted out the window, sending a shiver of yearning over Cecily's skin. All she had to do was close her eyes and he was behind her, on top of her, inside of her.

"Don't be absurd!" Estelle's mother chided him. "We're quite honored to meet such a celebrated hero. All of London is abuzz with news of your astonishing recovery. Is it true that you've completely regained your sight?"

"I still struggle a bit when dusk first falls, but those shadows are growing easier to navigate every day. My physician seems to think that my mind is just taking a little while to catch up with the progress my eyes have made."

Cecily pressed her own eyes shut, unable to resist casting a brief, but fervent, prayer of thanksgiving heavenward.

"I didn't come here today to talk about me," Gabriel was saying. "I was hoping you could help me with a personal matter. I'm searching for a woman who was recently in my employ and was once in yours—a Miss Samantha Wickersham."

"He's looking for you!" Estelle whispered, elbowing Cecily in the ribs hard enough to make her grunt.

"No, he's not," she replied grimly. "He's looking for *her*. Don't you remember? It was your idea that we give him a letter of reference from your parents. You were the one who forged your father's signature."

"But we assumed that if he tried to contact them, they would still be in Rome."

"Well, guess what? They're not."

"Samantha Wickersham?" Lord Carstairs was saying. "I don't seem to recall the name. Was she some sort of domestic?"

"Not exactly," Gabriel replied. "According to the letter of reference you provided her, she was governess to your children. For two years."

Lady Carstairs sounded even more bewildered than her husband. "I don't recall her or such a letter. That would have been several years ago, but I'm sure I'd still have some recollection of the name."

"Her employment would have to have been fairly recent," Gabriel said, the wariness in his voice increasing. "Miss Wickersham was a young woman, probably no older than five-and-twenty."

"Well, there you have it! That's quite impossible. Our son Edmund is at Cambridge right now, while our daughter is—Just a minute. Estelle, darling," her mother called toward the open windows, "are you still out there?"

Estelle shot Cecily a panicked look.

"*Go!*" Cecily gave her a frantic shove. "Before they come looking for you."

Estelle went stumbling out from behind the bush. She smoothed the white muslin of her skirt and gave Cecily one last petrified look before calling out cheerfully, "Yes, Mama. I'm right here."

As Estelle disappeared into the house, Cecily crawled through the bush and sat with her back to the brick wall beneath the window. She pressed her eyes shut, fighting the temptation to steal just one look at Gabriel. It was torture to be so close to him, yet a world away.

"This is our Estelle," Lord Carstairs was saying, the note of pride in his voice unmistakable. "As you can see, she outgrew her need for a governess several years ago."

"She's the perfect age to start filling up the nursery with babes of her own," his wife added with a nervous titter. "After we find her the perfect husband, of course."

Biting back a groan, Cecily banged the back of her head against the bricks. Just when she thought things couldn't get any worse, Lady Carstairs was trying to marry off her best friend to the only man she would ever love.

As Gabriel murmured a greeting, she tried not to envision him bending over Estelle's hand, tried not to imagine those clever lips of his flowering against its snowy softness. Unlike Cecily, Estelle rarely braved the sun without gloves and bonnet.

"So where's your little friend?" Lady Carstairs asked. "Weren't the two of you taking tea?"

Cecily's eyes widened. The slightest whisper of her name and she would be exposed for the liar and fraud she was.

"There's no reason we can't all take tea together with Lord Sheffield," Estelle's father boomed. "Why don't you go and fetch Miss—"

Estelle launched into a fit of violent coughing. Cecily slumped

against the wall in relief. After several rounds of concerned murmurs and slapping on the back, Estelle managed to choke out, "So
sorry! Scone must have gone down the wrong way."

"But you didn't have a scone," Gabriel pointed out.

"I did earlier," she replied, the wintry note in her voice daring
him to contradict her. "And I'm afraid you'll have to forgive my
friend. She's very shy. She bolted like a rabbit when she heard the
front bell ring."

"That's quite all right," Gabriel assured her. "I really haven't
the time for more introductions. And while I appreciate the hospitality, I'm afraid I'll have to decline your invitation to tea."

"I'm sorry we couldn't be of more help, Sheffield," Lord
Carstairs said, his chair creaking as he rose. "It sounds as if you've
been the victim of some unscrupulous character. If you still have
this forged letter in your possession, I'd advise you to turn it over
to the authorities immediately. They might be able to find this
woman and bring her to justice."

"There's no need to call in the authorities." The determination
in Gabriel's voice sent a shiver down Cecily's spine. "If she's out
there somewhere, I'll find her."

When Estelle emerged from the house a short while after Gabriel
had taken his leave, Cecily was sitting on the hill overlooking the
small duck pond. A mother duck drifted across the pond's serene
surface, seven tiny bits of brown and green fluff gliding in her
wake.

"I never dreamed he'd call my bluff on the letters of reference,"
she admitted as Estelle sank down in the grass beside her, arrang-
ing her skirts in a graceful bell. "He never even saw them." She
turned her anguished gaze on Estelle. "I don't understand why
he's still looking for me—for *her*! As soon as he regained his sight,
I thought he'd go back to the life he knew before we met."

"Which time?" Estelle asked gently.

Cecily hugged a knee to her chest, no longer able to bite back the one question she'd promised herself she wouldn't ask. "How did he look?"

"Quite scrumptious, I must confess. I always thought you were exaggerating his charms—blinded by love and all that rot—but I must say that he's a rather magnificent specimen of manhood. And I adore the scar! It adds an aura of mystery." Estelle shivered with delight. "It makes him look like some sort of pirate who might carry you off over his shoulder and ravish you within an inch of your life."

Cecily turned her face away, but not before Estelle saw the blush come creeping into her cheeks.

"Why, Cecily Samantha March, he's not the only one you've been keeping secrets from, is he?"

"I don't know what you mean."

"I think you do! Is it true? Were the two of you . . ." Throwing a glance over her shoulder, Estelle lowered her voice to a whisper. "*Lovers?*"

"Only one night," Cecily confessed.

"Only once?"

"No. *Only one night,*" Cecily repeated, carefully enunciating each word.

Estelle gasped, looking both delighted and horrified. "I can't believe you've done *that*. With *him*! You're very progressive, you know. Most women wait until after they're married to take a lover." She leaned closer, fanning herself with her hand. "I just have to ask. Is he as *accomplished* as he looks?"

Cecily closed her eyes as Gabriel's *accomplishments* came flooding back into her memory, sending a rush of hot desire melting through her veins. "More so."

"Oh, my!" Estelle fell back in the grass, her arms spread in a mock swoon. But she sat up just as abruptly, stealing a troubled look at Cecily's slender form. "Dear Lord, you're not . . . with child, are you?"

"I wish to God that I was!" The confession burst from Cecily without warning. "Doesn't that prove what a terrible person I am? I'd be willing to break my family's heart, suffer the censure of society, and risk everything if I could just have some small piece of him to carry with me always." She buried her face against her knee, no longer able to bear the weight of her friend's pitying gaze.

Estelle stroked her hair. "It's not too late, you know. Why don't you go to him? Tell him the truth? Beg his forgiveness?"

"How could I?" She lifted her head, gazing at Estelle through a mist of tears. "Don't you understand what I did? I nearly got him killed. I abandoned him when he needed me the most. Then, to try and atone for those sins, I tricked my way into his house and toyed with both his memories and his affections." A harsh sob tore from her throat. "How could he ever forgive me for that? How could he ever look upon me with anything but loathing?"

Even as Estelle gently drew her into her arms so she could cry out the tears she'd been holding in for the past two months, Cecily had another terrible thought. Now that Gabriel knew Samantha had been lying to him, how long would it be before he started to wonder if the night she had spent in his arms was nothing but a lie as well?

≈ Chapter 21 ≈

My darling Cecily,

One word from your lips and I would never leave your reach . . .

The stranger made his way through the crowded London streets, his expression so forbidding and his long strides so determined that even the beggars and cutpurses scurried to get out of his way. He seemed oblivious to the bitter October wind that cut through the shoulder-cape of his woolen greatcoat, the chill droplets of rain dripping from the curved brim of his tall beaver hat.

It wasn't the jagged scar marring his face that made the passersby hug their children closer and sidle out of his path. It was the look in his eyes. His burning gaze searched every face that passed, evoking a shiver in everyone it touched.

The irony was not wasted on Gabriel. He could finally see, but he was denied the one sight he most desired. Every sunrise, no matter how breathtaking its pinks and golds, only lit up the dark road ahead of him. Every sunset foretold the long and lonely night to come.

He stalked through the falling dusk, keenly aware that the

shadows were descending earlier every day. The year was growing older and so was he. Soon it wouldn't be rain falling to wet his cheeks, but snow.

Despite the generous retainer Gabriel had offered them to keep looking for Samantha, Steerforth and his Runners had been forced to admit defeat. After that, Gabriel had taken to the streets himself, returning to his town house in Grosvenor Square each night only after he was too chilled and exhausted to take another step. He'd visited every hospital in London, but no one remembered a former governess named Wickersham who had tended the wounded soldiers and sailors.

He had only one fear greater than not finding Samantha—what if he didn't recognize her when he did?

He had dragged Beckwith along with him for the first month of his search. The shy butler had looked equally miserable huddling in the corner of some squalid tavern or questioning the street vendors in Covent Garden. Gabriel had finally taken pity on him and sent him back to Fairchild Park.

Now, just like the men he had hired to find her, Gabriel was forced to rely on descriptions that varied depending upon whom you asked. As best as he could tell, he was searching for a slender woman of average height with thick auburn hair, delicate features, and eyes too often veiled by those homely spectacles she had worn. Some of the servants insisted they were green, while others swore they had been brown. Only Honoria believed them to be blue.

He knew it was insanity, but Gabriel had to believe that if he came face to face with Samantha, something in his soul would recognize her.

He turned down a poorly lit street that wended its way toward the docks. The crowds were thinner here, the shadows deeper. Whenever Gabriel explored the seedy underworld of Whitechapel or Billingsgate, he wasn't so much afraid that he wouldn't find Samantha, but that he would. The thought of her wandering some dark alley, heavy with his child, maddened him. It made him want to start kicking down doors and snatching up strangers by the throats until he found someone who could prove she wasn't a figment of his imagination.

His determination to find her had not wavered, but the doubts he'd suffered since his visit to the Carstairs estate still haunted him. He remembered the rainy afternoon when she had read to him from *Speed the Plough*. She had played every role with such conviction. What if she'd only been playing the role of a woman falling in love with him? But if that were so, how could she have given herself to him so generously? How could she have surrendered her innocence without asking for anything in return?

As he crossed a narrow alley, an elusive whiff of fragrance drifted to his nose. Halting in his tracks, he closed his eyes and drew in a deep breath, embracing the darkness instead of fleeing it. There it was again—an unmistakable hint of lemon verbena rising above the mingled aromas of scorched sausages and spilled ale.

Opening his eyes, he scanned the shadowy figures around him. A cloaked woman had just passed him on the other side of the alley. Through the mist of rain, he could have sworn he saw a strand of dark auburn hair escaping her hood.

Racing after her, Gabriel caught her by the elbow and jerked her around to face him. Her hood went tumbling back to reveal a nearly toothless grin and a pair of sagging breasts that threatened to spill out of her gaping bodice. Gabriel recoiled from the gin-saturated stench of her breath.

"Whoa, there, guv'nor, there's no need to get rough with a lady. Unless, of course, you like it that way." She fluttered her sparse eyelashes, looking less coy than grotesque. "For a few extra shillin's, I just might be willin' to find out."

Gabriel lowered his hand, barely resisting the urge to wipe it on his coat. "Forgive me, madam. I mistook you for someone else."

"Don't be in such a rush!" she called after him as he turned and began to hurry away, nearly trampling a cursing chimney sweep in his haste to escape. "For a pretty fellow like you, I might even give you a taste for free. I know I 'aven't got too many teeth, but some gents says that only makes it sweeter!"

Weary to his very soul, Gabriel fled the shadows of the alley, determined to seek the refuge of the carriage he'd left parked around the corner.

Turning the collar of his greatcoat up against an icy gust of wind and rain, he crossed the busy street, dodging a carriage stuffed with giggling belles and a ruddy-faced lamplighter. The urchin scampered from lamp to lamp, igniting the oil with the briefest kiss of his sputtering torch.

Gabriel might not even have noticed the shabby figure huddled on the sidewalk beneath one of those lamps if he hadn't heard the man call out, "Alms, please! Spare a halfpenny to help them that can't help themselves!"

"Why don't you crawl off to the workhouse and help us all?" a passing gentleman snarled, stepping right over him.

His cheerful smile undaunted, the man thrust his tin cup toward a hatchet-nosed woman who was trailed by a maid, a footman, and a beleaguered African page struggling to juggle a towering armful of packages. "Spare a halfpenny for a warm cup of soup, ma'am?"

"You don't need a warm cup of soup. You need a job," she informed him, jerking her skirts out of his reach. "Maybe then you wouldn't have time to harass decent Christian folk."

Shaking his head, Gabriel drew a sovereign out of his pocket and tossed it in the man's cup as he passed.

"Thank you, Lieutenant."

Those soft, cultured tones stopped Gabriel in his tracks. He slowly turned.

As the man lifted his hand in a salute, it was impossible not to notice his uncontrollable shivering or the glint of intelligence in his light brown eyes. "Martin Worth, my lord. We served together aboard the *Victory*. You probably don't remember me. I was only a midshipman."

Looking closer, Gabriel realized that what he had mistaken for rags was actually a tattered naval uniform. The faded blue jacket hung loose over a chest so bony it was almost skeletal. The dingy white breeches had been pinned up over Worth's legs—or what was left of them. He no longer had any need for stockings or boots.

As Gabriel slowly lifted his hand to return the salute, a hacking cough rattled up from somewhere in Worth's chest, nearly bending him double. It was clear that the damp had already settled deep into his lungs. He would not survive the coming winter.

Some men still haven't come home from this war. And some men never will. Others lost both arms and legs. They sit begging in the gutters, their uniforms and their pride in tatters. They're jeered at, stepped on, and the only hope they have left is that some stranger with an ounce of Christian charity in their soul might drop a halfpenny in their tin cups.

As that damning voice rang through his memory, Gabriel shook his head in stunned disbelief. He had been searching for Samantha for months, yet it was here on this unfamiliar street corner, gazing into a stranger's eyes, that he finally found her.

"You're right, Midshipman Worth. I didn't remember you," he confessed, dragging off his greatcoat and kneeling to sweep it around the man's gaunt shoulders. "But I do now."

Worth gazed up at him in open bewilderment as he beckoned toward the other side of the street and let out a piercing whistle, summoning his waiting carriage to their side.

"I can't believe I let you bully me into this," Cecily whispered as she and Estelle descended the polished parquet steps that spilled down into the crowded ballroom of Lady Apsley's Mayfair mansion. "I'd never have let you drag me to London at all if our parish didn't have a new curate."

"Unmarried?" Estelle asked.

"I'm afraid so. Although if my mother has anything to say about it, not for long."

"I gather from your glum tone that you don't find him a suitable prospect for matrimony."

"On the contrary. He's everything my family believes I should desire in a husband. Dull. Stolid. Given to long rambling dissertations on the charms of raising blackface sheep and curing tongue sausages. They'd be perfectly content for me to spend the rest of my days darning his stockings and raising his plump, placid children." She sighed. "Perhaps I should allow him to court me. It's no more than I deserve."

Not even Cecily's elbow-length gloves could soften the bite of Estelle's fingernails into her arm. "Don't even think such a terrible thing!"

"And why not? How would you prefer I spend what's left of my life? Crying on your shoulder? Mooning over a man I can never have?"

"I can't predict how you're going to spend the rest of your life," Estelle said as they reached the bottom of the stairs and began to wend their way through the crush of chattering guests, "but I do know how you're going to spend tonight. Smiling. Nodding. Dancing. And making scintillating conversation with besotted young men who care nothing for sheep or curing tongue sausages."

"So what esteemed occasion are we celebrating tonight? Did Lord Apsley's horse win another race at Newmarket?" Cecily knew as well as Estelle that the most renowned London hostesses were quick to seize upon any excuse to brighten the long, dull months between Seasons.

Estelle shrugged. "All I know is that it has something to do with Napoleon following through on his threat to blockade us. Lady Apsley decided to throw a ball in honor of some of the officers who are shipping out tomorrow to spare us the horrors of a life without Belgian lace and Turkish figs. Why don't you think of tonight as your sacrifice to support the noble cause?"

"You forget," Cecily said lightly to hide the sudden ache in her heart, "I've already done my duty for king and country."

"So you have." Estelle sighed wistfully. "Lucky girl. Oh, look!" she exclaimed, distracted by the sight of a liveried footman weaving through the crowd bearing a silver tray of punch glasses. "Since we haven't yet caught the eye of any prowling gentlemen, I suppose we'll have to fetch our own punch. Wait here. I'll be right back."

Cecily bit back a protest as Estelle melted into the crowd, the white muslin train of her gown flashing behind her.

She peered around the heavily thronged ballroom, fixing an awkward smile on her lips. Estelle had insisted that she twine a fetching ribbon that matched her peach gown through her silky curls.

Although the dancing had yet to begin, a string quartet was warming up on the balcony at the far end of the ballroom. Cecily had just caught the hopeful eye of a young militia soldier when a lone violinist began to pick out the plaintive notes of "Barbara Allen."

Cecily closed her eyes, remembering all too clearly another ballroom, another man.

When she opened them, the young soldier was making his way through the crowd toward her. She turned away, thinking only of escape.

It had been a mistake to let Estelle coax her into coming here. She scanned the crowd, but her friend was nowhere in sight. She would simply have to find their carriage and demand that the driver take her back to the Carstairs' town house immediately. He could return for Estelle later.

Glancing over her shoulder to find the soldier still pursuing her, she hastened toward the stairs, trodding heavily on a slippered foot.

"Watch it, girl!" a scowling matron bit off.

"I'm so sorry," she murmured, shouldering her way past a squat man with a bulbous red nose.

She finally emerged from the milling throng, nearly trembling with relief to find herself at the foot of the stairs. Only a few more steps and she would be free.

Already feeling as if a crushing weight were slipping from her shoulders, she glanced toward the top of the stairs, only to find herself gazing directly into a pair of mocking sea-foam-green eyes.

≈ *Chapter 22* ≈

My dearest Gabriel,

(There I have said it! I hope you are satisfied!)

Gabriel Fairchild stood at the head of the stairs, garbed in the full dress uniform of a Royal Navy officer. He wore a dark blue frock coat with brass buttons and a narrow ribbon of white piping around the lapels. A plain blue stock had replaced his ruffled cravat. His waistcoat, shirt, and knee breeches were a dazzling white while a pair of shiny black Hessians hugged his lean calves. His tawny hair was still unfashionably long and drawn back in a leather queue.

A flurry of murmurs and admiring glances greeted his arrival. Just as Estelle had predicted, the scar only added to his mystique, made him seem even more of a dashing and heroic figure. Only Cecily knew how much of a hero he really was. She wouldn't be standing at the foot of those stairs if he hadn't risked his life to save hers.

Her heart staggered beneath the blow of seeing him this way. She had expected him to resume the frivolous lifestyle he had enjoyed before they met at Lady Langley's house party. But this was an entirely different Gabriel—more somber, yet somehow more irresistible.

There was some reckless part of her that almost wanted him to recognize her as Samantha instead of Cecily. She'd rather see loathing in his eyes than have him look at her as if she were of less consequence than a stranger.

She stood frozen into place as he started down the stairs. But his graceful strides carried him right past her, almost as if he'd been struck blind all over again.

Her eyes widened. There could be no mistaking it. She'd just been given the cut direct with a rapier twist. She glanced down at her bodice, surprised to find that it wasn't stained with her heart's blood.

"Excuse me, miss?"

Cecily turned to find herself gazing into the eager young face of the militia soldier. "I know we haven't been properly introduced yet, but I was wondering if you would care to join the dance with me?"

From the corner of her eye, Cecily could see Gabriel greeting their hostess, smiling as he lifted her hand to his lips. A dangerous thread of defiance curled through her veins.

"I most certainly would," she informed the young man, tucking her gloved hands in his.

Fortunately, the sprightly notes of the country dance made conversation impossible. Even as they joined the rollicking line of dancers, she was keenly aware of every step Gabriel took, every hand he kissed, every hungry glance he received from some of the bolder women. It wasn't difficult to follow his path. He towered head and shoulders over most of the men in the room.

In all that time, he didn't seem to spare her a single glance . . . or a single thought.

She lost sight of him just as the musicians began to play the first tinkling notes of an old-fashioned minuet. After guiding them through an intricate set of figures, the music swept into a new key, signaling a change in partners. Grateful to escape the sweaty-palmed young soldier, Cecily gracefully pivoted.

Suddenly she and Gabriel were face to face, hand to hand, palm to palm. She swallowed hard, half expecting him to turn on his heel and cut her dead in front of the entire assembly.

"Miss March," he murmured, proving he wasn't quite as oblivious to her presence as he'd pretended to be.

"Lord Sheffield," she returned as they circled each other warily.

Even through her glove, she could feel the heat of the hand pressed to hers. She tried not to remember the tenderness with which he had once touched her, the shattering pleasure his hands had given her.

Her greatest fear was that he might recognize her voice. She had modeled Samantha Wickersham's stern tones after a spinster aunt. But she knew her natural voice had slipped through on more than one occasion—such as when she'd cried out his name in ecstasy.

"It's gratifying to see you looking so well," she said, deliberately affecting a breathy cadence. It wasn't difficult when she felt as if she were drowning in his crisp masculine scent. "I heard rumors about the miraculous recovery of your sight. I'm glad to learn they were true."

He surveyed her through hooded eyes. "Perhaps it was fate that brought us together tonight. I've never had the opportunity to thank you."

"For what?"

"For coming to visit me in the hospital after I was wounded."

Cecily felt her heart lurch as he gave the rapier another twist. For the first time, she almost pitied the French. This was not a man to lightly engage as an enemy.

Tilting her face to his, she gave him her most dazzling smile. "You don't have to thank me. It was no more than my Christian duty."

His eyes darkened. It seemed she had finally succeeded in getting a reaction from him. But her triumph was short-lived. Before he could make any sort of response, the musicians finished their song. The last brittle note of the minuet hung in the air between them.

He bowed over her hand, brushing his lips across her knuckles in a perfunctory kiss. "It was a pleasure to renew our acquaintance, Miss March, if only to remind myself how very little I ever really knew you."

As the quartet launched into the sweeping notes of an Austrian waltz, the other dancers began to drift off the floor, seeking gossip and refreshments. Nothing cleared a ballroom floor faster than a waltz. No one wanted anyone else to suspect that they even knew the steps of the scandalous dance.

As Gabriel straightened, Cecily fought a rush of panic. In another minute, he would turn his back on her and stalk out of her life forever. They had already attracted several curious stares. She saw Estelle watching them from the other side of the ballroom, her face nearly as white as her dress.

What did she have left to lose? Cecily thought. Her good name? Her reputation? Society might not know it, but she was already ruined for any other man.

Before Gabriel could move away from her, she lightly rested her hand on his sleeve. "Hasn't anyone ever told you that it's ill-mannered for a gentleman to abandon a lady who wishes to dance?"

He gazed down at her, his expression both mocking and wary. "Never let it be said that Gabriel Fairchild could deny a lady anything."

With those familiar words, he slipped one arm around her slender waist and drew her against him. As he swept her into the dance, Cecily closed her eyes, recognizing in that moment that she was willing to take any risk, pay any price, just to be in his arms again.

"I must confess that I was surprised to find you here tonight," he said as they whirled around the deserted floor, their bodies moving in perfect rhythm. "I thought by now you'd be wed to some country squire or gentleman farmer. I know you prize respectability in a man above all else."

She gave him a dimpled smile. "Just as you used to prize the quality of being easily seduced in a woman?"

"That was one quality you most certainly never possessed," he muttered, gazing straight over the top of her head.

"Unlike most of the women ogling you here tonight. Shall I step aside and let one of them take my place in your arms?"

"I appreciate your generosity, but I'm afraid I've no time for such dalliances. I'm shipping out on the *Defiance* tomorrow afternoon."

Cecily stumbled over her own feet. If he hadn't tightened his arm around her, she might have fallen. Fighting to keep her feet moving in the rhythm of the dance, she gazed up at him disbelief. "You're going back to sea? Have you completely lost your wits?"

"I find your concern touching, Miss March, if a bit belated. There's really no need for you to trouble your pretty little head about my fate."

"But the last time you sailed, you almost didn't come back! You were nearly killed! It cost you your sight, your health, your—"

"I'm perfectly aware of what it cost me," Gabriel said softly. As he studied her face, the last trace of mockery disappeared from his eyes.

Cecily desperately wanted to touch him, to cup his scarred cheek in her hand. But the jagged shards of broken promises and shattered dreams littered the space between them, making it impossible to breach.

She lowered her eyes to his lapel. "Why do you feel compelled to play the hero again? After nearly sacrificing your life on behalf of king and country, I should think you'd have nothing left to prove."

"Not to you, perhaps, but to someone else."

"Ah! I should have known there would be a woman involved." Although she knew she could hardly expect him to spend the rest of his life pining for a woman who had never existed, jealousy still rose up in her throat, more bitter than bile. It was agony picturing him in another woman's arms, another woman's bed, doing all of the tender, wicked things that he had done to her. "You always were willing to sacrifice everything for love, weren't you?"

The music ceased, leaving them standing awkwardly in the middle of the floor. Cecily could see the sidelong glances, hear the curious murmurs.

This time there was only pity in Gabriel's gaze. "I didn't even know what love was until I met—and lost—my Samantha. Forgive me for speaking so bluntly, Miss March, but you're not fit to polish her boots."

Offering her a curt bow, he turned on his heel and strode toward the stairs, leaving both Cecily and everyone else in the ballroom staring after him.

She stood there for a long time after he was gone before finally whispering, "No. I don't suppose I am."

Gabriel slammed his way into his town house, thankful the servants were long abed. He stalked into the drawing room. One of the footmen had left a fire burning in the grate to take the edge off of the November chill.

Shrugging off his damp coat, Gabriel poured himself a generous splash of scotch from the crystal decanter on the sideboard. As the smoky liquor scorched its way down his throat, he remembered another dark night when he had drunk too much scotch and contemplated ending his life. Samantha had come to him out of the darkness like an angel that night, giving him a reason and the will to live. It was the first time he had tasted her lips, held her warm body against his.

He tossed back the rest of the scotch in a single swallow. A carved dragon smirked at him from the pedestal of a glass occasional table. The room had been decorated in the Chinese style, but tonight the hangings of crimson silk, lacquered furniture, and miniature pagodas looked more ridiculous than exotic.

He didn't want to admit that seeing Cecily again could have put him in such a savage temper. He had thought himself immune to her charms. But when he had seen her standing there at the foot of those stairs, looking as lost and forlorn as a little girl, he'd felt an unexpected jolt.

She'd been thinner than he remembered. Her cropped curls had given him a start at first, but in some strange way they suited her. They gave her beauty a mature edge, made her graceful neck look longer, her luminous blue eyes even larger. It was the inexplicable sadness he had glimpsed in their depths that had jarred him the most.

Gabriel poured himself another glass of scotch. Perhaps he'd been a fool to believe seeing her again would have no effect on him. He'd spent countless nights at sea with nothing but her memory and her written promises to warm him. Promises she'd dismissed tonight with nothing more than a mocking quip and a dimpled smile.

He raked a hand through his hair. The scotch was only fueling the reckless fever racing through his veins. Once he would have sought relief for such a fever in the arms and bed of some skilled courtesan or opera dancer. Now all he had to console him were the ghosts of the only two women he had ever loved.

A knock sounded on the front door, startling him.

"Who in the devil would be calling at this hour?" he muttered as he strode through the foyer.

He flung open the front door. A woman stood there, cloaked and hooded. For one treacherous instant, hope beat wildly in his heart. Then she eased back the hood, revealing cropped honey-gold curls and a pair of wary blue eyes.

He searched the street behind her, but there was no sign of a carriage or hack. It was almost as if she'd materialized out of the swirling mist.

Gabriel's pulse thudded a warning. He should send her away, close the door in her lovely face. But the devil riding on his shoulder urged him to lean against the doorframe, to fold his arms over his chest and look her up and down with suggestive insolence.

"Good evening, Miss March," he drawled. "Have you come for another dance?"

She gazed up at him, her expression both wary and hopeful. "I was wondering if I might have a word with you?"

He stepped aside. As she brushed past him, he held his breath, deliberately trying not to inhale any of the floral scent that clung to her hair and skin. He escorted her into the drawing room, remembering all the times he had dreamed of being alone with her—a dream that had come true too late.

"May I take your cloak?" he offered, trying not to notice how perfectly the emerald green velvet offset the peachy glow of her skin.

Her slender fingers toyed with the silk frog at her throat. "No, thank you. I'm still a bit chilled." She perched on the edge of a chair covered in mandarin silk, nervously eyeing the pair of snarling dragons masquerading as hearth irons.

"Don't worry. *They* don't bite," Gabriel assured her.

"That's comforting." She peered around the room, taking in its lush decadence. "I thought for a moment that I'd wandered into an opium den."

"I have many vices, but partaking of the poppy isn't one of them. Would you care for something to drink?"

She drew off her gloves and folded her hands in her lap. "Yes, thank you."

"I'm afraid all I have here is scotch. If you'd like, I can wake one of the servants to fetch you some sherry."

"No!" She tempered her panicked outburst with a tremulous smile. "I should hate to trouble them. Scotch will be fine."

Gabriel poured them both a glass. He watched her face carefully as she took her first sip. Her eyes began to water. She choked back a cough. Just as he'd suspected, it was probably the first time she'd tasted the stuff. He expected her to politely set the glass aside, but instead she brought it back to her lips and drained the rest of the scotch in one swallow.

His eyes widened. Whatever she had come to say to him, it seemed it would require a stout dose of liquid courage. "Would you care for another glass or should I just bring you the entire bottle?"

She waved away his offer. The liquor had heightened the color in her cheeks, deepened the dangerous sparkle in her eyes. "No, thank you. I believe that should suffice."

Gabriel sank down on the end of the broad divan, rested his elbows on his knees, and swirled his scotch around in the bottom of his glass. He was in no mood to exchange pleasantries and small talk.

After an awkward moment of silence, Cecily blurted out, "I realize you may find my visit a bit unconventional, but I had to see you before you sailed tomorrow."

"Why the sudden urgency? You could have seen me at any time in the past year simply by calling at Fairchild Park."

Lowering her eyes, she fidgeted with her gloves. "I wasn't sure of my welcome. I couldn't have blamed you if you had set the hounds on me."

"Don't be ridiculous. It would have been far more efficient to simply have my gamekeeper shoot you."

She shot him a sidelong glance, as if to see if he was joking. Gabriel didn't even blink.

She drew in a deep breath. "I came here tonight to inform you that I wish to accept your proposal."

"Pardon me?" He leaned forward, believing he must have heard her wrong.

"You once asked me to become your wife." She lifted her chin, meeting his gaze squarely. "I would like to take you up on that offer."

He gazed at her in disbelief for a minute, then burst out laughing. The rich ripples of mirth poured out of him, forcing him to rise and lean against the mantel so he could catch his breath. He hadn't laughed like that since Samantha had vanished from his life.

"You'll have to forgive me, Miss March," he said, swiping at his streaming eyes. "I had forgotten what a wicked sense of humor you have."

She rose to face him. "I wasn't speaking in jest."

Gabriel abruptly sobered in more ways than one. He rested his scotch glass on the mantel. "Well, that's a pity, isn't it, because I thought I made it perfectly clear that you no longer have any claim on my heart."

"I believe your exact words were, 'I didn't even know what love was until I met—*and lost*—my Samantha.'"

He narrowed his eyes, coming as close to hating her as he ever could.

She began to pace back and forth, the hem of her cloak sweeping across the Oriental carpet. "There's nothing to stop us from being wed tonight. We can elope to Gretna Green just as you once begged me to do."

Gabriel turned his back on her and gazed into the leaping flames of the fire, no longer able to bear the sight of her treacherous and lovely face.

Her floral scent enveloped him, the same rich gardenia that had perfumed the letters he had carried next to his heart through all of those long and lonely months at sea. He felt her hand brush his sleeve. "You once wanted me," she said softly. "Can you deny that you still do?"

He whirled around to face her. "Oh, I still want you. Just not for my wife."

She took a step away from him, but he stalked her, backing her toward the center of the room one step at a time. "I'm afraid I'm no longer in the market for a wife, Miss March, but I'd be perfectly willing to make you my mistress. I could set you up in some handsome lodgings nearby and take my pleasure in your bed whenever my ship puts into port." Gabriel knew he was being a bastard, but he couldn't seem to stop. All the bitterness he'd hoarded in his heart since Trafalgar came welling up in one vitriolic rush. "You needn't worry about your material needs. I can be a very generous man—especially if I'm kept satisfied. Nor should you feel guilty for accepting my largesse. I can assure you that you'll earn every extravagant bauble, every diamond earbob and ruby necklace, either on your back"—he lowered his gaze to her trembling lips—"or on your knees."

Gabriel loomed over her, waiting for her palm to crack across his cheek, for her to denounce him for the bully he was and run screaming for the door.

Instead, she reached up and unfastened the frog at her throat, sending her cloak sliding off of her shoulders and onto the floor.

Chapter 23

My darling Cecily,

I shall never be satisfied until you are in my arms to stay . . .

Cecily stood before him in the firelight, wearing nothing but a silk chemise, gartered stockings, a pair of peach slippers tied with ribbons around her slender ankles, and a look of pure defiance.

She was absolutely exquisite, exceeding anything his imagination could have concocted—round of hip, slender of waist, high-breasted. The delicate chemise could have been woven by butterflies, so sheer was its gossamer fabric. The teasing hint of shadow at the peaks of her breasts and the juncture of her thighs made his mouth grow dry and his body grow hard.

He slowly circled her, drinking in the graceful arch of her calf, the plush curve of her rump.

As he moved back in front of her, their gazes locked and held. "Although the slippers are lovely, I must say that your bridal trousseau is somewhat lacking."

"Lacking for a bride, perhaps," she retorted, looking as

haughty as a young queen despite her scanty attire, "but not for a mistress."

Gabriel shook his head, still struggling to absorb this stunning new development. He had never expected her to call his bluff, especially not in such dramatic fashion.

He studied her face, fascinated by the emotions he saw warring in her beautiful blue eyes. "You didn't come here to marry me, did you, Miss March? You came here to seduce me."

"I was reasonably confident that if I couldn't succeed at one, I could at the other."

"Well, you were wrong," he said flatly. Retrieving her cloak, he swept it around her shoulders. He started for the door, determined to show her out before his resolve could weaken further. "I've already told you that my heart belongs to another woman now."

"She's not here tonight," Cecily said softly. "I am."

Gabriel halted, pressing his fingertips to his throbbing brow. "I should warn you, Miss March, that you're tempting both fate and my patience. Do you know how long I'm going to be at sea once I sail tomorrow? Those nights are very cold and very lonely. Most of the men under my command are probably going to spend tonight rutting like beasts. And they won't be particularly fastidious in their choice of bedmates. Any willing woman will do."

"Then pretend I'm any woman."

Gabriel slowly turned.

She stepped out of the cloak, gliding toward him like a vision from one of his more daring fantasies. "Or better yet, admit that I'm the woman who deserves to pay for breaking your heart. Isn't that what you've wanted ever since I ran out of the hospital that day? To punish me?"

No longer able to resist the temptation, Gabriel curled his hand around her throat, his broad thumb caressing the pulse beating wildly at its base. Oh, he would punish her, all right. Not with pain, but with pleasure. A pleasure such as she had never known. A pleasure such as she would never know again. A pleasure that would haunt her through all the nights—and all the lovers—to come.

He lowered his head, but before his lips could brush the softness of hers, she turned her face away. "Don't! I don't want you to kiss me. You won't mean it anyway."

He frowned, taken aback by her vehemence. "Most women require a certain amount of kissing before they'll allow a man to proceed to other . . . um, even more pleasurable pursuits."

"I'm not most women."

He raked a hand through his hair. "I'm beginning to realize that."

"I have two other requirements."

"Indeed?"

"Don't let the fire go out and don't close your eyes." She glared at him accusingly. "Do you promise you won't close your eyes?"

"You have my word as a gentleman," he replied, feeling less like one by the moment.

Her requirements demanded no great sacrifice on his part. She looked so beautiful in the firelight that he was reluctant to blink. It was one of his keenest regrets that his blindness had prevented him from ever seeing Samantha this way.

As Gabriel strode to the hearth, Cecily stood in the middle of the drawing room, trying not to shiver in her thin chemise and stockings. His shirt stretching taut over his broad shoulders, he wrested a log large enough to burn the whole night through from the firebox and shoved it into the flames. Dusting his hands off, he turned, eyeing her hungrily across the leaping shadows.

Standing before Gabriel in her chemise while he was fully clothed was an incredibly wicked sensation. Cecily felt like some sort of slave girl on an auction block whose very life depended upon her power to please her master.

Embracing that power, she drew the chemise over her head and tossed it aside, leaving her garbed in nothing but her stockings and slippers. Gabriel made a guttural sound deep in his throat. Then he was coming for her, his determined strides eating up the space between them.

"I'll never love you," he warned, even as he eased her beneath him on the divan.

"I don't care," she whispered fiercely, gazing deep into his eyes.

And she didn't. All she wanted was one more chance to love him before he sailed on the morrow.

He lifted his weight from her to drag off his waistcoat, tug the collar and stock from his throat. Then her hands were there, tearing at the studs of his shirt, spreading the linen so she could flatten her palms against the golden expanse of his chest, sift her fingertips through the crisp whorls of hair she found there.

As Gabriel's shadow fell over her, she turned her cheek into the pillow to remove the temptation of her lips.

"When you said you didn't want me to kiss you," he said, his voice a smoky murmur, "I assume you meant on your lips."

His open mouth glided down the column of her throat, sending gooseflesh dancing over every inch of her. She pressed her eyes shut against a tide of helpless longing.

"Don't close your eyes," he commanded, his voice as rough as his touch was tender. "I have a few requirements of my own."

She obeyed him just in time to watch him lower his mouth to her breast. Her nipple puckered beneath his swirling tongue, accepting both his kiss and the shivering pulses of pleasure it sent through her womb. He shifted his kiss from one breast to the other until they were both glistening and heavy with desire.

Only then did his skillful mouth glide lower, scattering whisper-soft kisses over the sensitive skin along her ribs, the curve of her hipbone, the quivering ribbon of flesh just above the honey-gold triangle of curls between her thighs. By the time he slipped to his knees on the floor and dragged her hips to the very edge of the divan, she was too limp with delight to do more than moan a half-hearted protest.

His big, warm hands parted her thighs, leaving her utterly vulnerable to him, utterly exposed to his hungry gaze. One of the logs shifted on the grate, lighting up the room with a shower of sparks. In that moment, Cecily almost regretted her careless demands. But she had been terrified that Gabriel would recognize the taste of her kiss, the tender rhythm of her body moving against his in the dark.

"You always were so damn pretty," he whispered, gazing down at her as if she were some sort of sacred treasure.

As he lowered his head, his tawny hair tumbling half out of its queue, she could not stop her eyes from fluttering shut.

"Open your eyes, Cecily." She opened them to find him gazing at her down the length of her body, his expression fierce, but not cruel. "I want you to watch."

She barely had time to note a few incongruous details like the fact that one stocking had slipped down to her ankle and she was still wearing her slippers before Gabriel touched his mouth to her, giving her the most forbidden kiss of all. Her whimper melted to a groan. Then there was nothing but the searing heat of his mouth, the maddening flicker of his tongue, the exquisite sensation of melting into a sea of rapture.

As those dark waves crested over her head, making her body shudder with delight and her toes curl inside her slippers, she cried out his name in a hoarse voice she barely recognized as her own.

Through a delicious haze, she watched him tear open the front flap of his breeches. Her breath caught in her throat as she saw how badly he wanted her. Still kneeling there between her legs, he spread her thighs wide and drove himself deep inside of her.

Gabriel heard Cecily's gasp, saw her eyes roll back in her head, not with pain, but with pleasure. Even as her tight body struggled to contain him, he had to grit his teeth against a savage pang of disappointment. He should be grateful that she was no innocent. That meant he didn't have to hold anything back; she was woman enough to take whatever he could give her. Curling his arms around her shoulders, he dragged her up and astride him.

Cecily wrapped her arms and legs around Gabriel, impaled on the rigid length of his staff.

I love you I love you I love you. The words ran through her mind like a ceaseless song. Terrified she was going to say them out loud, she buried her face against his throat, tasting the salty warmth of his sweat-dampened skin.

It was just as well that she had denied him her lips. He would have tasted those words in her kiss, just as he would have tasted the helpless tears trickling down her cheeks. She rubbed her face against him, drying them with his hair.

Gabriel slid back down to his knees on the floor, lowering her until she was straddling his lap, straddling the part of him that was buried to the hilt inside of her.

"Look at me, Cecily," he urged.

Trembling with emotion, she gazed deep into his eyes, seeing in their gilt-fringed depths an echo of the tender madness that had seized her own soul. Then he was moving inside her, she was moving over him, they were moving as one with the flames of the firelight licking at their golden flesh. And all the while, Gabriel never broke his promise, never closed his eyes or tore his gaze away from hers.

He held fast to his vow until the exact moment when the driving rhythm of his thrusts sent them both tumbling over the abyss of ecstasy into sweet oblivion. Only then, with his arms wrapped tight around her and his body surging at the very mouth of her womb, did he throw back his head and squeeze his eyes shut. Only then did a woman's name come roaring from his throat.

Cecily collapsed against him, awash in both pleasure and triumph. In that moment when Gabriel had surrendered to the darkness, it had been her name, not Samantha's, in his heart and on his lips.

Gabriel awoke with Cecily in his arms. Her tousled curls tickled his chin and each soft breath from her parted lips stirred his chest hairs. He had spent so many lonely nights imagining this moment, never realizing how bittersweet it would be when it finally came.

As a gentle snore escaped her, he sifted his fingers through her curls. It was no wonder she was sleeping so soundly. Her body was probably exhausted from his greedy attentions. He had made good on his vow not to waste a single moment of his last night on dry land. He had used Cecily's tender young body to indulge his darkest desires and her sweetest fantasies all through the long hours of the night. The huge log he had tossed on the fire was already crumbling to smoldering embers. But there was no reason to add another one. The muted glow of dawn was seeping through the gap in the heavy velvet drapes.

He reached down to draw her velvet cloak over her, just beginning to realize what a fool he had been. He had deluded himself into believing that the night had been about revenge, that he could punish her with pleasure, make love to her without loving her, then just let her go. But that was going to be much harder than he had anticipated. He touched his lips to her curls, wondering if it was possible to love two women at the same time.

She stirred and lifted her head, blinking up at him with drowsy blue eyes. "So how many diamond earbobs have I earned so far?"

"A king's ransom." He gently stroked her cheek, feeling a sharp twinge of regret. "I should have never said such a spiteful thing. I was only trying to frighten you off."

"It didn't work."

"Thank God," he whispered, tightening his grip on her.

But she slid out of his grasp, taking the cloak with her. The tantalizing softness of her breasts glided down his body. By the time they brushed his manhood, he was fully aroused. Again.

Tangling his fingers in her hair, he tugged her head up so she could meet his gaze, his breath coming short and fast. "What in the devil do you think you're doing, woman?"

"Trying for a ruby pendant," she murmured, smiling sweetly

before lowering her head to enfold him in those luscious lips of hers.

When Gabriel woke again, a dagger of sunlight was slanting through the gap in the drapes and Cecily was gone.

He sat up, his bleary gaze raking the drawing room. The fire had died to ash, leaving a stark chill hanging in the air. Except for the half-empty glass of scotch on the mantel and his own clothes scattered across the floor, the drawing room looked much as it had when he'd come home last night. There was no crumpled chemise, no velvet cloak, no Cecily.

If not for the taste of her lingering on his lips, he might have thought the entire night had been nothing more than a feverish, scotch-induced dream.

"Not again," he muttered, swinging his legs over the edge of the divan and burying his head in his hands.

What was he supposed to do now? Go out and comb the streets of London looking for her? Drive himself half mad wondering why she had loved him so tenderly, then left him without so much as a backward glance? At least Samantha had taken the time to leave a note before walking out of his life forever.

"Damn her." He lifted his head, feeling the chill in the air settle deep into his heart. "Damn them both."

Chapter 24

My dearest Gabriel,

There's no place I would rather be than in your arms . . .

Cecily gazed out the carriage window at the passing meadows and hedgerows, achingly aware that every revolution of the vehicle's wheels carried her farther away from London. And Gabriel.

Given that her last journey to Middlesex was made in a public coach with a squalling infant spitting down her bodice and a stout blacksmith standing on her foot, one would have thought she would appreciate the extravagant luxury of the Carstairs' town coach. But she was as oblivious to its plush cushions and brass fittings as she was to her friend's worried gaze.

Estelle's natural exuberance was no match for the shroud of gloom that enveloped her. As the coach rumbled over an arched stone bridge, it seemed only fitting that the low-hanging clouds would start to spit the first snowflakes of the season.

"I still can't believe you were bold enough to propose to him," Estelle said, shooting her an admiring look.

"I wasn't proposing. I was accepting his proposal. Unfortunately, it had been retracted."

"What if he had agreed to elope to Gretna Green? Just when were you planning on telling him you were his long-lost Samantha?"

"I'm not sure. But I'm certain the appropriate moment would have arisen someday. After the birth of our third child, perhaps, or while celebrating our fiftieth year together as man and wife." Cecily briefly closed her eyes, haunted by children's laughter she would never hear, joyful days in her husband's arms that would never come.

Estelle shook her head. "I can't believe he's going back to sea."

"And why is that so hard to believe?" Cecily asked bitterly. "He wants to be a hero for his precious Samantha. The last time he sailed, it almost cost him his sight. I wonder what it will cost him this time. An eye? An arm? His life?"

She leaned her cheek against the window, fighting despair. She had encouraged Gabriel to be a hero when she was the worst sort of coward. She had run away from his love in the beginning, afraid to trust in the steadfastness of his heart. Then she had run from the hospital because she couldn't face the consequences of her cowardice. She had run from his arms in Fairchild Park and now here she was, running again.

Only this time she would have to keep running for the rest of her life, even if it meant never getting anywhere.

"No more," Cecily whispered.

"Pardon?"

Cecily sat up on the edge of her seat. "Turn the coach around."

"What?" Estelle asked, still struggling to follow.

"Order the driver to turn the coach around! Right now!" Too impatient to wait for her friend to catch up to her racing thoughts, Cecily snatched up the cane in the corner and began to bang on the silk-lined panel at the front of the coach.

The vehicle rocked to a halt. The panel slid open and the driver's bewildered face appeared, his nose ruddy with cold. "What is it, miss?"

"I must return to London. Turn the coach around immediately!"

The driver shot Estelle a wary look, as if wondering if he should cart her wild-eyed friend straight to Bedlam.

"Do as she says," Estelle commanded, her own eyes shining with excitement. "*Whatever* she says."

He gave Cecily a reluctant nod. "Where to, miss?"

"To the docks at Greenwich. And hurry! A man's life may very well depend upon it!"

The coach lurched into motion, sending Cecily tumbling back into the seat. Desperately needing a thread of hope to cling to, she reached over to squeeze Estelle's hand, a tremulous smile curving her lips. "And a woman's life as well."

Lieutenant Gabriel Fairchild stood before the mirror in the study of his townhouse in his uniform. As he adjusted the dark blue stock at his throat, the forbidding slash of his scar drew down the corner of his mouth, a mouth that looked as if it had never known a smile.

It was not a face an enemy would care to see on the wrong side of a rifle, sword, or cannon. It was the face of a man born to make war, not love. No one would have guessed that those stern lips, those powerful hands, had spent most of the previous night tenderly coaxing a woman to one shuddering release after another.

"My lord?"

At the sound of iron wheels rolling across carpet, Gabriel turned. No one would have recognized the man sitting straight and tall in the invalid's chair as the emaciated beggar Gabriel had found in the rain nearly a month and a half ago. His lips had lost their bluish tint and both his cheeks and his chest had filled out. With his excellent penmanship and head for figures, Martin Worth had turned out to be the most able secretary Gabriel had ever employed. He completely trusted the former midshipman to manage his household while he was at sea.

Gabriel had been quick to brush aside Martin's effusive gratitude. If not for a quirk of fate, he could have been the one sitting there with only half his legs, the one destined to spend the rest of his life in an invalid's chair.

Swiping a shiny brown fall of hair out of his eyes, Martin said, "There's someone here to see you, my lord." Before Gabriel's heart could take a treacherous leap, he added, "A Mr. Beckwith and a Mrs. Philpot."

Gabriel frowned, unable to imagine what urgent errand could have dragged the loyal servants away from Fairchild Park. After trolling the city's dark underbelly with Gabriel while looking for Samantha, Beckwith had sworn that he didn't care if he ever set foot in London again.

"Thank you, Martin. Send them in."

A footman rolled Martin away and Beckwith and Mrs. Philpot came bustling into the study. After greeting him warmly, they sank down on a brocaded sofa, making a painstaking effort to keep a respectable amount of distance between them. Gabriel remained in front of the hearth.

Mrs. Philpot removed her gloves. "We weren't certain if we should trouble you about this matter—"

"—but you did tell us to keep you apprised if anything unusual was found in Miss Wickersham's bedchamber," Beckwith finished.

Miss Wickersham.

The name jabbed like a hot needle through the ice around Gabriel's heart. He locked his hands at the small of his back, feeling his jaw go taut. "I was going to send word that you were free to burn her belongings. She obviously has no intention of ever coming back for them."

Beckwith and Mrs. Philpot exchanged a dismayed look.

"If that's what you w-wish, my lord," Beckwith said haltingly, "but I think you should take a look at this first." He drew a folded piece of paper from the pocket of his waistcoat. "Hannah and Elsie were turning the mattress in Miss Wickersham's chamber when they found it."

Gabriel tried not to remember the night he had shared that ridiculously narrow mattress with her, the way it had forced their warm bodies to nestle together like spoons in a drawer.

He gazed down at the paper in Beckwith's hand, oddly reluctant to examine it. "Surely she didn't leave me another note. Her first was quite eloquent. It hardly required any embellishment."

Beckwith shook his head. "That's why we found it so peculiar, my lord. It's not a letter *to* you. It's a letter *from* you."

His frown deepening, Gabriel accepted the folded letter from Beckwith's hand. Bits of old wax still clung to the ivory linen. It was even more worn than the letters he had carried into battle next to his heart. It appeared the paper had been stroked often and lovingly by tender fingers.

Gabriel unfolded it, recognizing with a start his own bold hand, his even bolder words.

My darling Cecily,

This will be the last missive you will have from me for a very long while. Even though I cannot post them, please know that I will write words of love for you on my heart every night we are parted so I can read them to you when we are reunited.

Now that I have taken your counsel and signed away my vain and useless life to His Majesty's Service, I hope you will not laugh your merry laugh and accuse me of shipping off to sea only to prove to my tailor how dashing I can look in a uniform.

During the long months when we are parted, I will strive to become a man worthy of your affections. I've made no secret of my fondness for gaming. Now I am gambling to win the most precious stakes of all—your heart and your hand in matrimony. Wait for me, I beg you, and know that I will return to you as

soon as I am able. I carry your letters and all of my hopes for our
future next to my heart.

Ever your,
Gabriel

Gabriel slowly lowered the letter, surprised to discover that his hands were shaking. "Where did you get this? Did you find it somewhere inside this house, on the stoop outside?"

They both blinked at him as if he'd lost his wits.

"No, my lord," Mrs. Philpot said, stealing a worried look at Beckwith. "We found it exactly where we said we did. Beneath Miss Wickersham's mattress."

"But how did she come to be in possession of it? I don't understand . . ."

But suddenly he did understand.

Everything.

Closing his eyes against a rush of raw emotion, he whispered, "There is none so blind as he who will not see."

When he opened them, everything in his life was suddenly crystal clear.

Tucking the letter inside his coat, next to his heart, he gave Beckwith a ferocious scowl. "So tell me, Mr. Beckwith, when are you going to make an honest woman out of Mrs. Philpot here?"

Although they were afraid to look at each other, the two servants both began to blush and stammer.

Beckwith drew a handkerchief from his waistcoat pocket and mopped at his brow. "You know, my lord?"

"How long?" Mrs. Philpot asked, wadding her gloves into a tiny ball.

Gabriel rolled his eyes. "Since I was about twelve and spotted the two of you kissing in the apple orchard. I nearly fell out of the tree and broke my neck."

"Are we to be allowed to keep our positions?" Beckwith asked, growing bold enough to reach over and take Mrs. Philpot's trembling hand in his.

Gabriel pondered the question for a moment. "Only if you get married right away. I can't have you living in sin under my roof and corrupting the morals of my children."

"But—but, my lord . . . you don't have any children," Mrs. Philpot pointed out.

"If you'll excuse me, I'm off to remedy that." Gabriel strode toward the door, determined not to waste another minute.

"Where are you going?" Beckwith called after him, sounding more bewildered than usual.

Gabriel pivoted on his heel, grinning at them both. "I have a ship to catch."

Cecily was out of the coach before it even stopped moving.

"Run, Cecily! Run like the wind!" Estelle called after her as she lifted her skirts and took off down the narrow street that led to the docks. It was snowing harder now, but she barely felt the icy bite of the flakes. She had left her cloak behind in the coach, believing she could move faster without its encumbering folds.

As her feet flew over the planks of the docks, she could see the towering spars of the ships waiting to sail and could only pray that the *Defiance* was among them.

She darted past a group of men unloading merchandise from a freighter. Rounding a stack of crates, she crashed right into the chest of a sailor nearly as wide as she was tall.

"Whoa, there, lass!" he boomed, catching her elbow to steady her. His blue eyes were not unkind.

Cecily clutched at his arm, dangerously near tears. "Please, sir, the *Defiance*! Can you tell me where I can find it?"

"I most certainly can." He beamed down at her, revealing a mouthful of black and gold teeth. "She's right there. And a fine sight she is flying His Majesty's colors into battle!"

Her heart already beginning to pound with dread, Cecily

slowly turned to follow the direction of his pointing finger. A ship in full sail was gliding toward the horizon, its majestic masts nearly obscured by the gusting snow.

"Thank you, sir," she mumbled as the seaman doffed his cap to her, hefted a massive crate to his shoulder, and lumbered off.

She slumped against a barrel, both her toes and her heart going numb as she watched the *Defiance*—and all of her hopes for the future—disappear over the horizon.

"Looking for someone, Miss March?"

Cecily whirled around to find Gabriel standing on the dock a few feet behind her, his unbound hair blowing in the wind. Her heart leapt with joy. It was all she could do not to run into his arms.

He arched one tawny eyebrow. "Or would you prefer I call you *Miss Wickersham?*"

≈ Chapter 25 ≈

My darling Cecily,

My arms will always be open to you, as will my heart . . .

As Cecily met Gabriel's cool green gaze, a shudder of awareness rocked her. She presented her back to him, wrapping her arms around herself to hug back a shiver. "You may call me Cecily if you like, now that I'm no longer in your employ."

She heard his measured footsteps moving closer. He draped his coat over her shoulders, enfolding her in its juniper-scented warmth. "I hope you won't be expecting a letter of reference."

"Oh, I don't know." She lifted her shoulders in a careless shrug. "I think I performed my duties with admirable enthusiasm."

"That may be true, but I don't want you performing them for anyone else."

At the possessive note in his voice, Cecily turned to face him, her heart pounding madly. "How did you know I would be here?"

"I didn't. I came to inform my shipmates that I had resigned my commission. You can keep the coat. I won't be needing it."

She hugged the garment tighter around her, afraid to ask, afraid to hope.

"Perhaps it's just as well that I ran into you, because I believe I have something that belongs to you." Gabriel reached inside his coat, the backs of his fingers brushing her breast as he drew out a folded piece of stationery.

She took the familiar scrap of ivory linen from his hand, lifting her bewildered eyes to his. "How did you get this?"

"The servants found it beneath your mattress at Fairchild Park. Beckwith and Mrs. Philpot delivered it to me only this morning. When I gave you my letters for safekeeping, I never suspected you had a stash of your own."

"It must have fallen out of the ribbon the night you came to my room. I suppose I never should have brought them to Fairchild Park with me, but I couldn't bear the thought of leaving them behind." She shook her head disbelievingly. "I had no idea. I thought I gave myself away last night."

"Oh, you gave yourself away, all right." With the knowing look in his eyes, the smoky timbre of his voice, suddenly everything that had been between them in the night was between them again. "And I was only too willing to take advantage of your generosity. But, no, it wasn't last night that spoiled your absurd little masquerade."

She lifted her chin defiantly. "Not so absurd, I think. I fooled you, didn't I? But the only trouble was that I fooled myself as well. I told myself that I could somehow atone for everything I'd done by helping you adjust to your blindness." She gazed up at him, no longer trying to hide the longing in her eyes. "But the truth was that I would have risked anything, even your hatred, just to be near you again."

An old pain shadowed his eyes. "If you wanted to be near me that badly, then why did you run away from me at the hospital? Was I that abhorrent to you?"

She lifted a hand, touching a finger gently to his scar. "I didn't flee your bedside because I was horrified by the sight of you. I fled because I was horrified by *me*. By what I had driven you to, all in the name of some girlish fantasy. I wanted you to win my heart by fighting a dragon. I never realized that in the real world, more often than not, the dragon wins. I was appalled at what I had cost you. I blamed myself for scarring and blinding you. I didn't see how you could ever forgive me."

"For what? Wanting me to be a better man?"

"For not loving the man you were enough." She let her hand fall limply to her side. "I went back to the hospital the very next day. But you were gone."

Gabriel gazed down at her bowed head, her soft fall of golden curls. In that moment, she was Cecily, the girl he had loved. And Samantha, the woman who had loved him.

"You were right," he said. "I didn't love you. You said it yourself. I never really knew you. You were only a dream."

At Gabriel's words, Cecily felt her heart crack in two like a block of ice. She turned her face away, not wanting him to see her tears.

But he tilted her chin up, forcing her to meet his fierce gaze. "But now I do know you. I know how brave and silly and stubborn you are. I know that you're more clever than me by half. I know you snore like a baby bear. I know you have a wicked temper and a sharp tongue and can give some of the most magnificent setdowns I've ever heard. I know you make love like an angel and that without you my life is a living hell." He cupped her cheek in his hand, his eyes shining with tender yearning. "Before, you were only a dream. Now you're a dream come true."

As Gabriel touched his lips to hers, a dizzying rush of sweetness spiraled through Cecily's veins. She wrapped her arms around him, returning his kiss with an ardor that left them both trembling.

He drew away. "I have only one more question for you."

Her wariness returned. "Yes?"

He scowled down at her. "Have you really seen numerous men without their shirts?"

Cecily laughed through her tears. "Only you, my lord. Only you."

"Good. Let's keep it that way, shall we?"

She let out a squeal as he swept her up into his arms, cradling her like a baby.

As Gabriel's long strides carried them toward the street, she rested her head on his shoulder, feeling as if she'd come home at last. "Before we proceed, my lord, I really must insist that you clarify your intentions. Are you offering me a position as your nurse or your mistress?"

He tenderly kissed her nose, her cheeks, her parted lips. "I'm offering you a position as my wife, my lover, my countess, and the mother of my children."

Cecily sighed, snuggling deeper into his arms. "Then I accept. But I'll still expect you to shower me with extravagant baubles on occasion."

He leered down at her, using his scar to its most devilish advantage. "Only if you earn them."

She suddenly stiffened in his arms, her eyes widening in horror. "Oh, no! I just thought of something. What will your mother say?"

Gabriel grinned down at her in the swirling snow. "Why don't we go find out?" His eyes sobered. "This isn't just a dream, is it? When I wake up in the morning, will you still be here?"

Cecily stroked his cheek with loving fingers, smiling up at him through a mist of joyful tears. "Every day, my love. For the rest of our lives."

⥈ *Epilogue* ⥈

15 December, 1809

My dearest Lord Sheffield,

On this, our third anniversary as man and wife, I feel compelled to point out that you are as impertinent, insufferable, and arrogant as ever, perhaps even more so now that you are so often to be found swaggering about the mansion with your daughter on your shoulder. Despite the misgivings of both myself and my staunchest ally, your dear, sweet mother, you insisted upon christening her "Samantha," ensuring that both she and the dog come running whenever her name is called. For a while there, you could never be sure which one of them you would find chewing and drooling on your boots. Her table manners are remarkably similar to what her papa's once were. She disdains both fork and spoon and flings her porridge about with a wild-eyed enthusiasm that makes both Beckwith and Mrs. Beckwith shudder with horror.

I am also writing to inform you that thanks to your devoted (and quite frequent!) attentions, I am once again with child. Per-

haps this time I will give you a son with green eyes and golden curls. He can order the staff about with the high-handed imperiousness one would expect of a Fairchild heir.

Ever your adoring,
Cecily

16 December, 1809

My darling Lady Sheffield,

I should point out that our little cherub also shares many traits in common with her mother. She frequently likes to pretend she's someone (or something) else, whether it be a fairy princess or a garden toad. She also has a tendency to disappear just when one needs her the most. Only yesterday, while I was frantically waiting for my newly trained valet, Phillip, to tie my cravat for church, I found her fast asleep in my dressing room beneath an enormous pile of hats.

So now you intend to give me a son, eh? No doubt he will be every bit as vexing and as irresistible as his mama and sister.

You asked me once if I would still love you when your lips were puckered with age and your eyes were faded. I can assure you that I will still love you when I have only the strength (and the scant teeth) left to gum those puckered lips. I shall love you when your bones are sharp enough to pierce my fragile flesh. I shall love you when the light in my own eyes fades for good and yours is the last sweet face I see. Because I am and ever shall be . . .

Your devoted husband,
Gabriel